HER SEAFARING Scoundrel

The Crawfords Series

SOPHIE BARNES

ALSO BY SOPHIE BARNES

NOVELS

Her Seafaring Scoundrel
The Forgotten Duke
More Than A Rogue
The Infamous Duchess
No Ordinary Duke
The Illegitimate Duke
The Girl Who Stepped Into The Past
The Duke of Her Desire
Christmas at Thorncliff Manor
A Most Unlikely Duke
His Scandalous Kiss
The Earl's Complete Surrender
Lady Sarah's Sinful Desires
The Danger in Tempting an Earl
The Scandal in Kissing an Heir
The Trouble with Being a Duke
The Secret Life of Lady Lucinda
There's Something About Lady Mary
Lady Alexandra's Excellent Adventure
How Miss Rutherford Got Her Groove Back

NOVELLAS

Lady Abigail's Perfect Romance
When Love Leads To Scandal
Miss Compton's Christmas Romance
The Duke Who Came To Town
The Earl Who Loved Her

The Governess Who Captured His Heart
Mistletoe Magic (from Five Golden Rings: A
Christmas Collection)

CHAPTER ONE

THE EARLY MORNING SUN GLOWED gold against a vibrant display of reds and yellows. Standing on the quarterdeck of his ship as it slid through the water, Devlin Christopher Benjamin Crawford considered the view London offered as he approached: a black silhouette of historic buildings against the fiery sky of dawn.

It was ten months since he'd last set foot on English soil, and while he always dreaded returning to the memories still haunting him here, he looked forward to seeing his family with great anticipation.

To think six years had passed since his brother Caleb, the Duke of Camberly, had married Mary Clemens, and five since his other brother Griffin had married Emily Howard never ceased to amaze him. Both couples had since been blessed with a number of children, including a set of boisterous twins, and he, being the excellent uncle he was, had made certain to bring them each a gift.

"Right ten degrees rudder," Devlin told his first mate, Mr. Montgomery Quinn. "Let's bring her to port."

"Aye, aye," Quinn responded.

The ship swung to the side, lining itself up at just the right angle. "Steady now," Devlin ordered. Stepping forward, he gauged the distance to the quay, waited a good five minutes until it was at the right distance, and addressed Quinn again. "Ease your rudder." As expected, they slowed their progress while steadily sailing toward a vacant berth. "Keep her so."

"Very well, Captain," Quinn said, his eyes never wavering from his destination.

Confident Quinn knew what he was doing, Devlin turned to the mooring crew. "Prepare to throw the heaving lines!" The task was carried out to perfection one minute later, allowing the mooring lines to be securely attached to the bollards.

Devlin breathed a sigh of relief. Although he'd been through this countless times, there was always a risk that something would go wrong, causing the ship to crash into the quay. He gave his first mate a smile. "Welcome home, Mr. Quinn."

His friend of almost fifteen years grinned. "Thank you, Captain." Neither man veered from proper protocol while on board, but once they stepped onto land, they'd be Monty and Dev to each other. "It'll be grand to see my wife and children again."

"Frankly, I don't know how you do it," Devlin said as he climbed down onto the main deck and headed toward his cabin. Monty kept pace directly behind him, issuing orders to the occasional crew member as they went. "Being away from them for such long periods of time must be trying."

"It is," Monty agreed, "which is why our next voyage together will be my last."

Halting mid-stride, Devlin turned to face his friend. "You're serious?"

"I'm afraid so." Monty scratched the back of his neck and looked askance, his expression sheepish. "I was going to wait until we were back on land before bringing it up, but I suppose now's as fitting a time as any."

Devlin tipped his head to acknowledge Monty's reasoning, then turned back toward the ladder leading below deck.

"I can't keep leaving Laura and the children for such long stretches of time. It's too damn hard." The soles of his boots thudded against each step as he clambered down after Devlin.

"Which is why I have no intention of ever marrying," Devlin said as he opened the door to his cabin and stepped inside. He grabbed his journal and stuffed it into a leather satchel. "If I had a wife and children, I would be torn between settling down for their sake and chasing after my own dreams."

The last thing he'd want was the sort of marriage his parents had had where they hardly spoke to each other and lived apart most of the time. Of course, he knew it was possible to have the opposite. His brothers had proven as much. But Devlin couldn't quite envision himself in the role of domestic husband.

Monty, who'd stayed in the open doorway with his shoulder and hip propped against the frame, raised an eyebrow. "You make a fair point, but being the married man I am, I don't have much of a choice. And besides, the love I have for my family has made the decision a great deal easier for me." He snorted. "Hell, my youngest will have learned to walk and talk by now. That's a lot of time to have missed."

Devlin glanced at the man on whom he relied more heavily than the rest. The pensive frown he wore suggested this had not been an easy decision for him. He would miss sailing, but there was no doubt his mind was made up. Regrettably, Devlin knew it was time for him to start looking for a new first mate.

Still, it was difficult to relate, partly because he could not imagine loving a woman more than he loved the sea and also because he had no desire to make a home for himself on land. Not only because his soul was restless and constantly needed to stay in motion but because he couldn't stand remaining in England for too great a period of time. Too much here reminded him of things he'd rather forget, like the fight he'd had with his father the last time he'd seen him alive, and the tragic carriage accident he still felt responsible for.

He shuddered, then retrieved the trunk he'd packed the night before and placed it near the doorway. Straightening, he met Monty's gaze directly. "Why don't you head on home?"

Monty stared back. "I can't do that when the

cargo needs to be unloaded and stored."

"I'll take care of it," Devlin said. He tilted his head and grinned, not caring that he would be almost buried in work for the next two days without Monty there to help. "Take your children to Gunther's for an ice or something. Go for a walk in Hyde Park."

"Are you sure?" Monty looked skeptical.

"Quite."

It took a moment, but Monty finally nodded. "You're a good man, Captain." The edge of his mouth tilted. "There isn't a woman in England who wouldn't be lucky to have you."

Devlin chose not to answer. It was difficult to argue with a man who'd made vastly different choices – choices Devlin knew he himself could never accept. So he simply wished him well and went in search of Mr. Harris, the boatswain, who'd help him with the logistics of sorting and storing the goods they'd brought from India and China. There were Englishmen stationed out there who longed for things from their homeland. And there were Englishmen here who'd pay handsome prices for exotic fabrics, teas, and spices. So he made the ten month round-trip journey as often as possible, never staying more than four days at most in each port. Except in England where he had been known to remain for up to four weeks.

"I've sent letters out to all of our clients informing them their orders are ready to be collected," Devlin told Trevor Bronswick two days later. Trevor was the officer in charge of ensuring the right order went to the right person. He was also the quartermaster's son and eager to make a maritime career like his father. "Send for me if any of them gives you trouble."

Trevor promised to do so, then helped Devlin carry his trunk and satchel down to the dock where a hired hackney stood waiting. Half an hour later, Devlin knocked on the front door of Camberly House and was promptly admitted by Caleb's butler, Murdoch.

"Welcome, Lord Devlin, or should I say Captain?" Murdoch inquired with a hint of humor in his eyes. Slightly hunched and with thinning white hair, he looked like he might be nearing retirement.

"Whichever you prefer," Devlin told him with a smile.

"Lord Devlin it is then. It's good to have you home."

Devlin thanked him, removed his hat, and angled his head at the sound of footsteps hurrying along the upstairs hallway. A warm and wonderful feeling filled his chest and then he saw them: three tiny versions of Caleb and Mary, otherwise known as the five-year-old twins, Amanda and Richard, and four-year-old William.

"Uncle Dev, Uncle Dev," they shouted as they stampeded down the stairs in an untamed manner that would have been frowned upon in most aristocratic homes.

They were followed by Mary, who appeared at the top of the landing with two-year-old Susan in her arms. "I can see Richard was right when he told me he heard your voice."

The door to the study opened and Caleb strode into the hallway with a, "What the devil is—" he spotted Devlin and instantly grinned "—by God it's good to see you again!"

Devlin grinned right back while his brother's children attacked him with hugs. He might not care to live in England permanently, but damn if it wasn't good to be home, surrounded by this kind of affection.

"You too," he said. "I wasn't sure if you would be here or at Montvale."

Uninterested in leading the expected lives of a duke and duchess, Caleb and Mary had built a cottage for themselves on the grounds of their largest entailed estate. They'd turned the manor itself into an orphanage so they could continue the work Mary had once helped start together with her friends Emily, now married to Devlin's other brother, Griffin, and Lady Cassandra Moor, Viscount Aldridge's sister. At Clearview House in Cornwall, the three women had housed, fed, and educated five children to start with, including Cassandra's illegitimate daughter, Penelope.

"I had some bothersome duke business to attend to," Caleb said, "so I was forced to come to Town for a while."

"I'm glad," Devlin told him while mussing the tops of his nieces' and nephews' heads. "Saves me an extra day's travel, and since I've still some work to attend to at the docks, it really is more convenient this way."

"It also gave us a chance to see your favorite museum, Papa," Amanda piped up.

"The one with the miniatures?" Devlin asked. All the children nodded with great enthusiasm. "I like that one too."

A pair of footmen who'd been sent out into the street by Murdoch while the family had been talking returned with Devlin's trunk and satchel. When they started toward the stairs, Devlin stopped them so he could retrieve the gifts he'd purchased for the children.

"Let's see now…" he murmured, making a show of searching through all his belongings. "This is for you," he told Richard and handed him a silk-clad box containing a beautifully carved chess set made from onyx and bone. Amanda received a pair of exquisite tortoise shell combs, William a pair of silk pajamas Devlin had found in Hong Kong, and Susan a porcelain doll dressed like a princess.

The children beamed and hugged him while muttering thanks, but when Richard sat down on the floor and began setting up his chess set, Caleb intervened. "Please take your gifts upstairs. While we might not be the most civilized household, toys do not belong in the foyer."

Without argument, Amanda, Richard, and William grabbed their things and disappeared back the way they had come. Most likely to the nursery. The footmen carried Devlin's things to the guestroom he always used while in Town and

Mary made her excuses. "It was lovely seeing you again," she said, "but it is almost time for Susan's nap." As if on cue, the little sprite opened her mouth in a massive yawn. Her mother chuckled. "I will join you once she's asleep."

"Am I mistaken," Devlin said as he followed his brother into the parlor, "or is there another Crawford on the way?"

Caleb glanced at him over his shoulder, then moved to the sideboard and poured them each a measure of brandy. He handed one glass to Devlin. "You're not mistaken," he said with a twinkle in his eyes and a lopsided smile.

"Well congratulations, then. I'm happy for you."

"Thank you." Caleb crossed to an armchair and sat while Devlin made himself comfortable on the sofa. His brother took a sip of his drink and regarded Devlin for a quiet moment before saying, "It's not the worst, you know, having a wife and children to love. You might consider trying it."

Devlin sighed. There was never any chance of avoiding this subject when he and his brothers met. Having found their happily ever afters, they wanted Devlin to do the same. "We've been over this before, Caleb. I'm not the marrying type."

"Because you refuse to buy a house, settle down, and stop sailing?" When Devlin nodded, Caleb shrugged. "You don't have to do any of that if you don't want to. If you find the right woman, I dare say she'd happily go wherever you choose."

"Life aboard ship is hard and can even be dangerous at times."

"True, I suppose. But people can also succumb to all kinds of terrible fates without venturing far from their homes." Devlin shuddered. He'd caused such a thing to happen once and although it had been thirteen years, he still couldn't forgive himself for the accident that had cost a young man his life. "Worrying over what may or may not happen," Caleb continued, clearly oblivious to the effect of his words, "can stop a man from living."

"Trust me," Devlin muttered, "if I were to live any more than I already do, I'd probably perish from exhaustion." He deliberately smirked, affecting a carefreeness he didn't quite feel at the moment. "I get to see the world *and* I've bedded women on more than one continent, though I'll be the first to admit that they've all required payment. *But,*" he raised one finger to stop his brother from interrupting, "it's still been fun and sates whatever needs I may have. Beyond that, I have a loyal crew, most of them fast friends for whom I would risk my own life. The desire for anything more simply isn't there."

"I see your point, I suppose," Caleb said. "Although—"

The door swung open, but rather than Mary entering the room, Devlin's mother, the dowager duchess, did so. "I've told Murdoch to have some sandwiches brought up. Dear heavens, Devlin, you look like you haven't eaten in years."

"It's good to see you too, Mother," Devlin

said as he stood and went to embrace her. Some maternal instinct of hers always made her believe it was her duty to plump him up before his next trip. Releasing her, he waited for her to claim the vacant spot on the sofa before returning to his own. Caleb, who'd also risen upon their mother's arrival, sat as well. "I wasn't aware you were here. You haven't moved back in have you?"

"No, no," his mother replied. "I'm still at my townhouse on Cavendish Square, but I came to visit for the day and decided to take a nap after luncheon, which I must say was rather fortuitous as it allows me to see you straight away."

A maid entered at that moment, bringing tea and two plates of sandwiches and biscuits. Devlin's stomach made a rumbling noise, causing his mother to turn to him with an arched brow. She offered him the plate filled with sandwiches and encouraged him to take at least two.

"Your return to London," she said once she'd offered the plate to Caleb as well and proceeded to pour herself some tea, "could not have been timed any better if I'd engaged my secretary to do it."

Devlin stilled and began chewing more slowly. Something was underfoot and he very much feared it wouldn't be something he liked. He glanced at Caleb, who suddenly seemed incredibly interested in the ceiling.

"Your brother and sister-in-law will be hosting the first Camberly ball in six years this coming Saturday. And since you are officially the only remaining Crawford bachelor, you will—"

"No," Devlin choked. "Whatever it is you think you can talk me into, it isn't going to happen."

"Please, Devlin. It really is the least you can do after staying away as long as you have." She sniffed. "One would think you cannot abide your family's company."

He groaned and used the rest of his brandy to dislodge the chunk of sandwich wedged in his throat. "I refuse to be trotted out like some stallion seeking a mare."

"Dev," Caleb said, his tight voice conveying his censure.

"My apologies, Mama," Devlin said, "but you know I don't wish to marry. Everyone knows it and yet—"

"I'm sure it's just a question of meeting the right woman," his mother said. "Wouldn't you agree, Mary?"

Devlin jerked his head around and saw that his sister-in-law had arrived. He stood, as did Caleb, and waited to sit until she'd lowered herself to the armchair adjacent to her husband's.

"There are men who never marry," Mary said.

The dowager duchess looked like she might have crossed herself if she'd been Catholic. "Please don't say that," she groaned while Devlin silently thanked Mary with a smile. She had certainly been the right woman for his brother. No doubt about that.

"Although," Mary added, causing Devlin to frown, "I would have thought that a man who's experienced as much as you, Devlin, would want to share it with his progeny, as a legacy of sorts."

"All I ask is for you to put in an appearance, chat with a few young ladies, and dance," the dowager duchess implored. And then, to ensure his compliance, she gazed directly into his eyes and said, "It would mean the world to me, Devlin."

Only a horrid, selfish, ungrateful son who didn't love his mother could say no to such a heartfelt request. Even if he knew she'd laid it on a bit thick. He sighed and took another bite from his sandwich while mulling over the situation. It wasn't what he'd been hoping for. Hell, what were the chances of Caleb, who hated *ton* fanfare as much as he did, suddenly deciding to host a ball at a time when *he* just happened to be in town? It was deuced unfortunate was what it was.

"Very well," he sighed, acknowledging there was no way out if he wanted to please his mother. "I shall put in an appearance and talk to a few young ladies. But I am only dancing one dance, after which I intend to remove myself to the card room." He eyed Caleb. "There will be a card room, won't there?"

"Of course," Caleb assured him.

"And also," Devlin said, deciding to do something nice for Monty, "I'd like to invite my good friend and first mate, Mr. Montgomery Quinn, and his wife to attend. They're not upper crust, but they're respectable enough and—"

"Your friend will be most welcome," Caleb said. "I look forward to making his acquaintance."

Later that evening, after the children had been tucked into bed and kissed goodnight, Mary sat at her vanity table, combing out her hair. "Your mother is up to something," she said, watching Caleb in her mirror.

He removed his cravat and padded across the carpet, positioning himself directly behind her. Taking the brush from her hand, he continued what she'd started.

"Whatever gave you that idea?" he murmured in that low tone that did funny things to her insides. After years of marriage, the effect he had on her hadn't faded one bit.

"Oh, I don't know," she told him wryly. "Perhaps the fact that you and I weren't planning to host a ball this Saturday."

"There is that," he agreed.

When he frowned, she felt compelled to say, "We don't have to do it, you know. I'm sure I can think of some excuse to get us out of it if you don't want the *ton* invading our home."

He sighed. "No. I suppose a Camberly ball is long overdue." Finishing with the brush, he set it aside and placed one hand on her shoulder. Their eyes met in the mirror. "Will you have enough time to plan it though?"

"I think I can manage if Emily and Cass help me write the invitations."

Caleb bent to press a kiss against her cheek, then straightened and smiled. "You have to make sure she's at the ball."

Mary didn't even try to pretend not to know to whom her husband referred. Three friends, two of whom had each married a Crawford brother, made it reasonable to surmise that the third would marry the last. Although...

"Cass has no intention of getting married."

"Neither does Dev," Caleb said as he offered his hand to Mary and helped her rise. "So they already have that in common."

She grinned. "You're terrible, you know that?"

"Terribly handsome?" he asked right before he pressed a kiss to her mouth. "Or terribly wicked?" he asked as he pushed her silk robe off her shoulders.

Mary simply sighed and gave herself up to her husband's caresses. There would be more time for logical thought and party planning in the morning.

CHAPTER TWO

THE LAST PLACE CASSANDRA MOOR wanted to be was at a ball. Not only because she considered it to be a colossal waste of time, seeing as she wasn't looking to marry and frankly hated dancing, but because it was one of those grand affairs to which every member of the *ton* had been invited. Which meant her parents were in attendance.

Hovering near the refreshment table where she could be somewhat obscured by a pillar, Cassandra peered through the throng of guests at the spot where Fiona and Charles Moor, the Earl and Countess of Vernon, stood. Since they were conversing with friends, Cassandra doubted they'd noticed her presence, which was just as well. The last time she'd seen her mother, the lady had crossed the street in order to avoid an embarrassing encounter with her ruined daughter. While Cassandra could appreciate the fact that she had gone and done the unthinkable by getting herself pregnant outside of wedlock, she'd always believed her parents should have loved her no matter what.

"Who are you hiding from?" a familiar voice asked.

Cassandra turned in response to Mary's question and saw that both she and Emily must have approached without her realizing. Jutting her chin a little to the left, Cassandra indicated the spot where her parents stood. "Who do you think?"

A sympathetic glimmer touched Mary's eyes. "I'm sorry about that, but they are the Earl and Countess of Vernon. It would have been bad form not to invite them."

"I know," Cassandra grumbled. She turned more fully toward her friends. "Had it occurred to me, I would have stayed away."

"Then it's a good thing it didn't occur to you," Emily said with a smile. "The evening wouldn't be the same without you."

"Thank you. I suppose." Cassandra rolled her eyes when both her friends chuckled. "I'm not really in Town for this sort of thing, however, and in a way I feel as though I'm being too lavish by coming here. It did require purchasing a new gown."

"And what a lovely gown it is," Mary said.

"You're allowed to pamper yourself every once in a while," Emily added. "At Clearview you hardly ever get the chance."

That was a bit of an understatement, Cassandra decided. The last time she'd attended an event near Clearview that even remotely resembled something as grand as this was six years ago when Caleb had been staying with her, Mary, and

Emily under an assumed identity.

"Speaking of Clearview," Mary said, "have you managed to work out an agreeable arrangement for the twelve-year-old girl who wrote to you?"

"Yes. Her aunt has finally released her into my custody." Like most of the children Cassandra had cared for over the years, Rosemary Clarence was an orphan. She'd written to Cassandra two months ago to inform her that her life had become intolerable after her father died and that she hoped there might be room for her at Clearview.

Cassandra frowned at the memory of what she'd discovered when she'd first gone to visit the girl's home. "That woman treated poor Rosemary as if she were her slave, not caring one whit about me being there. I've never seen anything like it."

"Well, it's a good thing you managed to wrestle Rosemary away from her evil clutches then," Emily said.

"How did you manage to do it?" Mary asked.

"How do you think?" Cassandra gave them both a meaningful stare. "I paid her a handsome sum of money."

"Well. I'm sure it's money well spent," Emily said. She moved to where a large pitcher of lemonade stood on the refreshment table and began filling three glasses. "Clearview will be good for someone like Rosemary who's been treated unkindly."

"How are things at Clearview going by the way?" Mary took one of the glasses Emily had filled and handed it to Cassandra. "You've been so busy while in Town, we've barely managed to talk. Hence my reason for insisting you join us this evening." She added a smirk then sipped her drink.

"All is well. As you know, Katherine is a tremendous help." The daughter of the Marquess of Stanhope, Katherine Donahugh, had fallen for one of the footmen in her father's employ. A child, now five years of age, had been the result, along with Stanhope's assurance that he wanted nothing further to do with Katherine or her bastard child. And since Katherine's fate was so similar to her own, Cassandra had sympathized deeply with her plight and offered she come live with her.

Together, they'd continued helping orphans until they reached the age of fourteen and required a more demanding education than the two women were able to provide. At this point, the children would move to Montvale Manor where Mary and Caleb took over, assisted by the tutors they'd hired.

"It is always a relief to hear you say so," Emily said. "Leaving you at Clearview by yourself so I could go off and get married has always made me feel guilty."

"It shouldn't. If you'll recall, Katherine moved in before you moved out." Taking a sip of her lemonade, Cassandra glanced back at where her parents had been standing and instantly froze. "Oh dear God, they're coming this way."

Her friends looked in the same direction as she. "Whatever happens," Mary murmured, "you have our support. They won't be allowed to be anything but cordial, or they shall have us to deal with."

"And our husbands," Emily said, alerting Cassandra to the fact that Caleb and Griffin were almost upon them. They'd been approaching from an angle that hadn't been within Cassandra's line of sight.

"Are you talking about us?" Griffin asked with a devilish smile as he came to stand next to his wife.

"Only in the context of the two of you possibly having to give the Earl and Countess of Vernon a set down, depending on how the next five minutes play out."

"And where is Devlin by the way?" Mary asked. "He promised he'd be here."

Cassandra's mouth went instantly dry. "Devlin's back?" How she managed to pose that question in a normal tone was beyond her. But she was grateful for her ability to do so.

"Arrived a few days ago," Caleb said. He seemed to survey the room. "Speaking of missing people, I haven't seen your brother either, Cass, and he assured me he'd be here."

"He's danced the last two sets with Vivien," Cassandra said. She'd actually been hoping he and her sister-in-law would soon be done so she could ask them if they could go home. She was staying with them during her visit, so they'd come to the ball together by carriage.

Another swift glance toward the spot where her parents had been moments earlier caused a cold bite of angst to grip Cassandra's spine. They still hadn't seen her, but they were awfully close and now…now there was the added risk of running into Devlin – the only man in the world whom she had to avoid at all cost.

"Thank you for a lovely evening," she said as she took a step back. "It's been delightful. Really."

"You're not leaving already, Cassandra?" Mary looked slightly miffed, though not the least bit surprised.

"I'm sorry, but I have to go."

"Don't worry about your parents," Emily told her. "We won't let them hurt you."

As much as Cassandra loved her friends for being so protective of her, she rather feared it was too late. Her parents had hurt her more than she would ever admit to anyone. "Thank you. But I prefer not to give them the chance. Please let Robert and Vivien know that I've gone back to their house."

And with that she turned and hurried away, following the periphery of the ballroom until she knew her parents were somewhere behind her. Breathing a sigh of relief, she walked toward the open doorway, content in the knowledge that no one would try to detain her. After all, who would want to be seen in a fallen woman's company anyway? And if there was any doubt in her mind about whether or not those present might have forgotten who she was or the scandal that clung to her name, it was swiftly dismissed by the critical glances and muted whispers to which she was now subjected.

Behind the pillar, she'd been safe. Out in the open, she was prey for the vultures.

Doing her best to feign disinterest, she straightened her spine, pulled back her shoulders, and marched past the lot of them, happy to climb the two steps leading out of the room and into the hallway. Until she almost collided with the one person besides her odious parents she'd been hoping to avoid.

Devlin Crawford, who'd been entering the ballroom as she'd been trying to exit, came to an instant halt. "Lady Cassandra," he murmured, as if surprised to find her there. His eyes, warm and dark and with a slight hint of mischief, met hers.

And in that instant Cassandra was reminded of all the reasons why she'd been hoping not to run into him this evening, which she'd almost quite literally done. And really, when she put her mind to it, she had to admit all her reasons actually equaled one: the fact that he made her knees grow weak and her heart start to gallop, and lord, she was scarcely herself when in his presence. Which was probably why he was staring at her as if she'd lost her head.

Which she had. More or less.

"Lord Devlin," she said, quite pleased with the level tone of her voice. "I did hear that you had returned."

The edges of his eyes crinkled in a charming sort of way as he smiled. "Indeed." He was quiet for a moment, during which Cassandra wondered if she ought to step out of his way since she was, in fact, blocking his path. But then he said, "I hope you're not leaving just yet."

"Now that you mention it—"

"For I promised my mother I'd dance at least one dance this evening. And dancing it with you, a longtime friend of the family's, would be infinitely better than having to engage a young debutante."

Cassandra knew he didn't mean to insult her and that she shouldn't be hurt by his referring to her as a friend, but somehow the comment still stung. Which was part of the problem. Because she'd loved Penelope's father with all her heart and he'd loved her back. They'd made promises to each other and dreamt of the future they'd share once they were married. One indiscretion, the night before the wedding, hadn't seemed like a bad idea at the time. They'd wanted to be together and knew they'd be man and wife the next day. But rather than the joyous occasion they'd both been expecting, tragedy had struck in the worst possible way. And Cassandra had never recovered from the news that Timothy Dorset, Earl of Lemfield and heir to the Marquess of Sussex, the man with whom she'd hoped to spend the rest of her life, had perished on his way to the church.

Now, thirteen years later, she was just as aware as she had been back then that falling for anyone else would be a betrayal. So the guilt that sank its venomous teeth into her conscience each time Devlin made her cheeks flush or her skin start to tingle or her heart begin racing was what propelled her to keep her distance from him.

"I'd rather not," she said, then took a deep breath. "The last time we danced I stepped on your feet at least five times." She'd been out of practice and incredibly nervous.

He smiled – that lopsided smile she loved so well. It melted her bones. "That's a very long time ago," he said, offering her his arm, "and it really wasn't so bad."

Cassandra glanced past his shoulder, at the front door barely visible at the end of the hallway. In that moment it seemed so close and yet so horribly far away. "I really must go," she tried.

"And so you will. Right after this set."

And that was when she realized his insistence was based on more than his wish to avoid some young lady eager to snatch the last of the Crawford men. It also had a lot to do with the fact that their conversation was starting to attract attention. People were beginning to stare, which meant she could no longer leave without causing a stir or encouraging gossip. As it was, it might be too late, but at least she still had the power to ensure that the gossip remained positive and that it would not reflect poorly on any of the Crawfords.

"You owe me," she muttered between clenched teeth as she placed her hand in his and allowed him to lead her toward the dance floor. The moment she touched him a bolt of lightning raced up her arm. She groaned and wished she'd stayed at her brother's home for the evening.

"Duly noted," Devlin said in response to her comment. With the sort of elegance that ought to have been impossible for a man who was over six feet in height and possessed shoulders twice the width of hers, he spun her into position.

Cassandra instinctively gasped in response to the unexpected movement, and then the music began and she realized whatever nightmare she was currently living had just gotten worse, because this was no simple country dance or even a quadrille, cotillion, or reel. This was the waltz of all things and that meant close contact with one's partner and…

"Cass?"

Startled, she tripped and promptly planted her foot right on top of his shoe. "Sorry."

If she'd hurt him, he didn't let it show. Instead he tightened his hold on her hand and pulled her into a more secure position, bringing her shockingly close to his person. "Is something the matter?"

"No. Of course not. Why would you suppose such a thing?"

He gave her an incredulous stare. "Because you've been looking like a trapped rabbit since the moment I arrived."

"Well, I *was* trying to leave until you decided to stop me."

Inclining his head, he gave her a roguish smile while leading her in a wide arc that took them along the edge of the dance floor. "It's good to see you again. I probably should have mentioned that first."

She felt her cheeks grow warm and hoped he wouldn't notice her blush. "You weren't away quite as long as the last time, I don't think."

"Were you counting the days until my return?" He waggled his eyebrows and spun her sideways.

"Only so I could make sure to be out of Town by the time you dropped anchor." Which wasn't entirely untrue, though she did intend for it to be a joke.

He laughed, causing a pair of perfect dimples to form on either side of his mouth. Cassandra deliberately looked away. Her heart had belonged and always would belong to Timothy. To feel something even remotely similar toward another man was wrong. Plain and simple.

"I've always enjoyed our conversations, Cass." She liked the shortened version of her name, even though it was also used by everyone else who was close to her and therefore meant nothing beyond a familiar bond. "There's a straightforward openness to you along with a great degree of maturity and common sense."

She snorted. "Many would argue with you on that point."

"Why? Because you did something once that resulted in bringing a lovely little girl into this world?" When she gazed up at him and nodded, he smiled down at her and said, "I would never call that a lapse in judgment or a mistake. And those inclined to do so are fools."

Cassandra would have liked to say she got something in her eye at that moment, but the truth was that his understanding, most especially his acceptance of Penelope, practically slayed her. If she wasn't so determined to remain faithful to Timothy, she'd probably do something foolish like ask Devlin to marry her right then and there. At present, a nod was all she could manage, for her throat had turned into a giant knot, and she feared she might break down at any second and blubber all over him like a nitwit. Gracious, even her heart hurt, not with sadness but with overwhelming amounts of gratitude.

His expression had also tightened, as if the moment was affecting him emotionally as well. He cleared his throat and tightened his hold on her hand. "I'm sorry for all you've had to suffer. It isn't right."

"It's the way of the world," she managed to say once she'd taken a moment to compose herself. She tried to smile but it felt awfully strained.

"And part of the reason I try to avoid Society as much as possible." He snorted. "Once you've travelled to other countries and experienced other cultures, all of this – the rules that govern us British – seems utterly trivial."

"I've always envied you your ability to travel and see the world." She didn't miss the look of surprise in his eyes as she said it.

"Really? I would have thought you'd want to remain in England, more specifically at Clearview, considering all the children in your care."

"Well, of course." A chuckle escaped her when he surprised her by spinning her quickly around before settling into a steadier pace. "I can't actually go anywhere, but that doesn't mean there isn't a part of me that doesn't like to dream."

A flash of appreciation lit his eyes. The music faded and he guided her to a graceful halt. "Thank you for dancing with me," he said as he led her off the dance floor and toward the doorway through which she'd been planning to escape when he'd arrived. "I hope our paths cross again before I leave England."

"As do I," Cassandra replied, even though she had no intention of letting that happen. The feelings he'd stirred in her tonight were too powerful, too tempting, and entirely too dangerous. Which meant it would be best if she returned to Clearview as quickly as possible.

Devlin watched Cassandra walk away. He'd always found her pleasing to the eye, her curvaceous figure the sort that could capture a man's imagination for hours. She was also one of the prettiest women he'd ever known, with her lustrous brown hair, exotic green eyes, and a lush mouth that always seemed ready to smile.

But she was a close friend of Mary's and Emily's – the three were practically sisters – so chasing after Cassandra without the proper intentions would only result in him getting flogged by Caleb and Griffin. A pity, since he'd long believed she was equally drawn to him. For although she hid it well, her frequent blushes while in his company, the breathiness to her voice, and the way she always seemed to tremble whenever he touched her, revealed he was more than able to make her burn with desire.

"Devlin!"

He took a deep breath, expelled it while watching Cassandra exit through the front door, and turned. "Good evening, Mother." There was nothing like her to put an end to his improper thoughts.

"You cheated." Her arms were crossed and her brow knit in a disapproving scowl. "When I asked you to dance this evening, I meant with a debutante, not with Lady Cassandra, who's—"

"What?" Devlin felt the muscles in his back begin to bunch with annoyance. "Think very carefully before you finish that sentence, Mother."

Her eyes widened with what appeared to be shocked disbelief. And then she took a step closer to him so she could whisper, "Just so you know, I am extremely fond of Cassandra. It would never occur to me to speak of her disparagingly." She leaned back a little and sighed. "All I meant to say is that you might have tried dancing with a woman who'd be interested in marrying you."

"First of all," Devlin said, forcing his temper back under control, "you know perfectly well that I don't wish to marry. And second of all," he added before his mother had a chance to argue, "what makes you certain Cassandra wouldn't be interested?"

"Because," the dowager duchess explained with the patience of someone addressing an infant, "if she were, I believe you would have married her years ago."

"What the…" Devlin caught a look of interest from one of the guests and instantly turned his back on the nosy female. He lowered his voice even further and asked, "What on earth do you mean by—"

"Devlin. Mother." Caleb's well-rounded tone demanded attention. And so Devlin gave it to him. "You two look like a pair of conspirators, whispering over here in the corner. Care to tell me what's going on?"

"Not especially," Devlin grumbled, then added, "I'm sorry I'm late."

"No matter." Caleb glanced from one to the other then told the dowager duchess, "I believe your friend, the Duchess of Chitilla, is looking for you."

"In that case, you must excuse me." She gave Devlin a hard look. "One more dance, Dev. You owe me." And then she was off.

Owe her?

For what? Giving him life?

"I gather our dear mama wasn't pleased with your trying to placate her by dancing with Cass."

"She insists I give it another go."

"And will you?"

Devlin looked Caleb straight in the eye. "Of course not." He'd done as he'd promised, whether his mother agreed or not. Glancing away, he searched the room until he located Monty, then raised his hand to draw his attention. "Wouldn't mind a drink outside on the terrace though. Care to join me?"

Caleb nodded. "Certainly."

"Have you met my first mate and longtime friend, Mr. Quinn?" Devlin asked as soon as Monty had reached them.

"We exchanged a few words when he and his wife arrived," Caleb said.

Monty gave Devlin a nod by way of greeting. "One would think you'd be more punctual when you live at the place where the ball is held." The edge of his mouth pulled upward. "Was there a great deal of traffic between your bedchamber and the downstairs, Dev?"

"Ho, I like you," Caleb told Monty while Devlin did his best to maintain a serious expression.

"Mm…" Devlin muttered. "You wouldn't believe the sort of impassable pile-up that can occur on a landing." The three men laughed. When their mirth faded, Devlin said, "We were just discussing drinks on the terrace, Monty, and I thought you might like to join us."

"Sounds like a splendid idea to me," Monty said. He tugged at his cravat. "The fresh air would do me good."

"It's settled then," Caleb said. "Let's go."

They each snatched a glass of champagne from a serving tray as they went, then headed toward a pair of French doors made almost entirely of glass. Once outside, they removed themselves to a private spot a little off to one side where they could talk openly without too much chance of being overheard.

"So," Monty said in that way he so often did when he was about to broach an uncomfortable topic. "The woman you danced with…"

Devlin clasped his glass a bit harder. "What about her?"

"Is something the matter with her?"

"What?" Devlin almost spat the champagne he'd just drunk back out.

Monty shrugged. "There were a lot of whispers, so naturally I—"

"Lady Cassandra is a close friend of the family's," Caleb said, apparently sensing Devlin would more likely sputter than speak if he tried to say something else at the moment. "She's the Earl of Vernon's daughter, which made it all the more scandalous twelve years ago when she had a daughter out of wedlock."

"Could she not have married?" Monty asked. "Surely there must have been someone willing to take on the task of raising her child in order to gain an attachment to such a prestigious title."

"If she received any offers," Devlin said, "she turned them all down. As far as I know, she's content to be a spinster with a bastard child, however unusual that may be."

"*You* could have asked her," Caleb said. "After meeting her, that is."

Devlin frowned and took another sip of his drink. "I've as little interest in marriage as she does."

Monty made an "hmm" sound that clearly

demanded further investigation, but Devlin forgot all about responding the moment he heard a lady say, "I cannot believe the duke and duchess would think to invite her." The speaker had just stepped onto the terrace a few yards from where Devlin stood.

"It is my understanding that she and the duchess are dear friends," another voice gently advised.

"Well yes. There is that, I suppose. But to not consider the Vernons' feelings really is bad form." There was a small sniff. "Can you imagine having your scandalous daughter make a spectacle on the dance floor for all the world to see? I mean, honestly! She practically threw herself at him, poor man." There was an outraged snort. "As if Lord Devlin would ever consider marrying the likes of her. The mere thought of it is—"

"What?" Devlin asked stepping forward. He set his glass aside and faced the spiteful shrew. His head felt like it might explode at any given second. In fact, strangling the woman before him was not an implausible outcome. He stared her down while digging his fingernails into his palms. "The mere thought of me marrying Lady Cassandra is what, madam?"

"I…ugh…" The shrew gaped at him as if he were some sort of statue who'd suddenly come to life. And then she said, "I am Baroness DeVries. A lady of the peerage."

Devlin deliberately grunted, then proceeded to stare her down.

"I don't believe he cares about that," the baroness's friend muttered.

She was right. The only thing Devlin cared about at that precise moment was seeing justice served. Because Cassandra was one of the finest people he'd ever known and she deserved to be defended. Even if that meant forcing the horrid baroness to choke on her own words.

"Yes?" he inquired in an eerily quiet voice that managed to turn his own stomach. "You were saying?"

"Um…merely that…er…" She glanced at her friend while fidgeting with her gloves but when she found no help there, she surprised Devlin by raising her chin and looking him dead in the eye. "You are a duke's brother for heaven's sake and she is nothing but a—"

"Lady DeVries," Caleb snapped.

"—trollop," the baroness finished, punctuating her statement with a victorious smile.

What she couldn't see was the blood rushing through Devlin's veins or the tight strain of his muscles. Never in his life had he been so livid, and if Lady DeVries had been a man, he would have called her out by now so he could have the pleasure of shooting her dead.

"Devlin," Caleb murmured from somewhere nearby. "Don't do anything rash. I beg you."

But the middle-aged woman who stood before Devlin, dripping with smug maliciousness, had pushed him past all reason. "And what makes you so much better?" he asked.

Lady DeVries gasped. Her friend gulped, took

a step back, and then fled back inside the ball-room, abandoning the baroness to her fate. Caleb groaned and Monty managed to get in a weary, "For God's sake, Dev," before Lady DeVries recovered and said, "I will not be spoken to in such a rude manner. I deserve better."

"So does Lady Cassandra."

The baroness crossed her arms. "Don't be absurd. She might have been born into the nobility, but she threw all of that away the moment she chose to—"

"Madam," Devlin seethed, "I would advise you to choose your next words wisely."

"Or what?"

"Or I shall have to ask you to leave," Caleb said.

The baroness scoffed — scoffed! — in response to her host's statement, but Caleb apparently chose to let it go without comment. "Why am I not surprised?" she asked as she turned away and started toward the French doors leading back to the ball-room. But just when Devlin thought that might be the end of their quarrel, she turned back to face him with all the arrogance Devlin despised about the aristocracy. "Lady Cassandra is a fallen woman. When even her parents can see that, I don't understand why you find it such a hard concept to grasp."

"Oh, Jesus," Monty murmured.

Devlin speared Lady DeVries with his hardest glare. "You will not speak of her in that manner."

"As much as I respect your family, I hardly think it appropriate for you to advise me on how I may or may not refer to a person of such low moral standing as Lady Cassandra."

Maybe it was the fact that he'd just gotten off a ship after several months at sea, maybe it was the champagne—though he seriously doubted it, or maybe it was the fact that he'd really enjoyed seeing Cassandra again that finally made Devlin come up with something completely unplanned and, quite possibly, cataclysmic. What he did know was that he could think of only one way in which to give Cassandra the stamp of approval necessary to make this woman regret her words.

Blind with rage and as he'd later admit not entirely clear-headed, he ignored Caleb's words of warning and leaned toward the baroness. Meeting her gaze with all the hatred he possessed for her at that moment, he said, "It bloody well is when she is to be my wife."

CHAPTER THREE

THE SILENCE THAT FOLLOWED WAS such that Devlin could hear his own heartbeats. *Thump, thump. Thump, thump.*

Oh, dear mother of God, what had he done?

He blinked, startled by the words he'd heard himself speak. And Lady DeVries – her mouth kept opening and closing like a mackerel gasping for air. Which was probably the only reward he would get from his lack of restraint.

Devlin unclenched his fists and leaned back slowly. Now he would have to figure out what to do next. He glanced at Caleb and Monty. Both men stared at him as if he'd lost his mind. And they weren't entirely wrong. Within a few minutes, Lady DeVries had driven him to madness, and he, foolish man, had allowed her to do so.

"You and Lady Cassandra Moor?" the baroness screeched. Devlin turned to face her. A knot had formed at the base of his throat and his lungs felt horribly constricted. Unable to speak, he nodded.

"Well!" Outrage squeezed her features together in an ugly manner. "And to think I was hoping you'd give your attentions to my Lucinda." She sniffed with obvious disdain. "Thank you for inviting me here this evening, Camberly. Unfortunately, the company has proven too intolerable for my tastes. I shall see myself out."

"Please do," Caleb told her retreating form.

"I don't suppose there's a hope in hell of her never mentioning what occurred on this terrace?" Devlin asked once she'd gone.

"It's unlikely," Caleb said. "And even if she were to keep silent, the rest of the witnesses probably won't."

"What?"

"Did you forget we weren't the only people out here?" Monty asked.

Devlin turned and saw only his brother and friend. Until they tilted their heads to the left. Certain he was about to have his worst nightmares realized, Devlin looked toward the other side of the terrace. His stomach dropped and his heart stopped beating. Or at least that was how it felt. Because there, off to the side, were no fewer than ten guests, all staring at him in shock.

"Christ." His hands were trembling, no longer from anger but from panic. "What have I done?" The question kept repeating inside his head. He met Caleb's solemn expression. "What the hell have I just done?"

"You saved a friend's reputation," Caleb told him.

"But at what cost?" He looked to Monty, then back to Caleb. "She'll never forgive me for this." And who could blame her when he'd just gone and ruined her life?

"Let's think about it for a moment," Caleb suggested. His voice was calm, if a bit strained. "It might not be as terrible as you fear."

"Marriage can be a wonderful thing," Monty said, "and considering your longstanding friendship with the lady in question, she might not be averse to the notion of having you for a husband."

"I've actually always imagined the two of you ending up together one day. So has Mary." Hands in his pockets, Caleb rocked back on his heels and smiled. "Yes, this could quite possibly be a blessing in disguise."

Devlin could only gape at them both. Apparently Monty thought Cassandra might want this while Caleb had secretly been picturing a love match between him and Cassandra for God knew how long. Frustrated, mostly with himself, he raked his fingers through his hair. Soft, lyrical music drifted onto the terrace. Partially bathed in moonlight, it served as the perfect setting for a big romance, yet it had now become the scene of his greatest blunder.

"Don't forget," Caleb said, "giving Cass your name will also help Penelope."

There was truth to be found in those words. And yet…the optimism they stirred was fleeting. "I don't want to be tied to England, and that's precisely what a wife and daughter will do."

"Something you might have wanted to consider ten minutes ago before you announced your engagement," Monty said.

Caleb nodded. "Although you do have some options that don't require being tied down. For one thing, you could take Cass and Penelope with you. Or," he added when Devlin opened his mouth to protest, "you could leave them here while you head off to sea."

The second option might work, he supposed, even though he'd always sworn he would never abandon a wife and child for extended periods of time. Monty did it though, so maybe it wouldn't be nearly as hard as he imagined. Especially since he and Cassandra would not be marrying for love.

Devil take it, she didn't even know her fate yet.

Devlin swallowed convulsively. "I have to go to Aldridge House and—"

"What the hell are you playing at, Crawford?"

Devlin turned in response to the curt tone and found himself face to face with a very angry looking viscount. Not just any viscount though. This particular one was named Aldridge, and he was Cassandra's older brother. He was also one of Caleb's best friends, so Devlin generally addressed him by his given name, which was Robert.

"I, um…" Devlin wisely stopped himself before uttering something truly idiotic like, I misspoke. Instead he squared his shoulders and met the other man's hard gaze head on. "Your sister is a remarkable woman. I hold her in the highest regard and look forward to the prospect of marrying her."

Robert didn't move. His expression remained like stone, hardening even further when he spoke. "Is that why you chose not to ask my father for her hand? Because of how eager you are to make her your wife?"

His accusation struck Devlin firmly in the gut, but what was done was done and the only thing to do now was make the most of it. And frankly, the notion of asking Vernon for permission to marry his daughter would not have entered Devlin's mind even if he'd decided to do things properly. "Considering the lack of understanding your parents showed Cassandra when they learned she was pregnant, I hardly think either of them deserves a say."

"What about me then?"

"Well…um…" Devlin scratched the back of his head.

Robert narrowed his gaze. "She doesn't know about any of this yet. Does she?"

Devlin's shoulders slumped and he sighed heavily. "No."

"He was trying to defend her honor," Monty said.

"Lady DeVries was being disgustingly cruel," Caleb added.

"I won't bother asking how that could possibly lead to you announcing your engagement to Cass," Robert said to Devlin, "but you ought to know that I am not about to make her marry you if she doesn't want to."

Devlin stared at Robert. "But there will be talk if we don't go through with it now. Her reputation will be ruined."

"No more than it already is, I'll wager." Robert straightened his back. "You forget that when she refused to do as our parents suggested, which was to marry quickly so she could pass her child off as somebody else's, I supported her decision. I bought a house for her in Cornwall where she could live the peaceful life she desired. And as I understand it, she has been very happy there these past thirteen years."

"I will have to convince her then," Devlin said. An odd pain squeezed at his heart. Having recovered somewhat from his spur of the moment decision to do what he'd never intended to do, he rather liked the idea of marrying Cassandra. Curiously, the chance of getting out of it didn't excite him as much as it ought to. On the contrary, he was starting to hope she'd be amicable to the idea, which could only mean that the madness he'd suffered while facing down Lady DeVries still lingered.

"Do that and you'll have my blessing," Robert said. "I've always liked your family, so being related through marriage would not be the worst. As long as this is what Cass wants. Her happiness is paramount, Devlin. Understand?"

Devlin nodded and gave his agreement. He then shook hands with Robert and promised to call on Cassandra the very next day. He'd have to bring a cartload of flowers to make up for what he had done. And even then he feared it would not be enough.

"What on earth are you on about?" Cassandra

asked when she woke the next morning to find both her brother and sister-in-law sitting at the foot of her bed. The first words out of Robert's mouth the moment she'd opened her eyes had included marriage, Devlin Crawford, and a Baroness De Somethingorother. Yawning, she pushed herself into a sitting position, blew a stray lock of hair out of her eyes, and leaned back against the headboard. "I didn't think Devlin wanted to marry."

"There's still a chance he doesn't," Vivien said with a strange look of sympathy in her eyes. Robert shushed her, which was also incredibly strange.

"Then why would he get engaged to a baroness?" Cassandra asked. Her brain was slowly waking up, and she was starting to feel more herself.

Vivien and Robert shared a concerned look. Robert took a deep breath. "You misunderstand, Cass. Devlin isn't marrying the baroness."

"Oh. I see." She frowned, then shook her head. "Actually I don't. I thought you just told me—"

"He says he's marrying *you*!"

Cassandra stilled. And then she laughed, because really, nothing could possibly be more ridiculous than Devlin announcing he'd marry her of all people. At a ball, no less, without her there and without having gained her approval. Only, when her laughter died down and she looked at Vivien and Robert, neither was smiling.

A tremor of unease slithered down Cassandra's spine. "You are joking, are you not?"

"Sadly not," Robert said. "But if it is any consolation—"

"I cannot believe he would do such a thing!" Whatever humor she'd found in her brother's earlier words was gone. In its place was extreme irritation along with the awful feeling of having been used in some foolish show of masculine power. What else would compel a man to act so high handedly, without any thought to her wishes?

"Robert says he was trying to defend your honor," Vivien said.

"Ha!" Cassandra had climbed out of bed and was now selecting the clothes she would wear. "As if I am supposed to be grateful. Well, I am not. And you may feel free to tell him so the next time you see him."

"I expect you shall see him soon yourself, Cass," Robert said gently. "He did say he would call on you today in order to explain things."

"Then he will be disappointed since I have no intention of being here when he shows up." She stood, clutching a day dress and a shawl while Robert and Vivien stared at her expectantly. "I wasn't planning to go back to Clearview until tomorrow, but given what has happened, I shall have to depart right away."

"I suspected this might be your decision," Robert said. "And you should know that we support it wholeheartedly."

Cassandra's eyes began to prick most uncomfortably. She sniffed. "No other brother would be so understanding."

"Of course not," Robert said with an easy smile and a shrug. "I am without doubt the very best of brothers."

"And husbands," Vivien told him loyally. She stood and gave Cassandra a hug. "I'll ask Cook to pack a lunch for you and Penelope to share on the road."

"And I shall have the carriage readied," Robert said. He followed his wife out of the room, leaving Cassandra to wake her daughter and pack with haste. The sooner they left the house, the less chance there was of having to face Devlin Crawford.

It was just after nine o'clock when Devlin awoke. Ten, by the time he made it downstairs for breakfast. Caleb and Mary were still at the table, though their children, who were always allowed to join their parents for meals when only family was present, must have scampered off. Four empty plates with bits of leftover toast marked the spots where they'd been sitting.

"Good morning," Devlin said as he strode to the sideboard. The eggs and bacon smelled delicious.

Caleb and Mary returned his greeting. A rustling sound followed as Caleb set the newspaper he'd been reading aside and said, "I should congratulate you on making the headlines."

Devlin crossed to the table, pulled out a chair and sat. A frown strained his brow. "I didn't think my return to England was interesting enough to warrant so much attention." Because that was the only thing the newspaper could possibly have written about. Surely there wouldn't have been enough time for it to contain any news about—

"No, you dolt, it's about your engagement."

Devlin promptly choked on a piece of bacon. Coughing, he reached for his cup, which he'd not yet filled.

"Oh dear," Mary murmured. "Here, allow me." She poured some coffee and added enough milk to cool it down.

Managing a nod of appreciation between two more coughs, Devlin drank. "What," he croaked, "does it say?"

"Lord Devlin Crawford has announced his engagement to Lady Cassandra Moor," Caleb declared with a flourish.

Well, that wasn't too bad, Devlin supposed, although he would have preferred if the news had not gotten out for another day. It would have been nice if he'd had a chance to talk to Cassandra first. "I have to get over to Aldridge House right away." Hell, he'd probably have a fuming fiancée by the time he got there.

"I'd say." The newspaper crackled between Caleb's hands. "Because there is more to the article than the headline alone."

"Like what?" Devlin asked. He took a careful bite of his food to avoid it going down the wrong way again.

"It's not terrible," Mary said when Caleb didn't answer. She sipped her tea and then pursed her lips. "But I'm not sure Cass will be pleased."

"Of course she won't," Devlin muttered. "It must be quite shocking for her to wake up to the fact that she's to be married."

"Provided she wants to," Caleb reminded him. "Robert did say he'll let her decide what to do."

"Of course, but..." Devil take it, he was letting himself get distracted. He shook his head. "What else does the paper say?"

Caleb met his gaze for a second, albeit long enough for Devlin's nerves to contract with unease, then read, "Last night's ball at Camberly House has without a doubt been the most eventful one of the Season. Lord Devlin Crawford, having recently arrived home from one of his seafaring journeys, barely made his entrance before engaging the Marquess and Marchioness of Vernon's spinster daughter, Lady Cassandra Moor, in a dance. As a close friend of the Crawford family, this would not have been entirely shocking, if the dance in question had not been a waltz *and* if Lord Devlin had danced with other young ladies first. But," Caleb proceeded, not allowing Devlin to interject, "the greatest shock of the evening came after Lady Cassandra had taken her leave and Lord Devlin announced his intention to marry her. One has to wonder if Lady DeVries did not press the gentleman to reveal what has surely been a well-kept secret and how Lady Cassandra will respond to finding herself at the center of gossip and scandal once more."

"How," Devlin managed to spit out the moment his brother was finished, "is that not terrible?"

"Well, at least it is honest," Mary said. But her eyes were filled with the sort of concern that caused Devlin's insides to shrivel.

"I have to go," he said right before wolfing down the rest of his food and finishing off his coffee. He wiped his mouth with his napkin and stood. "As it is, Mother is going to kill me." She'd looked ready to do so last night, but he'd managed to make his escape before she had the opportunity to let him have it.

"Perhaps." Tilting his head, Caleb studied Devlin for a moment before asking, "Do you want me to come with you?"

Devlin considered his offer, then shook his head. "No. Thank you. I'll handle this on my own. But I would be grateful if there's a ring among the family heirlooms that you'll let me have."

"Oh, indeed!" Mary practically leapt to her feet. "I'll have the jewelry boxes brought down right away." She dashed from the room.

Caleb grinned, then turned to Devlin. "Don't look so glum. Having a wife and children is a blessing. You'll realize that soon enough."

Devlin wasn't so sure. There was, after all, a difference between marrying for love, as Caleb and Griffin had both done, and marrying out of necessity.

There was also a very big difference between a willing bride and an unwilling one, he learned when he was admitted to the Aldridge House parlor a little over an hour later.

"What do you mean she's gone?" Clutching the

impressive bouquet of roses he'd purchased on his way over, and with what he considered a stunning ring nestled securely in his pocket, Devlin stared at Robert. "Gone where?"

"Back to Clearview." Robert gestured toward a chair, inviting Devlin to sit, but Devlin's feet refused to move. "She left almost three hours ago."

When he'd just been starting to rise. Devlin scrubbed his jaw with his hand. "I thought she was going to be in Town for at least two more days."

"That was before she learned of last night's events."

This wasn't how it was supposed to go. Nothing was as it should be anymore, so perhaps…perhaps Cassandra turning him down was for the best. She would in all likelihood go on much as before since she rarely mingled with Society anyway. Clearview kept her busy. She didn't lack company or a purpose and she already had a child of her own, never mind all the ones she'd taken into her care. So what could he really offer?

He had no intention of staying in England, which meant they would mostly be living apart. Of course, while he was home, he'd take great pleasure in warming her bed, provided she'd let him. Devlin frowned. As much as making love to Cassandra appealed to him, there had to be a better reason for them to marry. The threat of scandal obviously wasn't enough, so then…

Something his brother had said last night came

back to him with a pang. It wasn't just about Cassandra. It was also about her daughter and the future she would have as an illegitimate child. He was a captain, accustomed to being responsible for others. The fate of those who depended upon him mattered. And while Cassandra might not need his help, he knew Penelope did.

Certain he was making the right decision, he handed Robert the bouquet of flowers intended for Cassandra. "I'm going after her then."

"Are you sure?"

"Yes, damn it, I'm sure." He and Cassandra had one thing in common and that was their dogged determination to see things through to the end. But it was also the sort of determination that could easily blind a person if one wasn't careful. Angered and possibly even a little hurt, Cassandra was acting purely on instinct by running away. But in so doing, she'd neglected to think of her child, which meant Devlin would have to do so for her.

CHAPTER FOUR

I T TOOK THREE DAYS FOR Cassandra to reach Clearview. Initially, she'd feared Devlin might show up at one of the inns she'd stayed at along the way, but in the end, the journey had been uneventful. Penelope and Rosemary, whom she'd managed to pick up on her way out of Town, had played several games to keep themselves occupied. In between, Cassandra had read to the girls from *The Swiss Family Robinson.*

"You're back sooner than I expected," Katherine said upon Cassandra's arrival.

"Only by a couple of days." Cassandra introduced Rosemary and was just about to suggest showing her around when Penelope grabbed the girl's hand and pulled her inside the house.

"We'll have tea and biscuits in the parlor in fifteen minutes," Katherine called after them.

Cassandra smiled. "I think she'll settle in nicely, don't you?"

"Oh, indeed."

They let the coachman help with the luggage and asked if he'd like to stay for some refreshments.

"Thank you, but I'd rather get to the village inn and rest before heading back to London in the morning."

Once he was gone, Cassandra followed Katherine into the kitchen. Laughter drifted toward her from other parts of the house and filled her heart with joy. As much as she loved seeing her brother and her friends, it was good to be home.

"What made you return so soon?" Katherine asked once she'd hung a kettle over the fire.

"Actually, if you can believe it—" Cassandra grabbed some cups and saucers and placed them on a tray "—Devlin Crawford announced his intention to marry me."

The tin can Katherine had been collecting from a shelf clattered to the floor. "I beg your pardon?" When Cassandra said nothing, Katherine scooped up the fallen tin and set it on the counter. She looked bewildered. "Since you're here ahead of schedule, I can only assume you turned him down."

"No. I did not."

"What?"

Cassandra sighed. "To do so he would have had to ask me to be his wife. Which he did not."

Katherine's mouth dropped open. She blinked, took a moment to collect herself, and then said, "I don't believe I can wait for this story until after the children have had their tea." She perched herself on the edge of a stool. "Can you give me a quick summary?"

Cassandra did – or rather, she related what the

details were to the best of her knowledge. Her friend said nothing until Cassandra finished with, "So there you have it."

"Well, in that case we should probably start preparing the cottage." Katherine added tea leaves to the tea pot and went to fetch the kettle.

Cassandra frowned. "Whatever for?"

She was met by a do-I-seriously-need-to-explain-it-to-you sort of look that ended with a sigh. "Because if Devlin Crawford is half as persistent as you have described him to be, then I'll wager he's on his way here right now."

Cassandra insisted this wasn't the case. She told herself repeatedly that only a man in love would behave so rashly. Yes, Devlin might have mistakenly said they would marry, but once he recovered from his blunder and realized she had no intention of going through with an actual wedding, she was sure he'd let the matter go. Of course, it might take a while for people to stop talking about what would now be labeled a broken engagement, but with Devlin away as much as he was, she doubted he'd be troubled by any additional gossip. As a man, it was far more likely he would go on as if none of this foolishness had happened.

It was an uplifting notion, though sadly one she was forced to dismiss the very next morning when she entered the kitchen and found him there, slouched in one of the chairs while his feet rested on another.

Too stunned to think or to deliberate over him being asleep, she blurted the first words to enter her heard with zero finesse. "What do you think you're doing in my kitchen?"

Devlin started. Uttering a series of short half-finished snores, he opened his eyes and scrambled out of the chair so fast he almost knocked it over. He cleared his throat and shook his head. His hair, Cassandra noted, was mussed while his eyes conveyed the bewilderment of someone who'd woken to unfamiliar surroundings. To her annoyance, there was a sheepishness about him that made him look rather adorable.

She placed both hands on her hips and glared.

"I…um…er…" He pushed a lock of hair away from his forehead. "I came to find you."

"Well, you've done so." Moving farther into the room, she began collecting the items she needed to start breakfast. "If you're hungry, I can give you something to eat before you leave."

"But…" He was silent a moment while she lit the fire and added water to the kettle. "Cass, I came here to talk to you."

"You needn't have," she said, her irritation with him increasing until it began transforming to anger. "My departure from London should have made clear my position on this idiotic scheme of yours."

"It isn't exactly a scheme," he grumbled, rubbing his eyes.

Lord, how she wanted to wring his neck, although upon further inspection, she wasn't quite sure she'd be able to get her hands all the way around it. She sighed with frustration and told him plainly, "If you put your boot in your mouth then that's your problem. Not mine." Doing her best to pretend he wasn't standing right there staring at her as if *she* were the one who'd lost half her brain, Cassandra cracked some eggs into a bowl and proceeded to whisk them with great ferocity.

"I'm sorry," he said once the eggs were cooking on a pan alongside some bacon. "I shouldn't have said what I did, but Lady DeVries made me so bloody furious." He blew out a heavy breath. "She insulted you, Cass, and I couldn't let it pass."

It was difficult not to sympathize a little when his intensions had been so noble, but it didn't make his actions any less damning. "So," she said, waving a spatula in his direction, "rather than simply arguing her point or offering a clever retort, you decided to head for the altar?"

"Offering my protection seemed like the best way to make the horrid woman shut up." His eyes bore into hers with the intensity of a man who'd ridden into battle for her and lived to tell about it. "I respect you too much to let anyone tarnish your name, Cass, and…now that I've had a few days to think matters through, I've concluded that getting married might not be so terrible."

A half strangled choking sound escaped her. Just when she thought he was starting to sound sensible, he went and ruined it with more foolish words. "Then I wish you luck finding a bride, Devlin, because—"

"I know it's a big decision." He took a step closer to where she stood, causing her to turn away and start slicing a loaf of bread. "Getting married was never part of my plan either, but the thing of it is, I like you and…I hope you don't take offense to me saying this, but I do consider you a friend and as such, I'd like to help."

The knife came down a hair's breadth away from her finger. "Help? How is springing a surprise engagement on me helping? How is having my name emblazoned on the front page of *The Mayfair Chronicle* with words like 'spinster' and 'scandal' immediately beneath it helpful? How is—"

"It's not just about you, Cass," Devlin murmured.

His voice was whisper quiet – frighteningly so – for it made her feel like an axe was about to come crashing down over her head. "What are you saying?"

"There's also Penelope to consider."

Cassandra gripped the breadknife while the blood flowing through her veins turned to ice. She was half tempted to go for Devlin's throat. Instead she held herself utterly still and forced back the tears now pricking her eyes. "Get out."

"Ca—"

"I said," she told him more firmly while taking a step in his direction. "Get. Out!"

"Cassandra, is everything all right?" Katherine's gentle voice was a stark contrast to Cassandra's trembling nerves.

Swallowing, she glanced toward the doorway where her friend stood and shook her head. "We have an uninvited guest," she gritted.

"I can see that," Katherine said with exasperating slowness. "You must be Lord Devlin."

Devlin smiled with a sickening amount of charm and executed a gracious bow. "At your service, Miss…"

Cassandra rolled her eyes. "*Lady* Katherine Donahugh."

"Enchanted," he murmured, his attention solely on Katherine, whose cheeks immediately turned a bright shade of pink. And then she giggled – *giggled!* – like a young girl who'd just received a posy from the boy she fancied. It was enough to make Cassandra gag.

"You should have told me how handsome he is," Katherine said without any attempt at lowering her voice.

Cassandra coughed and instantly went back to tending the eggs and bacon which were close to being done. "I didn't think it was worth mentioning," she grumbled.

"What was that?" Devlin asked.

"She says she mentioned it," Katharine chirped.

Cassandra spun around and came face to face with her friend, whose raised eyebrows and cheeky smile informed Cassandra that getting rid of Devlin would be no simple matter.

"Did she indeed?" he asked with a grin so bright it made Cassandra's mind go blank for a second.

"No," she exclaimed. "I would never think to do so." She waved her hand toward him as if he were some sort of mess in need of tidying. "Not when I've always considered your brothers to be better looking."

He pressed his lips together. A curious light danced in his eyes, causing them to sparkle. Cassandra couldn't look away. She knew what she'd said was a lie about his looks, but she wasn't feeling very charitable at the moment and certainly didn't want him to realize she found him attractive. Lord knew that would only make him think she might be swayed in her decision.

"You do realize we're triplets," he said. "Identical triplets," he added for increased clarity.

Cassandra ground her teeth and nodded. "Yes."

And then, for some ridiculous reason most likely born from a stubborn need to be right – to win this silly argument – she said, "Though there are differences. Slight ones perhaps, but noticeable enough to anyone who knows the three of you well enough."

"I suppose Griffin's scar does set him apart, doesn't it?" Devlin murmured. "And Caleb has that dimple at the left side of his mouth.

"While you," she began, then quickly stopped herself. Smiling tightly, she sniffed and went to collect some plates.

"I can do that," Katherine said, beating her to the cupboard. "Why don't you pour Lord Devlin a cup of tea instead?"

"While I what?" he asked. He raised one eyebrow and pinned her with a look of interest that did something funny to her stomach.

"Nothing," she said. Averting her gaze, she tried

to focus on the kettle, the teapot, and the cups the tea was meant to go into.

"Even so, I'd still like to hear it."

"Hear what?" Penelope asked, making her entrance with Rosemary and three younger children named William, Clyde, and Henry. Cassandra groaned.

"Your mother's opinion on what distinguishes me from my brothers," Devlin said as he went to give Penelope a hug.

For a moment, Cassandra forgot all about her annoyance with him. The affection he showed toward Penelope and the other children was both heartwarming and…enticing? She shook her head in bemusement, though not without noting the knowing look Katherine gave her.

"Oh, I can give you the answer you need." Penelope smiled up at Devlin as if he were some Greek god about to fulfill her every wish. "It's your nose and your hair."

Cassandra gulped. "Breakfast is ready," she announced and then hastily went about making sure all the children washed their hands. "Sofia and Jamie are missing. Perhaps—"

"I'll fetch them," Penelope said.

"And I'll take this tray to the dining room if you bring the eggs and bacon, Cass, and Lord Devlin agrees to carry the teapot."

"I'd be happy to," he said.

Deciding their battle would have to be put on hold while they ate, Cassandra did as Katherine suggested and picked up the dish filled with eggs and bacon. Although she avoided looking directly at Devlin, the heat of his gaze scorched the back of her neck as he followed her out of the kitchen.

Devlin had known he would not be welcomed with open arms when he arrived at Clearview. What he hadn't anticipated was how amusing it would be to see Cassandra, who was ordinarily so composed, lose her temper. Because of him.

While his brain had told him he ought to be insulted by some of the things she'd said and the way she'd said them, he'd also been strangely pleased by her reaction. It meant he was able to get a fiery response out of her, which wasn't the worst thing a man could incite in a woman. Least of all in one as desirable as she.

Rogue that he was, he made no effort to stop himself from admiring the sway of her hips or the alluring way her muslin gown moved over her backside as she walked. She was, after all, to be his wife, even if she'd not yet agreed. But she would. Of that he was certain. Because he had every intention of doing his utmost in order to convince her. Funny thing that, he reflected as he took his seat at the table. Four days ago he'd been completely opposed to marriage. Now there was no longer any doubt he wanted to be a husband – Cassandra's husband. Not after weighing all of the pros and cons during his ride to Clearview.

"I didn't know you had returned to England, Devlin," Penelope said with the familiarity of a child who'd known him so long she treated him like a blood relation. He liked that. "Did you, Mama?"

Cassandra kept her gaze carefully averted from Devlin's while helping Katherine serve the food. "Yes," she said. "I was aware."

"And you chose not to tell me," Penelope said with a hint of accusation in her young voice.

"Maybe it was supposed to be a secret," Rosemary said.

William, Clyde, and Henry all nodded. Sarah took a big gulp of milk from her glass, her large round eyes fixed on Devlin in an almost disconcerting sort of way. Jamie, the oldest of the boys, proceeded to wolf down his food with the gusto of a growing youth.

Penelope scrunched her nose in thought. She watched her mother pour tea and waited until she'd filled Devlin's cup before saying, "I find it odd that you would come here without your brothers. I mean, what could possibly be your incentive?"

"Perhaps he longs for a peaceful sojourn in the country," Cassandra suggested.

Penelope's fork stabbed at a piece of egg and then made its way to her mouth. She chewed. Her eyes narrowed with the sort of unrelenting inquisitiveness only a child can possess. And then she asked, "Why have you come to Clearview, Devlin?"

He smiled at her. This twelve-year-old girl had just given him the perfect opportunity to swing things in his favor. Penelope had always seemed to like him, and over the years he'd become quite fond of her. So with this in mind, he ignored Cassandra. He didn't have to look at her to know she was silently begging him to keep quiet.

Instead, he directed all of his focus at Penelope and said, "Why, to ask your mother to marry me, of course."

A clatter came from Cassandra's vicinity, along with some guttural utterance that wasn't the least bit feminine. He chuckled inwardly. If he listened hard enough, he'd probably be able to hear her grinding her teeth. And if he dared glance her way...

For the sake of self-preservation he avoided doing so, his attention fixed solely upon Penelope, whose lips were stretching into the widest smile he'd ever seen. His heart thumped with excitement.

"That is the best thing I've ever heard," Penelope said. "Oh, Mama, you must say yes, you simply—"

"Stop it," Cassandra snapped. Everyone stilled. Penelope's mouth moved but no words escaped. Eventually, she dropped her gaze to her food.

Katherine cleared her throat. "Go ahead and eat," she told the children gently.

Spurred into motion at the sound of her voice, the youngsters resumed eating; forks and knives began to scrape across plates. Chewing noises followed, only occasionally interspersed by the soft gurgling sounds produced whenever someone took a sip of milk or tea.

Between two bites of toast, Devlin hazarded a look at Cassandra. She appeared to be staring at the opposite edge of the table with eyes that seemed to see too much without seeing anything at all. Jaw tight, she ate with mechanical movements, her mind clearly preoccupied by an intricate puzzle, like figuring out how to kill him and get away with it.

He considered the sweep of her jawline, the angle at which it connected with her ear, and the elegant slope of her nose. Her lips, wide and full, were a bold shade of pink - an unusually bright color for anyone to have naturally and, Devlin reflected, deserving the envy of every pale-lipped woman in England.

It was curious really. He'd known Cassandra for years and during that time he'd recognized she was comely - the sort of woman who could easily stir his desire. He'd sensed an attraction, at least on his part, but he'd never taken the time to figure out what it was based on.

Now, looking at her, he saw she was more than a family friend whom he'd gotten used to, and certainly more than pleasant to look at. She was, in fact, stunning, and while her mouth was set in a rigid line at the moment, Devlin could not stop from imagining what it might be like to kiss it.

Which was yet another reason to marry, he mused.

Slowly, he took a sip of his tea. It was wonderfully hot and soothing. It also allowed him a brief moment of reflection in which to decide on the best strategy. He needed to get Cassandra alone so they could talk, and since gaining her compliance would likely be easier with witnesses present, he took one more sip of tea and said, "Perhaps the two of us can go for a walk after breakfast and discuss the matter?"

She turned her head very slowly and speared him with the sharpest stare he'd ever been subjected to. "As far as I am concerned, there is nothing to discuss. So please stop trying to force an issue in which I have no interest in playing a part."

Devlin took another bite of his toast and chewed on it while wondering how to proceed from here. Some men, he mused, might give up at this point. Few would bother trying to convince a woman as stubborn as Cassandra. Especially since he hadn't wanted to get married either until he'd learned she'd run off.

Apparently, her attempt to escape him and then try to send him packing had made him all the more determined to gain her agreement. Sneaking a peek at her while he mulled this over, he figured his own bull-headed nature must be to blame. Because the more she resisted, the more he wanted to win this strange battle of wills. Hell, it was almost a matter of pride at this point.

That, and the fact that he'd started to ponder the benefits of having her as his wife. He allowed himself a smug smile. If she kissed and made love with the same kind of passion she argued, then he'd be a fortunate man indeed.

"I think you should listen to what Devlin has to say."

Devlin blinked. Penelope had spoken softly and

yet so deliberately, it was impossible not to pay attention.

"Penelope," Cassandra murmured. "This isn't an appropriate subject of conversation for us to have at the table."

"Maybe not," Penelope grumbled, "but that doesn't make my point any less valid."

"I agree," James said, in response to which the rest of the children nodded like tiny members of parliament giving their opinions.

Cassandra sighed while Devlin did his best to hide the smile forming on his face. "Be that as it may, my position on the matter is firm."

"You say that as if this is all about you and what you want when—"

"Enough, Penelope." Cassandra's words sliced the air. Her daughter's mouth transformed into a tight line.

"Perhaps we should try to fly the kites after breakfast," Katherine suggested.

"You had a father," Penelope told her mother while jutting her chin up and straightening her back. "He might not have been a very good one, but I'm sure he was better than nothing at all." She shoved back her chair and stood, eyes shimmering with the threat of tears, her face a deep shade of red.

Devlin had to admire her perseverance and her courage. To stand up against a parent so publically when one had been raised in a world built on manners and etiquette required some serious resolve. Curious to see Cassandra's reaction, he returned his attention to her and saw she'd gone horribly pale. His heart stuttered slightly and his stomach made an uncomfortable dive. Penelope's words had clearly hurt her, and as much as Devlin appreciated having the girl as an ally, he could not let that pass.

"Penny," he said, his words too loud in the silence, "apologize to your mother."

"But—"

"Do it now, please." He caught the girl's gaze and held it, conveying to her without the use of words that he was grateful for her help but that he believed she'd crossed a line.

She swallowed and gave a quick nod. "Forgive me, Mama."

"Of course," Cassandra said, but she spoke as if her mind was no longer present.

"May I be excused?" Penelope asked.

When Cassandra didn't answer, Katherine gave her consent, upon which Penelope grabbed her plate and glass and quickly exited the room. The rest of the children eyed each other as if to discern the overall mood and whether or not it would be all right to speak.

Eventually it was Henry who said, "I think your idea to fly the kites is a great one."

"We could make it a competition," William said.

"Based on who can fly the highest or which one stays airborne the longest?" Sarah asked.

The conversation continued until everyone was done eating, the children's chatter growing increasingly boisterous as they began to plan out the teams. "But I don't want to be with Clyde," Henry grumbled as he followed the rest of the children out into the hallway later. "His kite crashed the last three times and…" The rest of his words trailed off as he disappeared to some other part of the house.

"Well, I suppose I'd best go and find those kites," Katherine said. She stood and picked up the tray filled with empty serving dishes. When Devlin started to rise, prepared to offer assistance, she shook her head discreetly and shifted her eyes deliberately toward Cassandra.

"I'll help," Cassandra blurted. She reached for the teapot only to have it whisked out of reach by Devlin who offered a wide open grin in response to her thunderous glower.

"I'd like to have another cup if you don't mind." And since his aim was to keep her from leaving, he deliberately poured for her while Katherine slipped quietly out of the room. The door closed with a soft click, leaving him utterly alone with a fetching virago.

CHAPTER FIVE

IT WAS DIFFICULT FOR CASSANDRA to describe precisely what she was feeling. So many emotions, from anger to disappointment, to heartache and humiliation, churned inside her, whipping up memories so long buried she was half tempted to board the next ship out of England and never return. Ironic that the man she wanted to escape the most had the power to make this wish come true. She looked at him while trying to figure out what exactly to say.

What could she say that had not already been said? She'd told him to leave, but he was still here, she'd asked him to drop the subject of marriage, yet he'd brought it up in front of everyone. The infuriating man had even managed to make an ally of Penelope, who was most likely upstairs right now in her room, crying because she wanted something Cassandra couldn't provide.

"You had no right," she said, the pain Penelope's words had caused like an open wound still raw to the touch.

"You're correct," he said, holding her gaze from across the table, "but it was the best way, perhaps even the only way, to make you listen."

She crossed her arms with a snort. "Has it never occurred to you that women don't like to be forced to do a man's bidding?"

"Certainly. But has it ever occurred to you that men don't like being ignored?"

"Ignoring you has been near impossible since you showed up in my kitchen of all places and promptly proceeded to try to talk me into something I don't want to do."

He tilted his head. The edge of his mouth lifted to form a somewhat roguish smile and heaven help her if her heart didn't beat just a little bit faster. "You blocked me at every turn, Cass, making it near impossible for me to make my case. Not to mention that you ran away, leaving me with no choice but to cross the greater part of southern England for what should have been a half hour chat at your brother's home in London."

Cassandra opened her mouth to protest, then stopped herself since she had to admit he did have a point. She huffed out a breath. "Very well."

He raised an eyebrow. "Very well?"

She pursed her lips, reluctant to show any hint of acquiescence and yet unwilling to be the difficult harridan she wished she was able to be at the moment. "Since you did travel all the way here, it would be badly done of me not to hear you out."

She was tempted to add, "Even though it's your fault we're in this mess," but chose to take the higher ground and refrain. As it was, she was rather exhausted from all the arguing she'd engaged in that morning.

"Thank you." He drummed his fingers lightly on the table while studying her in a way that made her skin grow uncomfortably tight. Eventually he stood, came around to where she sat, and extended his hand. "The outdoors will offer a more pleasant atmosphere for this conversation."

Cassandra stared at his hand, half dreading having to touch it. Unlike the night of the Camberly ball, he wore no gloves and neither did she. But to think of an excuse while he stood there expectantly waiting for her to accept his escort was impossible.

So she took a deep breath and placed her hand in his. An immediate shock of awareness shot up her arm and caused her to freeze. His fingers closed around hers with deliberate firmness, alerting her to the calluses he'd obtained from his work. Swallowing, Cassandra rose. She'd never thought of him as being the sort who engaged in manual labor the way Caleb did. As a captain, she would have expected those under his command to do the arduous tasks while he enjoyed a life more in line with Griffin's, whose passion was building clocks, mechanical toys, and music boxes.

"I like that color on you," Devlin said, allowing his gaze to consume her turquoise gown as he tucked her hand into the crook of his arm. "It suits you extremely well."

Heat rose to Cassandra's cheeks. A flutter of nerves caused her stomach to wriggle. She forced herself to be polite while hating how easily he could affect her. "Thank you."

"No compliment in return?" he asked when they'd gone a few paces in silence.

His voice was jovial, his scent a delicious combination of sandalwood and something earthy she couldn't quite pinpoint. She was rather tempted to lean in closer and breathe him in, but since she knew she'd despise herself for it immediately after, she kept herself firmly in check.

"Your boots," she told him, deliberately mentioning something safe that had nothing to do with the way he was able to quicken her pulse with one look. "They appear to be very well made."

"So they are." He spoke in a pensive tone underscored by a fleck of curiosity. "I ordered them for myself while I was in India. The leather is excellent quality."

"I see." Because really, what else could she say without delving into the intricacies of cobbling and the best sort of animal to use when crafting a pair of Hessians? Truthfully, she had no interest at all in such a subject, so she chose to say nothing more until they stepped out of the house.

Glancing up, she caught Devlin's gaze. The intensity she found there made her so uncertain and weak, she felt compelled to repeat what she'd told him earlier just to maintain some sense of stability. "Whatever it is you think you can say to sway me won't work. I have no intention of marrying anyone, Devlin. Certainly not for the sake of avoiding a scandal."

"Let's head in this direction," he said and steered her toward the lake.

"But—"

"It's such a beautiful day. Don't you agree?" His hold on her tightened a little – just enough to bring her arm flush against his. "Look at the way the sun's light spills across those flowers over there. Everything looks so vibrant and..." He inhaled deeply. "The air is wonderfully fresh and the birds are singing. There's life here, Cass, everywhere as far as the eye can see."

"It's the same at sea, is it not?"

He shrugged one shoulder. "In a way, I suppose. The seas and oceans are certainly full of life, but it's different when it's beneath you. One doesn't see that life or interact with it as one does on land."

"And yet you continue to leave." A couple of birds took flight as she and Devlin approached.

"I suppose I've developed a taste for travelling. Plus, a seafaring life does have its appeal."

"How can being confined to a single vessel for months on end be better than having the freedom to walk for as many miles as you wish, to enjoy a picnic with friends, to go for a ride or..." She twirled her free hand. "Or to simply know all these things are possible the moment you walk out the door?"

"You're only considering the time between places and even then there's a humbling vastness one tends to forget when one cannot see further than to the next village." His voice had taken on an almost dreamy quality that held her attention.

"But out on the water, the distance is endless and we so small, it opens one's eyes to one's place in the world. Then, once the destination is reached, a new world filled with unfamiliar sights, people, and senses beckons to be explored. And it becomes startlingly clear that we English, who pride ourselves on being so cultured and learned, are shockingly ignorant."

What he said made sense. "I suppose knowledge is limited to one's experiences, unless one takes the time to read about the experiences of others."

He frowned and twisted his mouth a bit as if in thought. "You're right, but you're also misunderstanding me." When she glanced at him in question, he explained. "I'm not suggesting the English don't know about other cultures or lack the ability to appreciate them. What I'm saying is that other cultures make our own look bloody ridiculous."

Cassandra's lips started to twitch and for some absurd reason, Devlin apologizing for his curse only made it worse. Within two more seconds, she was choking back laughter, without even knowing why. His comment hadn't been especially funny, yet something about his iteration, the use of profanity, and his facial expression made it hilarious. Imagining a haughty lady and gentleman worrying over afternoon tea or whether to stand or sit in each other's presence while fighting off mosquitoes in some foreign land also helped.

"Well, we do have a king and a very impressive flag," Cassandra told him dryly. "Apparently that's all it takes to conquer the world."

"I'd like to think there's a bit more to it than that," Devlin muttered. "Hong Kong has become an impressive city under our rule. Although I do sometimes wonder if we haven't benefited more than they have. Without a solid foothold in China, the English might not be drinking tea, and that, I daresay, would have changed our entire culture."

"One shudders to think of it," Cassandra said with mock horror.

Devlin chuckled. "Indeed." They crossed the grass leading down to the lake, following the gentle slope until Clearview sat a good hundred yards behind them, secluded by trees and rhododendrons. "I began traveling so I could escape my father and the life he insisted I lead. Later, I stayed away for other reasons."

"But never permanently."

"No." He smiled wryly. "My work invariably forces me home."

While his voice was light with humor, Cassandra sensed a hint of displeasure that suggested he'd rather be elsewhere.

"And while England does have its merits," he added, "nothing can beat a stroll along a tropical beach." Releasing her arm, he stepped in front of her so they could face each other. "Imagine swimming in turquoise blue water so clear you can see all the way to the bottom. Consider the pleasure of sitting beneath the shade of a palm tree while a warm breeze wafts lazily over your skin."

Cassandra's pulse quickened. Not because of

what he was saying, but because of the gleam in his eyes as they gazed into hers. And because his voice had dropped to a low, seductive timbre.

"Try to envision a place where you can have sweet, juicy pineapples every day, not to mention mangoes, bananas, and a whole host of other things Europeans consider a luxury."

"You make it sound like paradise."

His lips curled into a roguish smile. "It is, and I would love nothing better than to show it to you." He took a step closer, causing her to catch her breath. "Marry me, Cass, and I will take you to places you never dreamed existed."

"I already told you—"

"I know," he said, his gaze so intense it heated her blood. "But think of Penelope." He held up one hand to stave off her protest. "What prospects will she have as your bastard daughter?"

The question poked at a wound so deep, Cassandra instinctively turned away in anger. Her intention was to leave and be done with this aggravating discussion, but Devlin caught her by her elbow and pulled her back.

"Let me," she began, only to stop when she saw his somber expression.

"With my name," he said, "and the dowry I intend to give her, she has a chance of marrying well."

Cassandra swallowed convulsively. Until this moment she'd had no doubt about her ability to turn down Devlin's suit. But he was now offering something more than marriage - something so important she feared her resolve. Because when it came to Penelope's future, her happiness and wellbeing, there was little Cassandra wouldn't do to ensure it.

"My life is here, at Clearview," she told him weakly.

"It doesn't have to be."

A nervous shiver swept over her shoulders. "So Penny and I would go with you?"

"If you and I marry I'll not want to live apart, so yes, you and Penny will join me on my next voyage."

Excitement mixed with trepidation as she considered his words and what they implied. "I...I won't be the sort of wife you want or deserve." When he said nothing to this, she hastily added, "My heart will always belong to another."

"To Penelope's father, I presume?"

She nodded.

"I see no issue with that." When she stared at him blankly he said, "We're not marrying for love, Cass, but I do think the friendship we share will result in a happy union. Most importantly, I believe it will help with your reputation."

"But surely..." She looked askance at the ripples traversing the surface of the lake. Her heart knocked wildly against her ribs. How could she inquire about his expectations pertaining to the marital bed without—

"Surely what?" Somehow, he managed to sound both curious and charming.

Cassandra cleared her throat. "Well...um..." She

coughed. "If I agree to this, I would like for us to have separate beds."

"Separate beds?"

When she gave her attention back to him, there was something queer about his expression that she couldn't quite identify. So she nodded resolutely. "It is nonnegotiable as far as I am concerned."

He frowned. "Am I to understand that you and I will never—"

"Correct," she blurted, hoping to stave off the awkwardness.

"I see." He stared at her until her skin felt as though it might catch fire. "Since I did get us into this mess and my sole aim is to make amends, I shall accept your terms."

Cassandra's stomach launched itself into the air, did a somersault, and dove down into her feet. "You will?" she squeaked.

"Oh, indeed." He reached inside his jacket pocket and pulled out a sparkling object - a dazzling sapphire ring. "Will you consent to be my wife?"

Trapped by circumstance, Cassandra raised her hand with great reluctance and allowed Devlin to slip the ring on her finger.

Choosing to focus solely on Penelope's future, she ignored her own apprehensions. Instead she looked up into Devlin's face, and gave him her answer. "Yes."

His devilish smile should have warned her of what was to come, and yet he still managed to catch her by surprise when he pulled her against him and pressed his mouth to hers.

Stunned by the unexpected intimacy of the contact, the rough hint of stubble scraping her skin as he angled his head, and the press of his hand at her waist, Cassandra needed a moment to figure out what was up and what was down.

Her immediate focus was on the feel of his lips, both soft and firm, and on the solidity of his body now pressed against hers. Next, there was his masculine scent, more intoxicating now than it had been before, the warmth he emitted, and the guttural sound escaping his throat as he tightened his hold.

Devlin was a man - tall, broad shouldered and ready to conquer - while Timothy... Cassandra gasped and pulled away from Devlin's grasp. Her breath was coming fast and her cheeks felt flushed while her heart... Oh dear God, what had she done? She shook her head and took a step back while Devlin remained where he was, watching her with smoldering eyes.

"You promised," she muttered.

"Only that I wouldn't bed you."

She stared at him in horror. The tips of her fingers touched her lips. "We can't do this either." Hating herself for what had just happened, she stepped back further on trembling legs. She'd not only let Devlin kiss her, she'd actually liked it, and had almost forgotten the man she loved in the process. Timothy, with his honest blue eyes and boyish smile. He'd been nothing like this dark-eyed man she'd agreed to marry. And if she wasn't careful...

Her heart thumped and her lungs squeezed the air she tried to inhale. "Friendship," she gasped, "that is all I can offer – all you and I can ever have."

He didn't respond, but the way he looked at her, with the confidence of a man who was used to wearing down the most resilient opponents, made her very aware of the challenges she would face in the months to come.

Intent on hiding her concerns, she raised her chin, squared her shoulders, and walked away slowly.

She wanted to run from him as fast as her legs could carry her. Of this, Devlin had no doubt as he watched Cassandra make her retreat. He rather admired her for it, and he admired himself as well for not giving chase. Because that kiss they'd shared, while too brief for his liking, had lit a fire inside him he'd like to stoke and let burn to completion. Hell, he'd always known they had a spark of some sort between them, but he hadn't imagined it might turn into a blazing inferno.

Now, there was no doubt in his mind. The moment his lips had met hers, desire poured through his body like molten lava, pushing his need past the bounds of reason. She'd felt right, smelled right, and tasted divine. But...she was determined to keep him at arm's length.

Devlin shoved his hands in his pockets and sighed. Separate beds and no kissing. What a way to start a marriage. He shook his head and grinned. Somehow, he'd find a way to seduce Cassandra – a challenge he meant to focus on with diligence once they left England.

Until then, he'd let her believe he'd surrendered.

"That's fantastic," Penelope exclaimed when Cassandra told her she'd decided to accept Devlin's proposal.

"Are you sure?" Cassandra asked. After leaving Devlin she'd returned to the house and gone straight upstairs to her daughter's room. Penelope had been putting on her walking boots in preparation for the kite flying expedition when Cassandra arrived.

The first thing she'd done was apologize for her reaction earlier. A warm embrace had followed, after which Cassandra had told Penelope everything.

Cassandra gave her a direct look. "If you have any objections, I can tell Devlin I've changed my mind."

"Why would I object? We get to sail the world, Mama, to go on a real adventure." If Penelope looked any more excited she'd probably start glowing. "I think you marrying Dev is a smashing idea."

Dev?

Cassandra blinked and then uttered the only word she could think of. "Why?" When Penelope gave her a queer look, Cassandra said, "Besides the part about getting to go on an adventure."

To Cassandra's surprise Penelope didn't hesitate. "Because he's fun, charming, handsome, kind..." Penelope counted each characteristic off on her fingers. "Romantic, knowledgeable, atten—"

"Romantic?"

Color flooded Penelope's cheeks. "He chased after you, Mama, and fought for your hand even though it was obvious you did not want him to do so."

"That could just mean he lacks common sense and manners."

The arch look Penelope gave her seemed far too mature for a twelve-year-old to manage. "Either way, his persistence paid off."

"When on earth did you become so observant?"

Penelope grinned. "I've also noticed you haven't denied the part about him being handsome."

It was Cassandra's turn to blush. "Well," she said, "doing so would be rather dishonest, don't you think?"

Penelope's grin turned into a joyous smile. "I'm glad you're doing this." Having finished with her boots, Penelope stood, chin raised, and with a thoughtful expression suggestive of great insight. "Hopefully, it will give you the same kind of happiness Mary and Emily were able to find with Caleb and Griffin."

Cassandra had her doubts about that since her motive for getting married was entirely different from what her friends' had been. But she appreciated her daughter's words and most especially the blessing they represented. And now that she'd put her initial annoyance with Devlin aside, she agreed he wasn't the worst man a woman could end up marrying.

Half an hour later, while standing with Katherine on the edge of a meadow they'd carefully selected for their kite flying outing, or kiting, as the children liked to call it, she watched Devlin help unwind strings and show the youngest boys what to do. He knelt beside them in the grass, making gestures and offering explanations.

Katherine gave Cassandra a nudge when Devlin showed Henry how to hold the kite and run with it. "He'll make an excellent father one day."

Cassandra choked on her own breath and coughed until tears pooled in her eyes.

"Good heavens." Katherine patted her back. "Are you all right?"

"Mm...hmm." Cassandra took a deep breath, coughed once more, and finally felt her throat start to clear. "It's just...um...what you said."

Katherine tilted her head and gave Cassandra an odd look. A frown creased her brow and then suddenly, without any warning, her eyes grew wide. "Cass." Her expression conveyed a mixture of shock and sympathy. "He's going to be your husband. I mean, that man over there will be yours to..." She waved her hand.

Cassandra groaned. "I know, but I don't think I can."

"Because of Timothy?"

"I loved him with all my heart, Kathy. To... Oh, how do I explain this?" She blew out a breath.

Devlin was now running across the field with Henry, shouting instructions while the rest of the children looked on. And then the kite was released. It wobbled slightly until a breeze caught it and swept it up into the sky. Henry whooped and Devlin grinned while the rest of the children called for him to help them next. "I gave Timothy something I swore I'd never give anyone else. The night we spent together was magical, Kathy. I remember each detail, each precious moment, so vividly I can close my eyes and picture it with perfect clarity."

"And you worry this memory will fade or be overshadowed by new ones made with Devlin."

Cassandra nodded. "I feel as though I'm betraying Timothy by even marrying Devlin – by pledging myself to someone else before God."

Katherine reached for Cassandra's hand and gave it a squeeze. "I didn't know Timothy, but I cannot imagine he would want you to torture yourself like this. Don't you think he would rather you moved on and found someone else to share your life with?"

"Of course he would. But that doesn't ease the ache in my heart or stop the guilt from eating away at my conscience." Liking Devlin, being attracted to him, only made it worse. "I'm marrying Devlin for Penelope's sake. He's a friend, so I don't imagine it being so bad. But I won't give him children, Kathy. I cannot make myself do it."

"Is Devlin aware of this?" When Cassandra answered in the affirmative, Katherine looked stunned. "And he has agreed?"

"Until four days ago he had no intention to marry or have children, so I don't believe it's an issue, considering his motivation is based entirely on doing the honorable thing."

"I see," Katherine murmured. But the way she said it made Cassandra wonder if she might be pulling the wool over her own eyes. Devlin was, after all, a man in his prime. He would surely have needs. And if she didn't satisfy them, then he'd probably have to find someone else who was willing to do so.

She considered his lean body as he loped across the field to help Rosemary and Penelope with their kite. For some peculiar reason, her heart squeezed painfully at the thought of him being with another woman. But she supposed that was something she'd simply have to get used to since dishonoring Timothy wasn't an option.

CHAPTER SIX

"I HAVE TO RETURN TO LONDON," Devlin informed Cassandra the following day when he found her in the kitchen.

She met his gaze without any hint of how his comment affected her. "When do you leave?"

"Immediately after breakfast." Was that a flicker of disappointment in her eyes? He couldn't be sure, but he hoped she'd regret his absence a little. "I left in a bit of a hurry, you see." A hint of a smile tugged at her lips as she averted her gaze. "My quartermaster will be needing my help with the cargo we brought to England and then with readying the ship for departure."

She raised her gaze to his. "When do we sail?"

"In four to five weeks." Noting the way she bit her lower lip and wrung her hands, he asked, "Does that give you enough time to plan the wedding?"

"I believe so. We only need three weeks for the banns, and regarding the rest, I'm sure Mary and Emily will be happy to help, not to mention Robert and Vivien."

"Good." He was tempted to step forward and

kiss her cheek, but she looked so guarded, as if she wished there were a wall between them, that he decided it might be best not to. There would be time enough to romance her later, when she'd had more time to adjust to the idea of being his wife.

So he just punctuated his sentence with a nod and removed himself to the dining room, taking the tea with him as he went.

Four days later, standing on the deck of his ship, The Condor, Devlin informed his crew of his intention to marry.

Silence followed for a good five seconds after, then someone said, "Well, it's about bloody time!"

Another voice sounded from amidst the throng of hardy seamen. "Congratulations to ye, Captain! We'll drink to yer health tonight!"

"Aye, that we will," a third voice murmured amidst the ensuing cheers and well wishes.

"I should mention," Devlin added with a hasty glance in Monty's direction, "that my wife will be joining us on our next voyage."

He reckoned he actually heard one man gulp in response to that comment. The crew stared back at him as if he'd lost his head. Only one word followed, and it was a dumbfounded, "What?"

Devlin allowed his gaze to travel across each familiar face. "Should her presence aboard the ship trouble you, you're free to remain in England. All I ask is that you let me know now so I've time to find replacements."

Someone coughed and then a young deckhand stepped forward. "Begging your pardon, sir, but having a woman on board is deuced bad luck. I... um..." He scratched the back of his head and shuffled his feet.

"No need to explain, Sam." Devlin eyed the rest of the group. "Anyone else?"

A fair amount of grumbling followed, during which six more men gave their notice.

"It could have been worse, I suppose," Devlin told Monty while the two of them enjoyed a drink later in Devlin's cabin. "Though I will say I'm sorry to lose Big Jack."

Monty nodded. "He was a fine gunner and a great personality to have on board." He tossed back his brandy. "I'll miss him as well."

Stretching his legs out, Devlin crossed his ankles and swirled the amber liquid in his glass. "Would you consider asking Laura to come along?"

Monty shook his head emphatically. "That would mean bringing the children, which isn't something any of us would be quite prepared for." Considering Monty had six, Devlin supposed he made a fair point. "And besides, I've been married long enough by now to know that the last thing I need is to be trapped with a woman I can't escape for great lengths of time. At least on land, I can go for a walk or head to the nearest inn for a small reprieve."

Devlin frowned. "Considering your plans to quit sailing so you can spend more time at home, I was under the impression you love her."

"Of course I do, but that doesn't mean we don't need time apart on occasion."

Devlin wasn't sure he understood his friend's reasoning. Cassandra was first and foremost a longtime family friend. He'd always enjoyed her company and valued her opinions. Now that he would be marrying her, he couldn't imagine not sharing every aspect of his life with her.

It was, he acknowledged, one of the reasons why he'd been opposed to marriage – his knowing he'd be taking someone away from what she was used to and possibly making her miserable in the process. He could only hope to God Cassandra would be happy sailing the world. Because that was the sort of marriage he wanted, one where he and his wife forged a bond more secure than any knot in existence. And the only way to do so was through shared experiences, honest conversation, communication, and intimacy – all of which required being together.

"Don't you miss each other?"

"Of course we do. That's the whole point, isn't it?"

Devlin shrugged one shoulder and decided to leave the subject alone. Cassandra was accustomed to the challenge brought on by change. She was used to rolling up her sleeves and making the most of a difficult situation. Unlike most Society women, she'd had her fair share of trouble to deal with, but rather than play the victim, she'd found her strength and used it to help others. He admired her greatly for that.

Now, if he could only find a way to dispel her aversion to intimacy.

"I still can't believe this is happening," Caleb told Devlin three weeks later when they rode toward the church in one of the Camberly carriages. "Are you nervous?"

Devlin considered the question for a second, then shook his head. "Not at all. On the contrary, I'm really looking forward to this new adventure." He'd not spent much time with Cassandra in the weeks leading up to the wedding. They'd both been horribly busy – she with arranging for someone to take her place at Clearview, packing for the trip, having her wedding gown fitted, and managing other wedding-related chores, and he with taking new cargo on board and preparing the ship for departure. So it would be good for them to focus more on each other, as he imagined they would be able to do once they left England and things settled down.

"She'll make you an excellent wife," Caleb added. "I've always thought so."

"Even though I practically coerced her?"

"She might not have fancied the way you went about the whole thing, but on the other hand, I doubt the two of you would have gotten married without a little disaster to nudge you along."

"And by disaster, you mean my own stupidity."

"What? I thought it very gallant of you to defend Cassandra's honor," Caleb said with a glint of amusement in his eyes.

"Hmm…I'm not so sure she saw it that way."

"Nevertheless, there's no denying she likes you

– no, don't argue with me on this, Dev. I've seen the two of you interact over the years. There's definitely more between you than the connection you share to Mary and Emily, and I'd say that's a pretty good start."

Devlin glanced out the window. They were almost at the church. He frowned. "I hope I can make her happy." It hadn't even occurred to him until that second that he was afraid of not being able to do so.

"You will," Caleb told him quietly, "because of the man you are. I know you'll do everything in your power to make sure she doesn't regret becoming your wife. That's a lot more effort than most husbands make, of that I can assure you."

Bolstered by his brother's words, Devlin felt his confidence surge. This was the right decision for him and for Cassandra. Not because they loved each other or because they felt destined to be together, but because this was about more than them – it was about protecting a young girl's reputation and ensuring she'd have the future she deserved.

And as Devlin watched Cassandra walk up the aisle toward him later, he gave Penelope a quick glance and silently thanked her. Surprisingly, she'd turned out to be the key to a dream he hadn't even known he wanted. Even if the dream was a little pricklier than he'd have liked, he mused when it was time for him to kiss his bride. She deliberately moved her head at the very last second, ensuring his lips touched her cheek instead of her mouth.

"Vixen," he muttered when they drew apart and his eyes were able to lock onto hers.

Brazenly, she arched her brow and held his gaze. "I did say we couldn't do that ever again," she whispered.

Naively, he'd thought he'd be able to force the issue when they were standing in front of a whole congregation, but she, cunning creature that she was, had managed to sidestep the matter entirely. He was certain he ought to feel affronted, angry even, yet the only emotion swirling inside him was excitement – rather like the thrill one might feel when faced with a sport one had yet to master.

"Touché," he replied beneath his breath as he started leading her out of the church. His lips quirked with humor. If this was how she wanted it to be, then by all means, he'd play the game and do his utmost to win it.

The wedding breakfast, held at Camberly House, was a lovely affair with only the closest family and friends present. Cassandra's parents, however, were not in attendance. Although she had—most grudgingly— issued an invitation, they chose to remain absent. Not that she minded. In fact, she was relieved to know she would not have to face them on her wedding day.

"I must confess I'm a little jealous of you," Emily told her once they were finished eating and they'd adjourned to the parlor for tea and cake. "You get to travel the world and see things the rest of us only get to read about."

"It's so exciting," Mary agreed, joining the conversation. "Devlin has always brought back the most fascinating gifts from faraway places. Makes me wish I could go there myself and experience it all first hand."

"You could suggest a holiday to your husbands," Cassandra said.

"Yes. I suppose so. But it will have to wait a few years." Mary placed one hand on her belly. "I don't think it wise to veer too far from what I am used to with a young infant."

"Neither do I," Emily said with a twinkle in her eyes.

"What? You too?" Cassandra gasped.

"Shh…" Emily grinned while holding one finger to her lips. "We only just found out about it and wanted to wait with an announcement until later so as not to overshadow your big day."

"Thank you for that. And congratulations to both of you." Cassandra took another sip of her tea and tried not to wonder why Emily's comment caused her to look at Devlin. He was standing near the fireplace, conversing amicably with his brothers.

His eye caught hers and Cassandra's heart bounced. Heat flooded her cheeks and she instantly dropped her gaze. "It will be lovely for you to welcome another child into the family."

"Speaking of children," Mary said, "I had a word with Katherine earlier and have promised her that Caleb and I will be here to help with Clearview if she needs us."

"Thank you." Cassandra had managed to find a young woman named Felicity who was ready to move in right away, but knowing Mary – who was familiar with the running of Clearview – was also willing to assist was reassuring. "I believe Katherine's sister plans to visit with her for a while as well, so all in all, it should be all right." But it had been one of Cassandra's greatest concerns since Clearview had always been hers. Leaving it with no intention of returning to the life she'd had there was strange indeed.

"Of course it will be," Emily said. "You mustn't worry about that. Now is the time for you to enjoy yourself."

"I must confess I'm a little concerned about Penelope. I mean, she's terribly excited to travel, but what if it's not as wonderful as she's expecting?" Cassandra pressed her lips together, then added, "From what I gather, life on a ship can be difficult, and once we're on it, we can't exactly change our minds and decide to get off."

"That is true," Mary said, "but I also think you're worrying over something that's sure to turn out fine. Penelope has always loved reading adventure stories, and her favorite thing to do when she was younger was study the globe in the Clearview library. If she's keen on the idea of travelling, I'm confident she'll enjoy the experience. And consider all the things she will learn. It's truly incredible if you think about it."

"I suppose so," Cassandra agreed. She glanced across at Devlin again and could not help but notice how happy he looked. Apprehension tightened her stomach. Perhaps it wasn't so much her concern for Penelope that made her nervous. Maybe that was just an excuse and the real issue was the idea of having to keep Devlin's company for – she blinked – the rest of her life. Tamping down the panic that threatened to rise, she gave her attention back to her friends. "I went to the cemetery yesterday. I haven't been in a while." She'd hoped the visit would give her some peace of mind. Instead, it had made her feel worse.

"I cannot put myself in your shoes," Mary said. She placed her hand over Cassandra's. "If I were to lose Caleb, I'd be devastated. But having said that, I do believe in second chances. And I think this is yours, Cass."

Cassandra took a deep breath and returned her cup to its saucer. "Maybe." It was the best response she could give without torturing herself or her friends with her muddled emotions. She and Timothy hadn't been married, and he'd now been dead for over a decade. Most people would probably say it was past time for her to move on.

But it wasn't so simple. Not when she'd known Timothy all her life. Their parents had been close friends, and he'd attended Eton with her brother. As she'd grown older, what had begun as admiration for the older boy who could make coins appear and disappear as if by magic and who always had a joke ready to make her laugh had evolved into the fiercest kind of love she'd ever known. During the year leading up to their engagement, he'd become her best friend, her closest confidant, and the single most important person in her life.

Losing him would probably have killed her, had it not been for Penelope. So she thanked God for her daughter's existence, and every night before falling asleep, she whispered the pledge she'd made to Timothy while she'd been lying in his arms. *I am yours and you are mine, forever and always, no matter what.*

"Are you ready?"

Cassandra started. She'd been so lost in the past she'd forgotten her surroundings completely. She blinked and looked up. Devlin was standing next to her seat, waiting for her to respond.

"Yes. Of course." Aware all eyes were on her, she rose and accepted his escort. Together they took their leave of everyone before heading outside to the awaiting carriage. They would be spending the night at Mivart's Hotel while Penelope remained behind at Camberly House.

Devlin helped Cassandra into the carriage then took a seat beside her on the bench. As the conveyance rolled into motion, he reached for her hand. Cassandra tried to relax but her stomach fluttered like mad in anticipation of how the evening would unfold. Would he remember their agreement or would he expect her to do her wifely duty? He could force her if he chose to. He'd have every right. No one would fault him. But Devlin wasn't that sort of man, so she knew he'd respect her wishes eventually. She just didn't want to argue over it.

"It's been a busy day," he said, wrapping his fingers more securely around hers. "We've scarcely had time to talk."

"I know." She chuckled, the sound thinner than she would have liked. Hoping to hide the evidence of her unease, she quickly added, "Your mother's efforts paid off though. It was a beautiful party with excellent food." While Mary and Emily had both pitched in and Cassandra had done her part as well, the dowager duchess had been the driving force behind the wedding arrangements.

"I think she's very relieved to have married me off. And," he added with a hint of deep appreciation, "to the loveliest woman in the world, no less." Leaning closer, he told her softly, "You are an exceptionally beautiful bride, Cass."

"Tha—thank you." And now she couldn't speak properly. Taking a long slow breath, she tried to steady her nerves. "You made a handsome groom. That blue color suits you very well." She cleared her throat and fought the temptation to kick herself. Which would be a difficult feat to accomplish anyway since—

"I'm not going to press my advances, Cass."

"Wha—what?"

He squeezed her hand. "You're so tense right now I worry you might implode, and the only reason I can imagine for such a state is anxiety over what to expect. Am I correct?"

She shrugged one shoulder. "Maybe."

Grinning, he scooted away from her slightly. "We have an agreement, so unless you've decided to renegotiate…" He paused until she shook her head. "I won't force the issue. Which is why I've arranged for two adjoining rooms tonight instead of just one. If you're amenable to the idea, I thought we might talk, have some dinner, and maybe play a game of cards before retiring to our respective beds."

"That would be lovely, Devlin." Her voice cracked this time, not because of her nerves but because he'd managed to touch a place deep within her soul. Her eyes pricked, forcing her to turn her attention toward the window and the scenery beyond. "Thank you," she whispered, even though no words could convey the scope of her appreciation.

"Think nothing of it, Cass. My only concern from now on is to make you and Penelope happy."

The emotion filling her heart overflowed and tears spilled onto her cheek. Whatever doubts she'd had about marrying Devlin were swept away and replaced by assurance. He was the kindest, most selfless man ever to walk the earth, and she was the luckiest woman alive to call herself his wife.

After checking into the hotel, Devlin and Cassandra decided to take a walk through Vauxhall Garden instead of spending the entire evening indoors. They stopped to eat dinner in one of the supper boxes before going to watch the infamous Cascade and firework display.

At some point they even began discussing the

tactical errors Napoleon had made during the war. It wasn't the sort of conversation they'd ever engaged in before, and Devlin was impressed to learn that Cassandra knew her political history remarkably well. So much so he was loath for their discussion to end. But when they returned to the hotel and he escorted Cassandra upstairs, she slowed her pace as they approached their rooms.

"It's been a lovely day," she said. "The wedding was perfect and I've really enjoyed the time we've spent together this evening." They reached her door and drew to a halt. "You mentioned cards earlier, but I'm actually quite tired." She bit her lip before hesitantly asking, "Do you mind if I retire instead?"

"Of course not," It was in truth rather late and he was pretty exhausted himself. "Perhaps you'll share your views on the War of 1812 tomorrow?"

"Only if you're prepared for them to be controversial." She followed the comment with a cheeky smile, and he almost cheered because she'd obviously managed to relax in his presence.

The camaraderie they'd returned to and the additional gumption she'd revealed pleased him beyond compare. She was slowly making him realize she had a boisterous streak, permitting her to joke and tease in the best way possible.

"I wouldn't expect anything less," he said in response to her comment. An odd, not exactly uncomfortable but somewhat inquisitive pause followed. She bit her lip and he wondered whether to say something more. Eventually, he decided to raise her hand to his lips for a reverent kiss, after which he wished her goodnight and promptly removed himself to his own room.

Roughly twenty minutes later, he remembered that he'd forgotten to tell her to knock on his door in the morning when she awoke so they could go down for breakfast together. One glance at their connecting door and the sliver of light beneath confirmed she was still awake. So Devlin put his shirt back on and knocked.

It felt like eternity passed before he heard her voice on the opposite side. "Yes?' The question was muffled.

"I wanted to tell you to—"

"What?" He barely made out the word.

Raising his voice a notch, he said, "I wanted to—"

She said something he couldn't discern. Devlin sighed and stared at the door. He knocked again.

There was a pause and then the door handle moved. He took a step back, prepared to convey his idea the moment she opened the door completely, but the perfectly structured sentence he'd had at the ready stumbled and fell off the tip of his tongue like a drunkard as soon as he saw her.

He tried not to gape or stare or look like he'd never seen a woman before, but he feared he wasn't entirely successful. Although it wasn't exactly his fault when she stood before him dressed in the sort of nightgown designed to make a man want a hell of a lot more than friendship. Not that it was seductive, per se, but it was cut from muslin so sheer he could clearly make out the shape of her body beneath. Lord, how his fingers itched to reach out and touch her. Just a little.

"I…er…ah…" He cleared his throat and tried again while gazing at a spot on the wall behind her left shoulder. "I thought it might be nice to eat breakfast together in the morning."

"Um…" She sounded uncertain and slightly confused.

"You can knock on the door once you're ready."

"Oh. All right."

He frowned. Was he imagining things or was she having trouble with words as well? Hazarding a quick glance at her face, he noted she looked slightly dazed. Or tired. Hell, she'd probably fallen asleep with the oil lamp still burning only to have him jolt her awake.

"Good. I will see you in the morning then. Sleep well and don't forget to turn down the light."

She nodded. "You too. I mean, sleep well, that is."

The door closed between them, leaving Devlin to ponder their awkward exchange. He scratched his head. Something about it perplexed him though he couldn't quite figure out what. Sighing, he removed his shirt and the rest of his clothes, climbed into bed, and prayed for sleep to save him from the discomfort his wife was causing.

CHAPTER SEVEN

FOUR DAYS LATER, CASSANDRA WATCHED from the parlor window of Camberly House as her luggage was loaded onto the carriage that would take it, her, and Penelope to the harbor. To avoid difficult questions and explanations, Devlin had claimed he had a lot of things to attend to before departure and that he preferred spending the remainder of his days and nights in England on board the ship.

In a way, Cassandra had been glad to avoid sharing a bedchamber with him. After seeing him in only his shirt, gaping open to allow a clear view of his chest, she hadn't thought her brain would ever function properly again. A rush of heat settled over her skin at the memory of it, and she deliberately closed her eyes, desperate to block it out, but of course that just made it worse.

With a low groan, she turned away from the window and went to join Mary and the children, who'd all assembled for afternoon tea and strawberry tarts fresh out of the oven. Hopefully, they would be able to distract her from her body's betrayal and from the thoughts she had no business having. Devlin might be her husband, but only by law. When it came to her heart and soul, she belonged to Timothy and Timothy alone.

"Is something troubling you?" Mary asked once the children finished eating and all headed out for a walk with one of the maids. "You look more sullen than I would have expected, considering your newly married state and upcoming travels."

"I'm fine," Cassandra lied and immediately added, "it's just…" When her friend merely waited for her to continue, Cassandra confessed, "I'm not sure marrying Devlin was the right thing to do."

Mary's eyes widened. Her head tilted slightly to one side. "Why do you say that?"

Cassandra drew a deep breath and felt the air quiver across her lips. "Because I'll never be the wife he deserves. I…I told him I'd never be able to…to be more than a friend and that my only reason for marrying him was for Penelope's sake." Lord, it sounded terrible. "He accepted all of this, but I worry I did him a serious disservice by not turning him down. I was thinking of Penelope's future and now… I think I must be the most selfish woman in existence." She clasped one hand to her mouth. "Oh God, Mary, what have I done?"

"The right thing, that's what," Mary told her. "You're not a foolish woman, Cass."

"My parents would argue that point."

"They can go hang, if you'll pardon me for saying so."

Cassandra's lips twitched and then she was suddenly laughing instead of crying as she'd expected to do only two seconds earlier. "It's quite all right, Mary. I rather agree."

Mary gave her a pensive look that turned her expression more serious. "You married Devlin in order to safeguard your and your daughter's reputations. There is nothing wrong with that when the man himself was determined to make you do it."

"I suppose he did chase after me all the way to Clearview. And I did tell him what to expect."

"Then he has no reason to want something else. Does he?"

"Not really, I suppose." The real problem was that Cassandra didn't know if she could trust herself to stay loyal to a memory when a real flesh and blood man was hers for the taking.

Mary smiled and offered Cassandra a strawberry tart. "You should stop worrying and trust things to work out as they're supposed to."

It was good advice for someone with a simpler problem, but Cassandra didn't tell her friend that. Instead, she ate her tart and waited for the butler to tell her it was time to depart.

"Goodness gracious me," Penelope whispered against the glass pane of the carriage window when they rolled to a halt beside The Condor an hour later. "Is that it, Mama?" Cassandra peered over Penelope's shoulder. "Is that the one we'll be sailing on?"

"I believe so, my love."

The carriage door opened and the driver set down the steps. Cassandra helped Penelope alight and then glanced about at the mass of people bustling to and fro. It was an interesting blend of merchants, sailors, upper class gentlemen, and tradesmen. Only a few women were present, making Cassandra feel rather like a red apple among all the yellow ones.

She clasped Penelope's hand and turned to the driver. "Do we just go on board?" Perhaps asking Caleb to greet them on the quay so he could escort them would not have been a terrible idea. But Cassandra was used to handling things on her own, so she'd decided there wasn't a need to trouble him.

"I think that's your husband right now, coming to assist you," the driver said. Cassandra turned and immediately spotted Devlin. His warm gaze was fixed entirely on her as he ate up the distance between them, striding down the gangplank as if he owned the entire country.

"Dev!" Penelope squealed and yanked her hand free from Cassandra's so she could run toward her new stepfather. The driver chuckled, gave Cassandra a look of amusement, and went to unload her trunks and bags.

Cassandra remained where she was, unsure of how to proceed. For although she was pleased to see Devlin again, she wasn't sure how to greet him. Their relationship was unique – something slightly more than friendship, yet significantly less than a love match. In the end, her concerns were unfounded. Having given Penelope a hug and exchanged a few words with her, he took her by the hand, crossed to where Cassandra stood, and dropped a quick kiss on her cheek.

It was chaste and very polite, yet somehow... lacking. Cassandra knit her brow and tried to focus on something besides the fact that she wished he'd done something a little more daring. Although to be fair, she had no idea what that something could have been, considering all the stipulations she'd placed on their marriage.

She sighed, fully aware she wasn't being very fair to him and disliking herself for it more than she'd ever expected.

"You look well," he said with the sort of bright smile that did funny things to her insides.

"As do you," Cassandra murmured.

His eyes flashed with something akin to amusement, and then he asked Penelope, "Are you ready to see your cabin?"

"Oh yes. I can scarcely wait!" Penelope started forward, practically dragging Devlin along behind her. Cassandra hid a smile and followed.

"Have you remembered to pack enough fruit and vegetables?" Penelope asked in a rush of words.

Devlin gave Cassandra a hasty glance as if to make sure she was coming along before dropping his gaze to Penelope, "Why do you ask?"

"Well, from what I have read, eating fresh fruit and vegetables helps prevent scurvy. And since I do value my teeth, I think that's an ailment I'd rather not have to experience. According to Captain Cook – I started reading one of his books in preparation for this journey, you know – lemon juice also works. And since Mama does enjoy making lemonade and I have never had scurvy, I suppose he must have been on to something. And also…" They made their way across the gangplank. "I've been wondering about the risk of falling out of bed."

At this, Devlin started laughing. "You've certainly been giving a great deal of thought to life aboard a ship, Penny." He turned to help Cassandra down onto the deck. "To ease your mind, we have plenty of fresh supplies to get us to Portugal. We'll stop there for a couple of days in order to bring more fresh fruit like oranges and lemons aboard so we've got enough to get us to Cape Town."

"Oh!" Penelope clapped her hands. "That's the southernmost part of Africa." Her eyes widened. "Will we disembark there? Will I be able to tell my friends that I've set foot on Table Mountain?"

"Yes and no," Devlin said. He offered Cassandra his arm. "I don't recall her being so inquisitive before."

"She's very excited." And Penelope's excitement was infectious. Within the last fifteen minutes, Cassandra had begun looking forward to sailing across the world and exploring new places in a way she hadn't before. Standing on board The Condor made it real, and her daughter's questions encouraged her own desire to learn more as well.

"Go ahead and descend the ladder to your left," Devlin told Penelope, whose rapid footsteps had taken her on ahead. He nodded toward a crewman, who tipped his cap politely toward Cassandra before resuming his duties. "I'll introduce you to everyone once you've gotten settled. Tonight, we'll dine with my first mate, Mr. Montgomery Quinn, and my quartermaster, who's also the ship's physician, Mr. Lionel Bronswick. They'll be the ones you'll turn to for help if I'm not available, so getting acquainted with them before we sail in the morning is important. Now watch your head."

Cassandra grabbed the railing and bowed her head to avoid the lintel as she clambered down the almost vertical steps. Darkness swallowed most of the light, and a warm smell of dry pine filled the air. It was quieter below deck, allowing Cassandra to hear the soft creaks and moans the ship made.

"This way." Devlin directed Penelope and Cassandra through a narrow passageway straight ahead. He stopped at the second door on the right and opened it. "This is where you will be sleeping, Penny. It's not as big as what you're used to but—"

"I love it," Penelope cried, almost stumbling over her own feet in her haste to enter the space she'd been given. Cassandra watched as she rushed to the porthole and looked out before giving the rest of the cabin her attention. "There's a desk and a bed, which is more than I'd ever expected, to be honest."

"You didn't think you'd have a bed to sleep in?" Devlin asked with one raised brow.

"I don't know." Penelope frowned and twisted her lips. "I suppose I thought only the captain would have such luxury and that everyone else slept in hammocks."

Devlin laughed. "I can get you a hammock if you wish it and hang it up overhead."

"I…er… Do you think that's a good idea?" Cassandra asked.

He glanced her way, paused for a second, then said, "Maybe we'll stick to the bed for now, Penny. There's a bar on the side, which should answer your earlier question about falling out."

"How clever!"

"I'll let the craftsman who fashioned it know you said so," Devlin said in a conspiratorial way that made Penelope beam with pleasure. Cassandra's heart filled with warmth and appreciation. "But first I must show your mother to her quarters. Will you be all right here by yourself or would you like to come with us?"

"I'd rather stay here and wait for my things to arrive so I can start unpacking."

"Sounds like a plan," Devlin said. "We'll see you in a bit."

"Are you sure we should leave her alone right away?" Cassandra asked when Devlin gave her arm a tug. "I mean, she doesn't know anyone here yet. What if she wanders off and gets lost? What if—"

"This isn't the Louvre, Cass, and we're just one door away."

"We?" Cassandra dug in her heels without even

thinking and pulled back against him. "What do you mean, Dev?"

He gave her a toothy grin and halted. They'd only gone ten paces but they'd already arrived at the door at the end of the passageway, and he was presently reaching for the handle. "You've never called me that before."

"I…um…" Heavens. Why was he making her feel so flustered? Her face felt hot and her belly swirled around like a whirlpool. "I must have picked it up from Penny."

"Well, I like it." He opened the door and ushered her into an elegantly furnished cabin much larger than the one Penelope had been given.

The door closed with a click and Cassandra started. "These are *your* quarters."

"Undeniably," he murmured, so close she could feel his breath tickling her ear.

A shiver washed over her skin, and she took a step sideways, deliberately adding distance between them. "But you agreed to not sharing a bed, and after our wedding night I assumed and—" She tried to calm her frantic heartbeats only to fail. "You cannot go back on your word now, that wouldn't be fair. You—"

"Shh…" Devlin strode forward and pulled aside two opposing curtains to reveal the sleeping spaces behind them. "I had an extra bed installed so I would be able to keep my promise. You're free to choose whichever you prefer, Cass."

"I can't have my own cabin?"

"There isn't enough space to allow for that

and—"

"I could sleep with Penelope." Dear God, just the thought of having him so close by at all hours of the day was cause for panic. Not to mention possibly seeing him in a state of undress, as she would no doubt do if they shared a cabin. "Yes. Penelope and I will be fine together."

"Cass." Her name, or more to the point the way he said it – with a bluntness she'd never heard in his voice before – forced her to look straight at him. "I would rather not be embarrassed in front of my men." His gaze was intense and unyielding.

In a strange sort of way, he made her feel like a young girl who'd just been scolded for being naughty. She blew out a breath and considered the space in greater detail. Devlin was doing his best to adhere to her wishes, but he also had his pride and did not wish for anyone to know his wife didn't want him.

"Of course," she told him. There was nothing for her to feel guilty about. She'd explained things clearly to him before they'd married. Yet somehow she still felt like the villain in some horrendous tale with a tragic ending. "I appreciate your taking the trouble to make another bed. It was very thoughtful of you."

He didn't smile. He just sighed and offered a nod. "I'll go check on your luggage, make sure it doesn't wind up in the cargo hold by mistake."

It was an excuse to escape, she knew, and for some peculiar reason this hurt in a way she would not have expected. Not that she blamed him for wanting to be elsewhere. Somehow the easygoing friendship they'd shared on their wedding night and the morning after had vanished. In its place was a strained relationship balancing on the awareness that theirs would not be a simple marriage. And Cassandra knew she was to blame.

She waited until he'd left the cabin before dropping into a chair and burying her face in her hands. If he didn't resent her already, he eventually would. With time, the resentment would turn to hatred, and he'd finally wish he'd never saddled himself with a woman who would never be able to love him as he deserved.

And she dreaded the day that happened, more than she'd ever dreaded any other.

Seated at the head of the table in the small dining room adjoining his cabin, Devlin stabbed at a piece of meat and stuck it into his mouth. Monty and Bronswick were busy regaling Cass and Penny with tales of their travels, from an abandoned vessel they'd once discovered in the Pacific to a treasure chest they'd managed to haul on board after one of the sailors had spotted it during a swim. Devlin never had learned what happened to the crew of El Duque, but he was fairly sure the treasure chest hadn't been anything more than a discarded cargo box.

Deciding to keep silent so as not to ruin the stories, he concentrated on his food and wine. He realized he'd won a small victory today. Getting Cassandra to share his cabin was an essential part of the plan he'd made to seduce her. He'd known she'd resist, but he hadn't thought her reluctance to room with him would feel like a stab to his heart. In every scenario he'd imagined, he envisioned himself laughing it off while she wasn't looking. Instead, he'd spent the rest of the day in a mood, snapping at people who'd done nothing wrong and feeling rotten to the core.

"Perhaps the captain will let you help steer the ship one day," Bronswick said when they'd finished the meal.

"Do you think so," Penelope asked.

"Of course I will," Devlin told her. "I'll even let you help keep a lookout for pirates."

Penelope's eyes widened. "Have you ever met a real pirate, Dev? Have you killed one?"

"Goodness, Penny," Cassandra exclaimed. "That really isn't the sort of question a young lady ought to be asking."

Devlin couldn't quite hide his smile when Penelope rolled her eyes and sighed in response to her mother's censure. He was immensely fond of the girl and looked forward to playing a larger role in her life. "Thankfully, I cannot claim to have met or killed one."

What he refrained from mentioning was the time pirates attacked his ship, but his gunners were a talented bunch who'd sunk the other vessel before a single crewmember managed to board. He gave Monty and Bronswick the sort of look he knew would keep them silent. No sense in worrying Cass or Penny without good reason. "But that doesn't mean it isn't wise to keep an eye out."

"If you will excuse us, gentlemen," Cassandra said when the conversation trickled to a halt. "Penny and I should probably retire for the night so we can get some rest." She rose to her feet and gestured for Penelope to do the same. Devlin and his friends followed suit. "It has been a pleasure."

"The pleasure has been entirely ours," Monty said.

"I'll be along shortly," Devlin assured her, in response to which Cass turned such a bright shade of red, Devlin's temperament instantly shifted toward a more positive one.

With a nod, she turned away and made her exit. He stared at the closed door for a second before resuming his seat and turning his attention back to his friends. Both were smiling like a pair of idiots.

"What?" Devlin asked.

"You're a lucky man," Monty said. "I know I told you so at your wedding, but now that I've spent more time with your wife, I can understand your reluctance to leave her behind."

"You'll be the envy of every man on this ship, Crawford." Bronswick grabbed three glasses and poured them each a measure of brandy. "Having a woman like that to keep you warm at night is a bloody luxury."

"God help us," Monty muttered. "My cabin's right next to yours, so I do hope you'll keep the noise down."

"You needn't worry," Devlin said. He tossed

back his drink and gestured for Bronswick to pour him another. "We'll be completely silent."

Both men burst out laughing. "I've always loved your dry humor, Dev, but this… Oh Christ," Monty said as he wiped his eyes with the palm of his hand.

"I'm so glad I'm able to amuse you," Devlin said. "Now if you're finished, perhaps we can take a quick look at the charts? With Cass and Penny on board, I'd like to avoid some of the rougher waters we've sailed through before."

"Does that mean you no longer plan to cross the Indian Ocean?" Bronswick asked.

"It'll double the length of our voyage if we don't," Monty said. "Reaching Australia will take forever."

"I'm not deciding anything yet, just trying to figure out what our options are."

"Well, we probably won't know in advance. Storms can come out of nowhere and they can even occur in the most unexpected places. Although, if we follow the coast of Africa back up toward India, it shouldn't delay us by more than a month. I shouldn't think."

"And a half," Monty said. He went to collect the relevant charts and began spreading them out on the table. "You know, it's not too late to leave them here where you know they'll be safe."

As if Devlin hadn't considered the option a thousand times already. But his relationship with Cass could only improve if they were together. Apart, she'd never make room for him in her heart. And besides, sailing wasn't so dangerous. He'd been doing it half his life and just wanted to make the experience as pleasant for her as possible. Although…

Oh dear God, what if she couldn't swim?

"Of course I can swim," Cassandra told him when he returned to his quarters and asked about her aquatic abilities. She'd selected the bed on the right and was sitting half propped up against a pillow. A book rested in her lap, but what got Devlin's blood rushing was the fact that she appeared to be wearing the same damn nightgown she'd worn at Mivart's. Or at least one like it. Which meant the moment she got out of bed or the covers slipped slightly lower, he'd be doomed to another restless night.

"What about Penelope?" he asked, deliberately wrestling his brain back to the subject of conversation.

"She can swim as well, but…" She gasped and sat up straight, which caused the blanket, which had thus far been protecting her modesty, to slide down to her waist and in so doing, reveal the most perfect outline of well-rounded breasts he'd ever seen.

His fingers moved, involuntarily gauging the shape and fullness and how they would fit in the palms of his hands. His mouth had gone dry three seconds ago, and his throat felt like sandpaper.

Still, by some miracle, he managed to ask, "But what?"

Cassandra stared at him. She tilted her head to

one side and frowned. "Is something the matter?"

"No." He shook his head and went to sit on the edge of his bed. "Why do you ask?"

"You look slightly ill all of a sudden."

"I feel fine." He yanked on his boot, taking his frustration out on the fine leather. Once it was off, he dropped it onto the floor and started on the other. "What were you going to say before? When you gasped?" He dared a hesitant glance in her direction and was relieved to see she'd pulled the blanket back up.

"I wondered why you would worry over whether or not Penny and I can swim, and it occurred to me that the only reason you'd do so was if you feared we might find ourselves in a situation where we'd have no choice but to swim. And the only scenarios that came to mind where something like that might be the case were if we fell overboard or if the ship started sinking. Both possibilities are rather frightening."

He'd removed his hose during her talk and now unbuttoned his breeches. Standing, he pushed them over his hips, folded them neatly, and placed them on the chair behind his desk. "I'm sorry to have worried you, Cass. It was thoughtless of me to do so when you're not in any danger. As long as neither you nor Penny decides to climb the rigging, there's no chance of either of you falling overboard. And as for The Condor taking on water and sinking, something would have to cause a hole for that to happen, and since I've no intention of taking you through any treacherous water with sharp rocks hidden beneath the surface, I don't see how that would happen."

"A cannonball from an enemy ship could do it."

Devlin couldn't help but laugh. Cassandra raised her gaze from her lap, which she had been studying since he'd started removing his hose. Her eyes widened a fraction and color rose to her cheeks. She opened her mouth as if intending to speak, then promptly shut it again and dropped her gaze.

Devlin allowed himself a smirk. More so when he turned his back and saw her reflection in the mirror that hung on the wall. She was watching him discreetly out of the corner of her eye.

Well then...

"You've a vivid imagination, Cass." He swept his shirt up over his head so the only remaining clothes he wore were his smalls. "But The Condor is fast and agile." Another look in the mirror confirmed her eyes were still on him. The awareness was deliciously thrilling and immensely satisfying. Knowing he'd piqued her curiosity also made him hopeful. He cleared his throat, took a deep breath, and turned. "If another ship looks like trouble, we'll steer clear of it, and that way they'll never be able to catch us."

"Sounds like a solid plan."

He had to applaud her for looking as innocent as she did. With both eyes fixed firmly on the wall now, nothing about her suggested she'd just been ogling him. It was quite impressive and useful, he supposed, for it stopped her from seeing precisely how much he wanted to ravish her right now.

Climbing into bed, he pulled the covers over himself. "May I turn down the light?"

"Yes." She set her book aside and he reached for the oil lamp.

"Sleep well," he told her as darkness settled around them.

"You too."

Silence crept in, filling the space. He closed his eyes and attempted to clear his head. A low whisper caught his attention, and he realized Cassandra was saying something. What, he had no idea. But for some peculiar reason, he knew the words weren't directed at him. They also weren't repeated, so he decided to let them go without comment.

She was entitled to privacy. And if she found comfort in prayer, he certainly wouldn't intrude.

CHAPTER EIGHT

IT WAS ONE OF THOSE mornings where awareness took its sweet time to rise to the surface. With a yawn, Cassandra snuggled further into her pillow and pulled her blanket up around her neck. The warm cocoon she'd created for herself was so comfy it almost lulled her back to sleep. She yawned again and opened one eye. The room she was in was bright, flooded by sunlight, and not the one she usually occupied at Camberly House or at Clearview.

Pushing herself up onto her elbow, she swiped a hand across her face and blinked the sleep from her eyes. When she opened them properly, her gaze immediately landed on a pair of men's trousers which were laid out on the opposite bed. She blinked as all the events from the previous day and the weeks before came tumbling back.

She was on board Devlin's ship and judging from the brightness of the cabin, it had to be at least ten o'clock. She'd overslept – something she'd never done before – but it was because…because…

She flopped back against her pillow with a groan and stared up at the white wood planking overhead. It had taken forever to fall asleep last night, and it was all because of him. Her husband clearly had no qualms about undressing in her presence. So he'd paraded about, removing his breeches and then his shirt as if he'd no care in the world.

And she'd looked. How could she not when he'd practically filled the cabin with his masculinity? Besides, she hadn't thought there'd be much harm in taking a little peek. But she'd been wrong. The moment she glimpsed the muscles straining across his back, her brain had turned to mush. All she could do was stare. And keep her mouth shut so she wouldn't start drooling. Her pulse had quickened, the tips of her fingers had started to tingle with some crazy need to reach out and touch him, and hot little embers had danced with wild abandon across her shoulders.

By removing his clothes, Devlin had managed to instill a feeling she hadn't experienced in years. And as it had gripped her, sending sparks spiraling through her, she'd known it for what it was.

Desire.

The worst part had not been her inability to look away or even the fact that she'd realized she wanted her husband with quite a surprising force. Most disturbing had been her inability to stop herself from comparing him with Timothy. But Timothy was the only other man she'd ever seen in a state of undress, so it had been a reflexive reaction completely beyond her control. Unlike Devlin, however, Timothy had had the body one might expect from a man of leisure— lean and elegant. He'd also been only two and twenty when he'd died, his frame still waiting to be filled out.

By comparison, Devlin looked like the sort of man who engaged in physical work on a daily basis. His wide back, flexing and straining with every movement, tapered toward a narrow waist. Arms, rippling with muscles of varying sizes, looked strong enough to wield the mightiest sword. And then, of course, there was the rest of him.

She'd closed her eyes and listened while he made his way to bed. Guilt had curled its crooked fingers around her heart and squeezed without remorse. Devlin had snuffed out the light and they'd said goodnight to each other.

"I'm yours and you're mine, forever and always, no matter what."

Tears had burned in her eyes as she'd whispered the words, because she'd known that by feeling desire for Devlin, she'd betrayed Timothy in a way she'd sworn she never would.

A heavy sigh pushed its way out of her lungs. She scrubbed one hand over her face and tried to push the unpleasant feelings aside.

Knowing she had to get on with the day and worried Penelope might be waiting for her, Cassandra got out of bed and gathered the clothes she would wear that day. It took only ten minutes for her to finish with her toilette, set her hair in a simple knot, and put on the sage green dress she'd picked out. Years of not having a maid to assist her had made her pick clothes she could put on alone, which was, she reflected, quite practical.

Grabbing a shawl, she left the cabin and went to knock on Penelope's door. When there was no answer, she pushed down the handle and looked inside the small cabin. Finding it empty, she made her way to the deck. A cool breeze hit her face as she climbed the ladder, so she pulled her shawl tight across her shoulders and tied the two ends in a knot to keep it from flying away. Shouts overhead made her look up. Two men, so high above her she couldn't make out their features, were balancing on a beam of wood that went across the mast while managing one of the sails. One wrong move and they would plunge to their deaths.

Cassandra sucked in a breath and looked away. The deck itself was full of activity. Teams of men pulled on ropes while a middle-aged man named Mr. Harris, whom she now knew to be the boatswain, appeared to be checking their work while assessing the ship's overall condition. Unfamiliar words and phrases like, "Give her sheet," "Tail on," and "Keep your luff," were shouted with clear precision.

She shielded her eyes against the sun with the palm of her hand and looked out across the water. They were sailing adjacent to the coastline, gradually adding distance as they crossed the English Channel.

"Good morning, Mrs. Crawford."

Jolting slightly, Cassandra turned. "Good morning, Mr. Quinn."

Placing his hand on her elbow, he steered her

toward the side of the ship. "It's probably best not to stand in the middle of the deck. And I'd suggest you keep your wits about you all the time in case one of the riggers drops something."

"Riggers?"

Mr. Quinn pointed at the men who balanced so high in the air they made her feel dizzy. "Doesn't happen too often, but you don't want to be in the way of an item falling from that kind of height if it does."

"Of course not. Thank you." A lock of hair had come loose in the breeze so she pushed it aside, trying in vain to secure it behind her ear. "I don't suppose you've seen my daughter?"

Mr. Quinn grinned. "Indeed I have. She was up bright and early. Helped us haul anchor." He winked. "Won't be long before she's commanding the ship herself."

Cassandra laughed. "I'm sure you're right."

"You think I'm joking, aye?" When Cassandra pursed her lips he chuckled and jutted his chin toward a spot behind her. "Just take a look for yourself, why don't you? She's standing right there."

Cassandra turned. She hadn't seen Penelope because she wasn't on the main deck. Instead she stood on the quarterdeck with Devlin, her hands on the wheel while he issued directions. A wide grin the likes of which Cassandra had never seen was painted across her face. On her head was a tricorn so big it almost covered her eyes.

A surge of warmth filled Cassandra's heart. She

smiled, a little undone by the appreciation Devlin instilled in her. He was making Penelope feel at home by giving her something important to do. "May I go up there?" she asked Mr. Quinn.

"Of course. I dare say those two will be glad to see you." The sly look in his eyes made her cheeks feel slightly warmer than before. "Come on. I'll escort you."

What Cassandra hadn't noticed, however, when she'd looked up from the main deck was Devlin's attire. Gone were the fashionable London clothes he usually wore, replaced by a beautifully tailored uniform that fit him so snuggly she almost forgot how to think. Cut from royal blue wool, his tailcoat was lined with gold cording. Matching epaulets adorned each shoulder and two rows of gold buttons followed a vertical line on each side. Beneath it, he wore a white waistcoat, shirt, and breeches. Polished black boots and a saber attached to his side finished off the ensemble.

"Monty," he said as soon as he spotted Cassandra and Mr. Quinn, "can you please take over?" He patted Penelope on her shoulder. "Just keep her steady and you'll be fine."

"This is the best thing ever, Mama! Can you believe I'm actually steering a ship?"

"I've always told you that you can do anything you set your mind to," Cassandra informed her. "Though I must admit I never imagined it being this."

"You must be hungry," Devlin said as he linked his arm with hers and began escorting her back down below deck. "Did you sleep well?"

"Very." Watching her step, she descended the ladder. "You should have woken me sooner though. I can't quite believe how late it is."

"I thought it best to let you get the rest you need. But I'm glad you're up." Having joined her, he gave her a sly smile. "I can't wait to give you a proper tour, starting with the galley."

To Cassandra's horror, her stomach responded with a low rumble, but if Devlin heard it, he pretended not to, for which she was immensely grateful. Instead, he grabbed her by the hand and pulled her through a narrow doorway next to the ladder. What had been a small crowded area before suddenly opened up to encompass the width of the ship.

"That's the lower part of the capstan." Devlin gestured toward a cylinder as thick as the trunk of an oak. "The top half – the part that sits on the main deck – has spokes in it. We use it for winding rope. And this," Devlin continued, pulling her through a square doorway, "is the gun deck."

Cassandra gasped in astonishment. Gleaming black cannons – eight on either side – were evenly placed between tables and benches. Buckets and knotted ropes hung overhead and against the bulkheads, while polished wood barrels stood as if strategically positioned along the length of the deck.

"It's beautiful and so incredibly clean." She caught her lower lip between her teeth and gave him a quick glance to see if he'd taken offense.

"What did you expect?" His eyes shone brightly with mischief. "That I would tolerate scruffiness?"

"No. I suppose not. But it really is impressive."

He responded with a grin. "Come on." His fingers curled more securely around her hand. "I'll show you where Mr. Talbot works his magic."

Mr. Talbot was the cook. Cassandra remembered him from yesterday when Devlin had asked his entire crew to line up on deck so they could be introduced to her.

"How does an omelet sound?" Mr. Talbot asked after greetings had been exchanged.

"I've never tried one before." Cassandra gave Devlin an uncertain look. "Is it good?"

"One of Talbot's many specialties."

"Ah," Cassandra smiled. "Well, then, I suppose I must try it."

Mr. Talbot beamed. "You won't be sorry." He began gathering eggs, an onion, and a tomato, as well as a small bunch of chives. "Will you be eating as well, Captain?"

"It would be rude of me to let a lady eat alone," Devlin said as he studied Mr. Talbot's ingredients with wolfish anticipation. "So I won't say no to a small portion."

"This is delicious," Cassandra told Devlin a short while later. She stuck another piece of omelet in her mouth and savored the flavor. "I don't suppose he could teach me how to make it?"

"You like to cook?" The question came with a hint of surprise.

Cassandra shrugged one shoulder and ate two

more bites. "It gives me satisfaction. Not that I'm especially good at it, mind you. Emily's the one with the culinary talent, but I'd still like to keep at it. Especially if I'm able to improve my skills." There was something curious about the way he looked at her and a thought struck her. "You think I should be above such things, don't you? As an earl's daughter, you—"

"Stop right there." He'd spoken abruptly, in a manner that put her slightly on edge. Setting down his cutlery, he pushed his plate aside and crossed his arms on the table so he could lean forward and stare straight into her eyes. It was unnerving, the way her heart leapt in response. Not out of foreboding, but with the thrill of being the center of such intense focus. It was both terrifying and wonderful all at the same time.

And then he spoke. "What can I possibly have said or done to make you think I'd ever prevent you from doing something that makes you happy?"

Unable to think, Cassandra could only cling to what she knew of the world she'd grown up in, which happened to be the same one as his. "Women of my rank don't perform household chores."

He raised one eyebrow.

Accepting his challenge, she rolled her eyes. "Unless, of course, they've allowed themselves to be ruined, run off from home, and decided to live life on their own terms. But," she added, raising one finger to stop him from interrupting, "that doesn't mean I should not try to be the respectable wife you deserve."

"While I appreciate your willingness to give up on something you like for my sake," he said, "I should probably point out to you at this point, since you do not seem to have realized it on your own, that I'm not your average gentleman."

"Because you'd rather work for a living even though I'm sure you don't have to?"

He was the son of a duke, after all, and brother to one now. Cassandra had no doubt in her mind that he or Griffin would ever suffer financially.

But rather than nod, Devlin shook his head and grinned. "No. It is because I told my father he could sod off, if you'll pardon my French, when he insisted I follow a path I did not want for myself. I left London, much as you did, aware that my father considered me to be a great disappointment."

"So what you're saying—"

"Is that you are free to keep doing as you please without any judgment from me." He frowned, then amended, "Provided you don't put yourself or anyone else in danger."

It was hard not to like him when he was being so agreeable. Not that Cassandra wanted to *dis*like him per se, but it would have been easier for her to keep an invisible wall between them – to convince herself he was wrong for her – if he'd been just a little ill-tempered or contrary. It would have been easier for her to stay true to her beliefs.

"If you're done with your food," Devlin said,

breaking into her thoughts, "I'll show you where we keep the chickens."

Cassandra almost spat out the tea she was in the process of drinking. "Chickens?"

"Well," he told her, eyes gleaming, "we do need to get the eggs for our omelets from somewhere and having chickens on board seems like the best solution." He stroked his chin as if in thought. The edge of his mouth lifted. "Catching seagulls is devilishly hard, you know, and only possible when—"

He broke off, most likely because of Cassandra's sputtering laughter. She didn't dare ask how one would even attempt to catch a seagull while on a moving vessel. Did one have to wait for it to land and then creep up on it, or did one attempt to harpoon it from the deck of the ship. Every option she envisioned was more ridiculous than the last and only increased her laughter.

"I see," she eventually managed between inhalations. Needing to get herself under some measure of control, she drank the rest of her tea, aware Devlin was smiling at her, his expression one of pure satisfaction.

"Bronswick, together with his son, Trevor, built the coop," Devlin said once they'd climbed down to the lower deck. Square hatch-like windows that could be closed with the quick tug of a rope offered a reasonable amount of daylight. "What do you think?"

"Penny will love this," Cassandra said as she watched the chickens strut about, pecking at the corn someone had strewn out for them to eat. To one side was a closed off section inside which straw had been piled. "That must be where they sleep?"

"And where they lay their eggs."

Cassandra straightened. "I once considered getting chickens at Clearview, but I worried we might forget to put them inside one evening and wake up to find them eaten by a fox."

"No risk of that happening here," Devlin said with a chuckle. "And they're actually surprisingly easy to take care of. Here, you should try holding one."

"I don't think so," Cassandra said and took a step back, but Devlin had already opened the gate allowing him entry. He scooped a chicken up into his arms and returned to Cassandra. She stared at it, unsure what to do, for although she might have been living in the countryside and wasn't completely unfamiliar with livestock, her experience with animals was limited to Raphael, the Clearview housecat.

"Come on." Devlin leaned in closer and offered a wry smile. "I promise it won't peck off your fingers."

"Good God, I should certainly hope not," Cassandra muttered. She considered the chicken and she considered Devlin. One was clearly more anxious for her to go through with this than the other. Well then…

Deciding she wanted to prove herself capable rather than a coward, she reached for the mass of feathers comprising the chicken and almost dropped it when it started flapping its wings in protest.

"Remind me why I am doing this?" she grumbled once she'd gotten a better hold of the bird.

Devlin crossed his arms and gave her a broad smile. "To satisfy my curiosity." When she narrowed her gaze at him he added, "I've always wondered what you would look like holding a chicken."

"Really?"

He shrugged. "It also means you can't hit me once I tell you that Penelope may have requested a sibling and that I may have assured her I'd do my best to accommodate her wish."

Cassandra's stomach plummeted. "What?"

"I'm sorry, but she looked at me with those big brown eyes and the words popped out by themselves. It really didn't have much to do with me at all, now I think of it."

He was right. She did want to hit him. Right over his head, except that would mean whacking him with a chicken. Cassandra glared at the man she'd married. "You've just gone and promised her something she'll never have, Devlin." It felt like a knife had been plunged straight into her belly. "How could you?"

His expression sobered. "I couldn't very well tell her the truth, Cass. If anything, she'll just think we can't conceive."

"Take this, would you?" She held the chicken toward him. When he hesitated, she blew out a frustrated breath. "I promise not to hit you."

"All right." He took the chicken from her and returned it to the coop.

The moment he straightened, she punched his shoulder as hard as she could.

"Ow!" His brow furrowed. "You promised you wouldn't hit me."

"Well, I lied." She brushed past him and headed toward the ladder. "It isn't so nice, is it?"

He muttered something she couldn't hear. Not that she cared. She was too upset with what he'd done, not just because he'd lied to Penelope, but because she felt he'd betrayed her trust – like he was secretly planning to get her with child one way or another, even if it meant involving her daughter.

Disgruntled, she headed back up to the main deck, hoping to seek out Penelope. They had some lessons to get through together, but when Cassandra saw that Trevor was teaching her how to fish, Cassandra returned to her cabin instead. Mathematics and French could wait a while. There were other things a young girl could learn that were just as important, and so far The Condor seemed to be a first-rate schoolroom.

That night, after giving her ample time to prepare for bed by claiming he had a few things to attend to before he was able to retire, Devlin entered their cabin. "I need to make some notes in my log." He closed the door and turned, that same tortured look she'd seen on his face the previous evening enveloping his features the moment his gaze found her. Before she could discern the cause or question him about it, he cleared his throat and went to sit at his desk. "I hope you don't mind."

"Of course not. I'm in the middle of an excellent book, so I can easily read for the next hour or so." Propped against her pillow, she reclined in bed with the blanket up to her waist. Her hair, which she'd undone and combed, hung loosely over her shoulder.

They'd made peace with each other that afternoon when he'd apologized for what he'd done. She'd admitted to overreacting a little and the conversation had happily ended with a fun game of chess, during which their friendship had been restored. Saying nothing further, Devlin retrieved his writing utensils. There was something strangely comforting about hearing the tip of his quill scratching across the paper as he wrote. Cassandra smiled and turned the page of her book, so engrossed in the story she did not notice when Devlin eventually stood and began to undress.

Until he asked, "Which book are you reading?"

She looked up and was instantly glad she was sitting down, because if she'd been standing, she probably would have fallen right over. As it was, keeping her mouth shut and not gaping was incredibly hard when confronted with his gorgeous perfection. Last night, she'd only glimpsed his back from the corner of her eye and had found it difficult to sleep after. Now, she was faced with his naked chest and abdomen, with muscles she'd thought existed only on sculptures.

Maintaining a vacant expression was extraordinarily difficult, yet somehow, inexplicably, she believed she managed to do so quite well.

Unfortunately, she could not for the life of her recall his question and ended up uttering a somewhat confused, "What?"

Devlin's lips twitched. "Your book."

"My book?"

A knowing smile seemed to envelope his features. It almost felt like his eyes might swallow her whole. "What's it called?"

Cassandra stared at him blankly for a good two seconds, until, to her utter mortification, she was forced to check the cover because he'd made her forget the title.

"*Autobiography and Letters,*" she said, more sharply than she'd intended. "By Mary Delany." It bothered her to no end that he had the power to turn her into a blithering idiot.

"Hmm..." Having already removed his boots, he shucked his trousers and padded across the floor, dressed only in his smalls and hose. Cassandra ground her teeth in frustration. "I haven't read it myself. Perhaps I can borrow it when you're done?"

"You would be interested in reading a woman's autobiography?"

"If it is interesting, I see no reason why I shouldn't."

"Um. Right. Of course." She cleared her throat. He got into bed and pulled his blanket over himself. She stared at him. He gave her a questioning look. Eventually she sighed. "Will you not be putting on a nightshirt?"

"No." Lying on his back, he tucked one arm beneath his head, offering her a direct view of the hair protruding from his armpit.

"No?" Although she tried to use a mild tone as a means by which to convey indifference, she heard the irritation in her voice the moment she spoke.

"I don't wear nightshirts, Cass." He reached for the oil lamp. "May I put out the light?"

Cassandra put her book aside. "Yes." The cabin transformed into infinite blackness. Closing her eyes against it, Cassandra pondered his comment and finally decided to address it by asking, "Have you never worn them?"

"Obviously I did as a child." He sounded annoyed.

She bit her lip, dissatisfied with his answer. "So one day you simply decided that from now on you would only wear your smalls to bed?"

A rough exhalation preceded his next comment. "I cannot imagine why you're so interested in my nighttime attire."

"Because it's unusual."

"Not that unusual," he grumbled.

"Don't you get cold?" She heard him expel a weary sigh, but he didn't answer her question. For some bizarre reason, she could not seem to let the subject rest. It had hooked itself in her brain, causing her to say, "It really wouldn't do for you to catch a chill. Not when you're the captain and—"

"Cass." Her name seemed to be forced from somewhere deep in his throat. It sounded raspy. "Would you please stop trying to manage me?"

"Bu—"

"I won't catch a chill. I never have before. At least not from the lack of a night shirt since I'm used to wearing considerably fewer clothes to bed. So will you please stop worrying and go to sleep?"

Cassandra barely managed a weak, "Good night," because all she could think of now was a naked Devlin and that was not an image conducive to sleep. It also wasn't the sort of thing a woman wished to contemplate when she was trying to remain faithful to another man. Add to that the patience and attentiveness he was showing Penelope, and she knew her heart was in trouble. Because when it came to Devlin, there was so much more than a physical attraction.

There was the man himself.

She'd always known him to be a fine person, but watching him work with his men and interact with Penelope really cemented this awareness.

Forcing her thoughts back to Timothy, she whispered her vow to him as she'd done for the last thirteen years. But somehow, the words didn't feel as honest. They no longer seemed to carry the weight they once had.

And nothing could have terrified her more.

CHAPTER NINE

THEY DROPPED ANCHOR IN LISBON on August fifteenth, ten days after leaving London. Having left Cassandra and Penelope to prepare for an outing on land, Devlin helped Monty gather the items, letters mostly, they'd be delivering to some of the Englishmen stationed there. Truthfully, he was glad to have something to keep his mind busy and away from his lovely wife. She was, as it turned out, proving to be an inconvenient distraction. And considering they still had several months left of their voyage, he wasn't quite sure he'd be able to keep his sanity unless he spent less time in her company.

Which, he had to admit, would not be conducive to his courtship.

What bothered him most was that she didn't seem to share his need for more than friendship. After being trapped on a ship together for almost two weeks, he would have thought her position on this would have started to change, if even a little. But that did not appear to be the case.

Oh, he knew he was able to affect her – the deep pink tones flooding her cheeks every evening when he undressed and got ready for bed proved it. But she was apparently more determined than he'd imagined to keep a barrier between them, and he was not the sort of man who'd ever resort to forcing a woman against her will. Which put them at a sort of impasse.

"Can you see to it that these are delivered?" he asked Monty once they'd filled a satchel with four letters and two small parcels bound for the British embassy. "I'd like to show my wife and daughter some of the sights since this is their first time travelling abroad."

My daughter.

It was the first time Devlin had referred to Penelope as such. But it felt right. Everything about marrying Cassandra felt right. Apart from the fact that she did not want his touch or his kisses or any of the other intimacies a man and wife should expect from a marriage.

"Of course." Monty put on his hat and grabbed the satchel. "Heaven knows you deserve to enjoy the early days of your marriage for as long as you can."

Although he did not feel the lighthearted fervor he ought, Devlin knew his friend had a point. Once they left Lisbon and headed for Cape Town, he'd be in higher demand on deck and have less time to spend with Cassandra and Penelope. So he wished Monty luck and went to find his wife. It wasn't her fault his heart was weighed down by concerns for their future. She'd been honest with him from the start – had made no pretense about what he might expect from her in marriage – and he, foolish man, had believed he'd easily change her mind.

He'd believed the spark he'd felt between them right from the start simply needed stoking. Considering Cassandra's past and everything she had told him, he ought to have known better. And it was now ten bloody days since they'd spoken their vows. Ten nights of him parading around half naked in the hope of…what exactly? That she'd melt in response to his tempting physique and beg him to take her to bed?

She obviously wasn't going to and he was starting to think he was proving to be the biggest idiot to ever walk the earth for even supposing such a tactic might work. Wearily, he climbed the ladder leading onto the deck, took a deep breath of fresh air, and expelled it slowly. He was so damn tired of constantly wanting, his body strained and needy in ways it hadn't been since he was a lad still dreaming of his first tup.

At least if he'd listened to her from the start, they wouldn't be sharing a cabin, and he wouldn't have to see her lying there, no more than two yards away, dressed only in that provocative nightgown of hers. Hell, he'd not even seen her naked, and yet the fantasies stirring his mind and body were so damn creative at this point, he wasn't sure what to do.

With the sort of rigid control he'd never believed he possessed, he forced himself to think of his father's parting words. *You're just like Caleb*

*and Griffin. Utterly useless and a disgrace to this family.
You'll never amount to anything. Do you hear!*

Devlin's hands shook as they always did in
response to the memory. But it did the trick. He
was on deck now, damn it, surrounded by his
men and with Cassandra and Penelope standing
right over there by the railing. It really wouldn't
do for any of them to witness the effect his lusty
thoughts were having on him.

"If you're amicable to the idea," he told Cassandra after exchanging a couple of words with Mr.
Harris, "I thought we might spend the day ashore
so you and Pe—"

"Oh yes," Penelope exclaimed with an enthusiastic bounce. Clasping her hands together, she
turned to Cassandra. "Oh please, Mama. It will
be so much better than remaining on board all
day, and I can already tell from here that there's
so much to see, and I've never been to Portugal
before, and—"

"All right," Cassandra grinned, her eyes bright
with the pleasure her daughter's eagerness gave
her. And then she smiled at Devlin – as if he'd
worked a magnificent miracle – and it was all he
could do not to pull her straight into his arms and
kiss her beautiful mouth. Her next words however, were a wonderful alternative. "I can think
of nothing better than to explore a new land with
the two of you."

So he offered her his arm, which she accepted.
He then looked directly at Penelope and said,
"Lead the way, Penny. It looks like adventure

awaits us."

With a squeal of delight, Penelope spun on her heel and marched toward the spot where a rope ladder had been secured to the side of the ship. Two rowboats had already been readied and lowered into the water, one transporting some of the crew to land while the other began maneuvering into position the moment Devlin gave the order.

"Wait," Cassandra warned, her voice filled with worry, when Penelope prepared to clamber over the side as if she'd been born on the ocean. "You should let Devlin help you."

Warmth seeped beneath Devlin's skin, spreading outward along each limb on account of her words. She wasn't just including him, she was trusting him with her daughter's safety in a way that made him feel capable of practically anything. Not that there was much he could really do to help since using a rope ladder didn't required much practice, but he made sure to instruct Penelope on how to move her hands downward gradually in accordance with her feet, to not make any sudden movements that might cause the ladder to swing and, most importantly, to be careful.

Once she'd reached the rowboat and found a seat on one of the benches, Cassandra breathed an audible sigh of relief. "Thank you."

"You're welcome." He gestured. "Your turn now."

"Right." She bit her lip, took a hesitant step toward the ladder, and peered over the side. "Dear lord."

Devlin couldn't help smiling. "Afraid of heights?"

"Of course not," she grumbled.

"Your daughter did it without hesitation."

Her brow creased. "She also leaps into the lake at Clearview from trees."

It took some effort not to laugh when an unbidden image of Cass doing that entered his head. "Well, we can climb down together. Which is probably the best thing for us to do anyway since it will allow me to stop your skirts from billowing out." When she stared at him blankly, he leaned in and whispered, "Wouldn't want to give my rower the sort of view he'll never forget."

She sputtered something that made no sense and turned a deep shade of red. "Perhaps I should—"

"Come on," he told her bluntly the moment he heard the hesitation in her voice. His hands went to her waist before she could comment, and then he was lifting her up and over the side of the ship. "Grab the rope."

"Dev!" Her voice was filled with indignation but at least she followed his orders.

Satisfied, he climbed onto the rung directly below the one where she stood and held on to the rope on either side of her.

Because of their difference in height, having her slightly higher up on the ladder brought their faces to the same level. So he pressed in close, pretending he had to adjust his position for the sole purpose of savoring the rare proximity their current positions allowed.

"Relax. I won't let you fall." His voice was low, deliberately soothing, and perhaps a little seductive as well. It couldn't be helped really. Not when he could feel her warm body against his own and smell the fresh scent of soap along with a hint of rosewater on her skin. "We'll climb down together. When you're ready."

"I'm ready," she said much sooner than he'd hoped. Then again, they couldn't remain where they were too long, dangling from the top of a rope ladder while Penelope waited for them in the boat below.

Scoundrel, he told himself silently as they descended. *Reprobate and unforgiveable rogue.* One thing was certain however, and that was the fact that his crew might have to lock him away before they reached Australia, all because of a woman who'd likely drive him to madness.

It was a sad state of affairs indeed when a man's own wife made him a prime candidate for Bedlam.

The sights and smells of Lisbon were exotic and so different from those Cassandra was accustomed to. She could not stop from turning her head in every direction or sniffing the air as they walked.

"The air is so much fresher here than in London," she said as they made their way through a series of narrow streets. The houses on either side weren't necessarily nicer than those in England. Most were plainer and narrower, squeezed together in a way that ought to have seemed overcrowded. But the varying array of colors added character and the sunshine bathing the walls provided a cheerfulness London homes lacked.

"I believe the ocean carries away all the unpleasant smells," Devlin commented. He drew Cassandra to a halt so they could wait for Penelope, who'd stopped to admire a shop window. "Not that there's much to complain about in that way to begin with. Lisbon isn't as industrial as London. There are fewer factories, less smoke, cleaner air." He glanced in Penelope's direction and smiled. "Do you see something you like?" Releasing Cassandra's arm, he went to look at whatever it was that had caught Penelope's attention.

Cassandra watched the pair while trying to ignore how bereft she now felt. She'd liked having her arm linked with Devlin's and missed the sense of security his touch had provided. When she'd gotten onto that rope ladder earlier, against her will, as it were, she'd been terrified until he'd joined her. It hadn't mattered that their combined weight had probably increased the chance of the thin rope snapping and both of them plunging into the sea. All she'd known in that moment was the strength he'd offered and the certainty she would be safe as long as he didn't leave her.

An ache bloomed in her breast, and she swallowed the pain that had been her constant companion for so many years. Devlin was already proving to be an excellent father for Penelope and the thought of Penelope viewing him as such – of Devlin being the only father she'd ever know—

made Cassandra's eyes flood with unexpected tears.

With only good intentions, he'd stolen the role that should have belonged to Timothy. It was a stupid observation to make. Cassandra realized this and hastily brushed the tears aside before anyone had the chance to see. But she couldn't stop the sense of loss or despair from tunneling through her. Everything Timothy had been, every promise she'd made him and every stride she'd taken to preserve his memory, was slipping between her fingers.

Penelope pointed at something Cassandra couldn't make out. Before she was able to move in closer and see what her daughter was so enthralled by, Devlin had taken her hand and entered the shop with her.

"We'll be right back," he told Cassandra with scarcely a glance in her direction. Which was just as well since it gave Cassandra a much needed chance to compose herself before either returned.

They did so within five minutes and with Penelope wearing a big bright smile.

On her head, she wore a stunning bonnet of pale green silk, tastefully decorated with braided cream ribbons along each edge. It was the first bonnet Penelope had ever owned and something about it – about all of it – made Cassandra react in a way she would later regret for at least twenty reasons. But in that moment, all she could do was stand there and stare while hot anger began to swirl inside her, growing and rising until there was nothing else for it but to allow it the freedom it craved.

"What," she asked, her voice not her own but belonging to some horrid woman she'd rather not be, "do you think you are doing?"

Devlin's expression immediately sobered and Penelope's smile fell away. They stopped, both of them watching her cautiously. It was clear to Cassandra that neither knew what they'd done to upset her, which made perfect sense since she hardly understood it herself.

"We bought a bonnet," Devlin told her as if he were speaking to someone who needed her head examined. "Penelope liked it so—"

"So you decided to get it for her without bothering to consult me? Even though I'm right here?" She spread her arms out, aware she was seconds from making a scene and also knowing she ought to thank him for being so generous. But she couldn't. The knot in her chest and the guilt continuously dogging her made her unreasonable. Which only increased her annoyance. "I'm right here, Devlin. I'm not...I'm not..." Her throat closed on a partial sob, forcing her to turn away in order to hide her mortification.

Silence followed until a soft voice spoke. "It's just a bonnet, Mama." Cassandra felt Penelope's much smaller hand clasp her own. "I can return it if you like."

Cassandra's heart twisted as she stared down into her daughter's face. It broke her to see how ready she was to abandon her own happiness for no other reason than to appease a mother who ought to be able to act with more dignity and understanding.

"No." She could not allow Penelope to give up on something she wanted – something Devlin was willing to give her – just because she herself was being irrational. It wouldn't be fair. She squeezed Penelope's hand. "I'm sorry."

"It's all right, Mama. I understand."

"You do?" It was a wonder since Cassandra herself was thoroughly confused by all the riotous thoughts and emotions she'd just experienced.

Penelope nodded. Her eyes were too wise and far too serious for a girl her age. "You want to hold on to the past, the present, and the future all at the same time. You want Papa to come back and for no other person to take his place." She glanced sideways to where Devlin stood a short distance away before returning her gaze to Cassandra. "Except he's not coming back. Not ever. So it's time for you to let go and move on or you'll never be truly happy. And I'd really like for you to be happy, Mama. I want it more than anything else in the world."

It was impossible not to cry when faced with such youthful clarity. "I know. I'm sorry." She swiped at her eyes with the back of her hand.

"What for?"

"For putting you in this position, I suppose." When Penelope gave her an odd look, Cassandra explained, "I should be giving you advice and life lessons, not the other way around."

Penelope's face brightened. "Does that mean I said the right thing?"

"It certainly does. I'm very proud of you, you know. Of how grown up you're becoming." Although it might not be the thing to do in the middle of a public street, Cassandra pulled Penelope into her arms for a tight embrace. "I love you."

"I love you too, Mama." They stepped apart. Penelope nibbled her lip. "So can I keep the bonnet?"

Cassandra immediately laughed. "Yes, Penny. You may keep the bonnet."

Penelope clapped her hands together and did a few twirls, reminding Cassandra that she was still just a child, no matter the insight she'd just delivered as if she had decades of experience behind her.

A handkerchief materialized in front of Cassandra.

Offering Devlin a grateful smile, she snatched it up and dabbed her eyes. "I must apologize to you for my behavior. It was unjust of me to criticize you as I did without good reason."

"On the contrary," he murmured, "I believe you had every reason, Cass." A startled gasp escaped her, and she instinctively looked up into his dark brown gaze. "Perhaps, when you're ready, you'll explain it to me so I might understand?"

"It's terribly difficult."

"And very important, I reckon." He held out his elbow and she placed her hand in the crook of his arm. "Perhaps a small reprieve is what's called for. Penny! Turn right up ahead." He lowered his voice to a more conversational tone and told Cassandra, "There's a restaurant I'd like to show you."

Set in a rustic courtyard where tables and chairs stood between a series of orange and lemon trees, La Primavera created a leisurely atmosphere where time appeared to stand still. It was exotic and romantic, appealing to all the senses with the intoxicating perfume of citrus and spice, of unevenly plastered walls and smoothly worn cobblestones, and a fountain gurgling at the center.

They dined on sardines, mussels, and a flavorful combination of rice, meat, vegetables and shrimp. Cassandra and Devlin shared a small jug of fruity red wine, the grapes of which were reputedly harvested by the establishment's owner, while Penelope enjoyed a glass of freshly pressed apple juice.

"Dev," Penelope spoke beneath her breath while eyeing the neighboring table. "Are those people eating snails?"

Devlin discreetly glanced sideways while sipping his wine. "It appears so."

"That's disgusting," Penelope muttered, scrunching her nose. "They might as well be eating worms."

"Some people do eat worms," Devlin said, earning a horrified look of revulsion from Penelope and causing Cassandra to snort as she did her best to swallow her laughter. "They're actually considered a delicacy by the indigenous people of New

Zealand."

"Really?" As revolted as Penelope looked, she must have been slightly intrigued as well for she quickly followed her question with another. "What other strange things do people eat?"

"Snakes, frogs, insects…though I'm not sure they themselves find it strange. And neither would you if it were your usual fare." Devlin helped himself to a few more mussels. "In South Africa there are often vendors with baskets full of big, fat, juicy caterpil—"

"Ew!"

"Penelope," Cassandra chastised, even though she understood her daughter's outburst perfectly and almost felt compelled to reprimand Devlin as well for inappropriate conversation during a meal, "That's enough. Remember your manners and concentrate on eating the rest of your food."

Penelope stared down at her plate where her half-eaten fish lay waiting. "I think I've lost my appetite."

"You ate several mussels though," Devlin pointed out. "They're not so different from snails in terms of—"

"Can we please discuss something else?" Cassandra asked, her patience with both of them wearing thin.

Instead of looking sorry, Penelope and Devlin just grinned like a pair of scoundrels who'd secretly conspired to tease her all along. It brought into sharp focus the bond they'd forged not only during the last ten days, but over the course of their six year acquaintance. There was more between them than friendship alone – a fondness that promised to turn into love.

Swallowing against the knot forming in her throat, Cassandra forced a smile. She envied what they had, hated the acuteness with which it reminded her of what she'd lost, regretted not having the courage to try and secure something similar for herself, and loathed the fact that she was so petty she actually wished Penelope wouldn't enjoy Devlin's company quite so much.

"All right," Devlin said. If he noticed her tight expression, he chose not to comment. "How does a visit to some of the town's historical monuments sound? The Romans built a theatre and several temples as well as a bath. Then there's the Muslim influence if that has your interest, several churches, some castles and…well, we probably can't see it all in one day, so if you're amicable to the idea, I'll take you to the places I like the best."

Cassandra found that to be an excellent plan. Emotionally drained from the sentimental attack on her soul, she needed something besides sad memories and heartache to blot out the pain. Penelope wanted to see her happy. It was in fact her greatest wish, so it was time for Cassandra to do what she could in order to make that happen. Exploring Lisbon more closely seemed like a good beginning. It would offer a wonderful distraction and maybe, hopefully, help create new memories with Penelope and Devlin for her to look back on later with pleasure.

CHAPTER TEN

"I WAS WONDERING IF I MIGHT be able to tempt you with an evening walk on the deck," Devlin said to Cassandra two days later. They'd sailed from Lisbon that morning and were just finishing their evening meal. Devlin knew it was probably underhanded of him to make the suggestion with Monty, Bronswick, and Penelope present since it would make it harder for Cassandra to decline. But devil take it, he wanted her company. In private, for a change. Without her lying in bed, tormenting him with lusty thoughts.

"I, um…" She cleared her throat, sipped her port, glanced at Penelope, and took another sip of her port. Was her hand trembling? "I should probably help Penny prepare for bed."

"I can do so myself, Mama," Penelope said.

Devlin hid a smile.

"But what about the story we're reading together?" Cassandra asked.

"You can read for me after your walk, if you like."

"But—"

"And if I happen to fall asleep before you return,

we can read the next chapter tomorrow instead."

It was difficult not to laugh, but Devlin forced his most inscrutable expression to the surface since he wasn't convinced Cassandra would appreciate him finding humor in the situation. Discreetly, he mouthed words of thanks to Penelope. He could kiss her for taking his side and knew this was what she had done when she suddenly winked at him from across the table.

If Monty and Bronswick thought it odd for Cassandra to try and avoid Devlin's company, they gave no indication. Most likely because they were both, much to Devlin's relief, engrossed in a conversation about men's boots – a subject Devlin felt had been exhausted at least ten minutes earlier.

"Well then," Cassandra murmured, her voice conveying the defeat she most likely felt. She looked straight at Devlin and graciously inclined her head. "A bit of fresh air would be welcome."

"Excellent." Pleased with himself, he ate the remainder of his dessert, waited for everyone else to finish as well, and stood. "We can see you to your cabin first, Penelope. If you like?"

"Unless the young lady would rather remain here with us for a game of cards," Monty said.

"Oh. I'd love to." Penelope looked to her mother for approval. "May I, Mama?"

Cassandra nodded. "Of course." She gave her attention to Monty and Bronswick next. "Just as long as the two of you don't teach her how to gamble."

"Oh, we would never," Monty began.

"Didn't even cross our minds," Bronswick said.

"Until you mentioned it, that is," Monty said, then hastily waved one hand and added, "but our game will be quite innocent. Truly, Mrs. Crawford, you can trust us implicitly."

"They're going to teach her how to gamble, aren't they?" Cassandra asked once she and Devlin had exited the dining room and were making their way through the passageway toward the ladder.

"Most likely," Devlin confessed.

To his surprise, Cassandra smiled. "That's all right. Sharing a secret with Monty and Bronswick will make her feel more at home."

Agreeing, but choosing to keep his opinion to himself, Devlin followed Cassandra up onto the deck. The air was still, the sky entirely black save for the smattering of stars, gleaming like flecks of silver overhead. A few strategically placed lanterns offered enough light for the crew to see, but for tonight, Devlin decided it served an additional purpose, the golden hue lending a romantic touch to the overall atmosphere.

Turning, he raised one hand in acknowledgement of the sailor who presently maintained the course, then offered Cassandra his arm and escorted her slowly toward the prow. He'd spent little time in her company since their outing in Lisbon. With a schedule to keep, the previous day and the evening prior to that had been spent on logistics, on packing fresh fruit and vegetables, completing his ledgers and updating his log. Because of the longer stretch of open water ahead, he'd also spent several hours in Bronswick's company, ensuring all was in order, that there were no cracks in the wood, no hint of insects in any of their supplies, and not a frayed rope in sight. So it was nice to feel her arm press against his as they walked, their strides slow and measured – a light scrape and tap in the otherwise silent night.

"Do you remember when we first met?" He glanced down at her, pleased to catch a smile on her lips before she answered.

"Of course. You arrived home during a dinner your brother was hosting at Camberly House." She gave him a slight nudge. "It was a very brief introduction since you chose not to join the party. Instead, you requested a tray be brought up to your room, as I recall."

"You've an excellent memory. I wasn't even thinking of that but rather of our next encounter at the Huntingham ball."

"I suppose it was the first time we had an actual conversation with each other."

He grinned, liking the easy journey they were taking into the past. "I had no intention of dancing that evening. Not because I'm averse to the exercise, but rather because I was out of practice. Caleb insisted, however, and I ended up partnering with you."

"So you did." Her eyes twinkled in the light from a nearby lantern. "And you were actually rather good."

"Only because you put me at ease by pointing out the guests who were doing things they weren't supposed to when they thought no one else was looking."

She laughed. "Like Cakesneaker, Slippertosser, and oh, Bottompincher?"

"I cannot believe you recall the names." He grinned and shook his head, then dropped his gaze toward hers. The air thickened with the sense of camaraderie they'd always shared, but with something else too – something that seemed to tug at his heart. "Do you regret marrying me?"

He hadn't meant to ask such a question. On the contrary, he'd meant to compliment her hair, which looked particularly pretty tonight. But then he'd wondered if she would appreciate such a compliment, which had made him wonder why he would even have cause to worry about such a thing. And he'd realized he did have cause because, damn it all, she didn't want him to touch her or kiss her or do the things he so desperately wanted to do.

"No. It was the right decision. Not only for Penelope, but for me as well. I just…" She turned away so she could stare at the endless blackness beyond the ship's railing. He waited for her to continue, until he was tempted to prompt her or shake her or something. And then she turned back, her eyes meeting his with bold intensity. "You are a wonderful man, Dev. The best man there is, I believe. And I am sorry I'm being so difficult. It's not fair to you at all when you have been nothing but patient and kind. But I…I…" She shook her head as if to inform him she'd lost the words to explain, and because he sensed what she required right now more than anything else was friendship, he pulled her into his arms for a hug.

It took a moment before she responded, but then her arms came around him as well, with a fierceness that surprised him. Somehow, for whatever reason, she needed to be held and comforted, to know she wasn't alone as she may have felt for so very long.

Yes, she'd had Mary and Emily to help her at Clearview, but when it came to Penelope, the reality was she'd been a single mother who'd lacked the support and love she should have received from her own parents. She'd lived through tragedy at much too young an age and been forced to shoulder problems no young woman of eighteen should have to bear.

Warm and soft and smelling of roses, she pressed her face against his chest and held on as if she were drowning.

"Sometimes," he murmured against the top of her head, "it can be freeing to talk about the things that plague us." When she didn't pull away, he smoothed his hand against her back and gently added, "Keeping it bottled up inside can cause it to fester until it destroys our soul."

Aware of the risk he took by pressing the issue – the chance of her walking away and leaving a gorge between them – he leaned back and tipped up her chin. Eyes haunted by pain and guilt and heartache stared back, causing his own heart to shudder with grief. And he knew that the only way forward was for him to be more transparent with her than a pane of glass.

So he eased her away just enough to take her hand and lead her toward a couple of crates. "You loved Penelope's father a great deal." It was curious how in all of their conversations and all the years they'd known each other, the man's name hadn't come up. Gesturing for her to sit, he waited for her to do so, then sank down and placed one arm around her shoulders. "I cannot imagine what it is like to lose someone so close, but that doesn't mean I do not understand the anguish death can bring. Especially when it takes a person before their time."

Her eyes were impossibly bright, like moss right after the rain. "You lost someone too."

"Not in the way you did. But yes." Devlin closed his eyes for a moment and forced himself to remember the details he'd struggled so hard to forget. "His name was Luke and he was a crew-member – a lad no older than sixteen years of age – and we'd just returned to London from Athens. It was my first voyage as captain and..." He blew out a deep, agonizing breath. "I sent Luke up the mainmast to make sure the sail had been prop-erly secured before disembarking, but it started to drizzle the moment he stepped out onto the topgallant yard – that beam of wood you see up there – the second one from the top."

He pointed toward it even though it was hard to make out in the dark. Cassandra still gasped, perhaps because she'd discerned the direction the story was taking. "I shouldn't have issued the order. I should have sent someone with more experience up there and…and I should have paid better attention to the condition the ropes were in. But I had a different boatswain back then. As it happened, the rope Luke grabbed hold of was damaged. It snapped the moment he checked its strength, but I'm not sure he would have fallen if it hadn't been for the slickness of the beam beneath his feet."

"Dear God."

"I did my best to catch him. Broke my arm in the process. But it wasn't enough, though I daresay it might have been best if I'd done nothing at all." When she stared back at him with incomprehension, he had no choice but to say, "The fall didn't kill him straight away. It took a while, during which he suffered tremendous amounts of pain."

"Was there nothing to be done?" Her hand had somehow found his while he'd been talking.

"I tried. The physician I usually brought along with me had family near Dover, so I'd dropped him off on the way and continued to London without him, confident I wouldn't need him for the remaining distance. So I ordered Quinn to fetch a physician post haste."

"But Luke didn't make it. Did he?"

Too agitated to remain seated, Devlin stood and clasped his hands behind his back. "No. He died before Quinn returned." But that wasn't all. There was more to the story – the reason he no longer drove past St. James's. He just couldn't seem to get the rest of the words out.

And then she suddenly stood and her hand found his cheek, and whatever else he'd meant to confess was completely forgotten. "Guilt is a wretched emotion. I'm sorry you've had to live with it for so long."

He stood, transfixed by the unshed tears causing her eyes to shimmer. Most people would have said they were sorry Luke had died or that Devlin wasn't to blame. As captain, however, he was responsible for the ship and its crew. So it *had* been his fault and he knew this, had lived with it every single day since. Which probably explained why he appreciated Cassandra's lack of finesse, because there was honesty in it.

"It won't go away."

She lowered her hand, leaving his skin more sensitive to the cool night air than before. "No," she whispered, "it won't."

And just like that he knew they were no longer speaking of him or of Luke, but of something else entirely.

Remaining perfectly still, so still he realized he held his breath in anticipation, he waited for her to explain. It wasn't easy. In fact, the brief moment of silence between them felt like the longest he'd ever endured. The temptation to prod her, to shift his weight impatiently, or blurt out one of the many questions he had about her and Penelope's father was horribly tempting. But he sensed that even the slightest sound, like clearing his throat, would cause her retreat.

So he waited. Waited until he was ready to shake her.

Until he began to worry she'd change the subject or find an excuse to go back inside.

But then, so softly he scarcely heard her at first, she said, "Timothy and I grew up together. He was my brother's best friend and..." Her lips formed a wistful smile. "He thought me a pest when we were little and used to tease me relentlessly. I always dreaded his visits."

"He must have liked you. Even then."

"He put jam down the back of my dress!"

Devlin grinned. "And I would most likely have done the same, had I known you back then." When she gaped at him he shrugged and told her plainly, "Boys don't tease girls unless they're interested in them." Belatedly, he realized what he'd said and how it might sound and all things considered, the last thing he wanted right now was for her to think he'd been pining away after her for years when she'd never pined for him and...

He coughed and quickly nudged the conversation back into motion by saying, "But then you got older..."

"Yes." She gasped the word as if startled. "There was a summer during which everything changed. We hadn't seen each other for a couple of years because he'd gone off to travel the Continent after completing Oxford. In fact, he left the same year I had my debut, but that didn't matter. None of the other young men made an impression. In retrospect, I suppose I was waiting for Timothy to return. We hadn't come to an understanding at that time, and I'm not sure I even realized what I felt for him until he came back." She smiled and Devlin's chest tightened. "My parents were hosting a ball, and I'd just finished dancing with Mr. Vreeland when Timothy arrived, perfectly attired and looking more handsome than ever. And I knew, before he reached me and asked me to dance, I just knew he and I would marry, because of how much I loved him."

Devlin clasped his hands tightly behind his back and fought the urge to retreat from the conversation. It would be cowardly when he himself had pressed for it and besides, he had no reason to feel jealous. Did he? It wasn't as if he'd fallen in love with Cassandra. So why should he care if she'd given her heart to Timothy so long ago?

Perhaps because he knew he *could* love her if she'd let him. And possibly also because the idea of loving her if she couldn't return the sentiment didn't appeal. "You still love him," he said, torturing himself with the reminder that a dead man would always have something he wouldn't – Cassandra's heart.

"Of course. He was my closest friend and Penelope's father. I shall always love him, Devlin. That won't ever change."

Unwilling to focus on the fact that he'd likely go to hell for wanting to curse the day she and Timothy had met, Devlin clasped his hands tighter and forced himself to say what was necessary. "I'm not trying to take his place." When she didn't respond, he added, "When we were in Lisbon and I bought the bonnet for Penny, you reacted as if you're afraid I'm trying to leap in and steal something from you, whether it be Penny's affection or the memories you have of Timothy or…or something else entirely."

"Devlin, I'm sorry. You deserve so much better than me and—"

"None of that matters when you're the woman I want." There. He was being as honest as he knew how, and she was now staring at him as if he'd grown horns. Well, it wasn't as if their marriage could get much worse, so he might as well explain. "It's always been you, Cass. Before I even realized. And then Lady DeVries gave me the perfect excuse to make you mine and I took it."

Her eyes widened. "Are you saying you deliberately trapped me?"

Put that way, it didn't sound very good, did it?

Devlin scratched the back of his head, aware he was stalling. "In a way. I suppose. Although I wasn't really aware of what I was doing. It was only later, at Clearview, that it occurred to me." He attempted a grin to lighten the mood, but it just felt flat and empty. "I knew you weren't looking to marry, that you still mourned Penny's father, and yet I foolishly believed in a mutual attraction between us." Needing to touch her, he reached for her hand and slowly stroked his thumb across it. "I'm sorry. You told me not to expect a conventional marriage but I ignored you. I told myself all we needed was time, that eventually you'd let me kiss you and once you did that we would end up in bed and our marriage would be as it should be. But you clearly don't want me with the same desperation I want you and…" Feeling like a proper idiot, he yanked his hand back and raked his fingers through his hair. "Christ, I've been so blind and stupid. I—"

"No." She spoke softly but surely, wielding the word like a blade to halt his self-deprecation. A ragged series of breaths followed. Devlin's heart began pounding with a curious awareness of impending change. "You're neither blind nor stupid."

"What are you saying?" He asked the words in a low gravelly voice he scarcely recognized.

Her throat worked and she glanced away. Clearly, she found their conversation difficult, the words hard to get out. But then she said, "The attraction is mutual. It always has been. And it scares me to death."

The knot in his chest loosened, allowing him to take a deep breath. Mutual attraction. Well, there was a start. But rather than let instinct guide him and do as his body demanded – which was to pull her fiercely against him and crush her mouth with his – he chose to focus on the last part she'd said.

"Because you think acting on it would be disloyal?" When she nodded he felt his heart break for her. Was she even aware of how much she was sacrificing for a love that could no longer be?

"If you'd been widowed at an older age, I might understand, but you weren't even married and your courtship was brief. Cass…" She stiffened and gave him her back. "I know you loved him, how could you not when he'd been a part of your life for so long? When you chose him to be the man you'd grow old with, the man who would father your children?"

Her shoulders began to shake, alerting him to the tears she was shedding. Nothing made him feel worse, but there was more to be said, so after giving her a brief reprieve, he quietly continued.

"Are you happy living like this, without being held or cherished as you deserve?" A small shake of her head was her only response. Devlin drew a deep breath and forged straight ahead. Moving closer, he placed one hand on her shoulder and carefully said, "Let me help you, Cass. Let me care for you as I swore I would do before God. Let me be the husband I know I can be. Let me… please, Cass, please…let me kiss you."

It was one of those moments where a simple response would determine the future. Cassandra felt this deep in her bones. She sensed that if she walked away from Devlin now – if she refused him – he'd never reach out to her again in this way, and she would most likely lose her chance to have a proper marriage forever. Because then it would be up to her to change things between them, and she knew she wouldn't have the courage to do so.

So she turned, in spite of the tears streaming down her cheeks and the guilt ruthlessly clawing away at her heart. Because his words had struck a chord, reminding her of the loneliness she always felt even when she was in a crowded room. It followed her everywhere, even though she'd been blessed with a daughter and friends who were like sisters to her. In spite of it all, something was missing, and as she gazed up into Devlin's expectant face, allowed her eyes to lock onto his, she knew without hesitation what that something was. It was the need to be held, touched, comforted, and adored, but also a burning desire to return the favor.

Shuddering slightly, perhaps from cold or possibly from her petrified nerves, she forced herself to reach for change by leaping off the proverbial cliff and straight into the awaiting abyss.

Of course it wasn't quite so dramatic. All it took was one nod and she was in his arms. A tiny gasp of surprise was forced from her throat and sensation took over. There was strength in his embrace and warmth as well, and lord, it felt good to be held by a man once again. It had been so long. Too long. And it hadn't occurred to her until right now the extent to which she'd missed it.

But it was also different, as she'd known it would be since the first time she'd watched her husband undress. He was much larger than Timothy had been, completely lacking the slimmer build of a younger man whose body had yet to mature. Instead, all she felt were the hard muscular planes and powerful limbs of a capable man. And as she pressed her cheek to his chest and felt his heart beat in response to her touch, she inhaled him, an enticing scent of sandalwood mixed with the wool of his jacket and an added hint of the wine he'd enjoyed during his meal.

She felt his hand settle carefully against the small of her back, holding her to him while the other reached under her chin, tipping it up until his face filled her vision. He stroked his thumb lightly over her temple, the callused pad adding a touch of abrasion she would have presumed uncomfortable. But it wasn't. Quite the opposite, in fact.

Eyes locked with hers, he slowly lowered his head, allowing her the chance to retreat. The thought did cross her mind and for a split second her brain screamed for her to run, to flee this man who could give her the life she'd been meant to have with another – a man she already cared for so deeply she worried she might one day grow to love him.

And what then? Would she not be dishonoring Timothy's memory by opening her heart to another? Would she forget how much he'd meant to her and how perfect things had been between them? Would what they'd once shared be overshadowed, buried a little bit deeper, with each new experience Devlin gave her? And if that were the case, could she live with herself, knowing she'd turned her back on the vow she'd once made?

Before she was able to answer the questions, she felt Devlin's lips on her own—soft, but certain –

just a gentle press of affection, or perhaps a test of how willing she'd be. A low whimper filled the air, and she realized she'd made the sound. Why, she wasn't entirely sure. It could have been either from pleasure or pain, a culmination of all her desires and fears.

"Cass," he murmured, so low his voice vibrated through her, offering life to parts of her body and soul that had been dead for so many years. Her hand caught his shoulder to steady herself as he kissed her again, this time at one corner of her mouth. And then at the other.

He placed another kiss on her lips and then drew back, just enough to gaze down into her upturned face. "I wouldn't mind if you kissed me back."

Confused, she blinked a couple of times. "What?" The word was scarcely a whisper.

The edge of his mouth lifted to form a wry smile. "You're like a statue, Cass." And then he frowned, loosened his hold, and seemed about ready to let her go. "Perhaps you'd rather we stop?"

"No. I like this, Dev. I like you and being with you in this way." Unsure of how to explain what was happening to her, she closed her eyes briefly and took a deep breath. When she opened them again, she was met by a desperate need for under-standing. So she told him as honestly as she was able. "This isn't easy. As much as I want to be the wife you deserve and to make you happy, I'm haunted by the past at every turn, and I just can't seem to let it go. Not completely."

"I'm not asking you to. I'd never do that. You

loved another man with everything you were, Cass, and I accept that. But that doesn't mean you and I can't have something new and uniquely ours." He cupped her cheek. "I believe a person can find love more than once in a lifetime. And one does not have to exclude the other."

"Love?" His dark eyes gazed down at her with fierce intensity, the fire burning within almost making her lose her footing. "But you don't, and I don't, and—"

He kissed her again, stopping her chaotic thoughts from swirling out of control. And this time, the added possessiveness of it prompted her to respond. Driven by some primal instinct she thought she'd forgotten, she arched against him and parted her lips.

A growl, elemental and utterly thrilling, leapt from his body and straight into hers as he deepened the kiss. She swallowed it with a helpless moan and wound her arms more securely around his neck. Because, dear God, her husband had sparked a flame inside her that threatened to turn into quite the inferno. How had she survived for so long without this?

The only reasonable answer was she'd forgotten how good it could be when a man and a woman shared a mutual desire. Her grief and the responsibility she'd had to raise her daughter had made her ignore her own needs. And heaven help her she needed this – needed Devlin – more than she needed her next breath.

"Christ, you taste good," he whispered near her

ear moments later after kissing a path along her jawline. He nipped her lobe, causing a series of shivers to dart through her body. "And you feel incredible." As if to illustrate this, he lowered his hand to her bottom and pulled her flush up against him.

"Dev!" Her tone surprised her, for it didn't convey the outrage she knew she ought to show in response to the blatant proof of his lust. Instead, it was raspy with need and an urgent yearning for him to help her block out the past. She didn't care how, she just had to feel, to let him take her away from the awful memories in which she'd been drowning for so very long.

"God you're stunning." His voice was hoarse – strained even. And then he crushed her mouth with his and kissed her hard, replacing every thought in her head with the knowledge that she was wanted.

It was impossible for her not to bask in all the glorious sensations he stirred in her body.

Shuddering with pleasure, she returned Devlin's kiss with equal fervor, allowing him to know she was just as needy as he.

And yet, she could not allow them to take this further. Already, there was no denying he'd likely be left in a state of discomfort unless they retired to their cabin and she let him claim her. Only she wasn't quite ready for that – wasn't sure when, or even if, she would be. And that piece of stark awareness made her feel awful. Because she'd used him for her own satisfaction, without any thought to the consequences and without considering him or his feelings.

Selfish. That was what she was. Horrible. Without a doubt the most awful person she'd ever known. And still, she continued to kiss him until he leaned back and pulled her roughly against him, holding her tight.

"I'm sorry," she muttered against his shoulder.

"Whatever for?" A choked laugh escaped her. Was he really going to force her to explain? She tried to formulate the right words, but then, before she had a chance to answer, he said, "I'm not sorry for any of it, Cass. If anything, I'm delighted to learn how well you respond to my touch."

"But you probably…um…I mean…er."

The horrid man actually chortled. *Chortled!* "You needn't worry. I'll never insist you do something for which you're not ready. And I have a feeling it may be a while before you are ready for everything I have to offer."

He dropped his gaze for a second, then returned it to hers and raised an arrogant brow.

Cassandra pursed her lips. "You're incorrigible. Do you know that?"

He nudged her and jutted his chin toward the other end of the ship. "You should probably go and check on Penelope."

"But what about you? I mean, aren't you coming with me?"

He snorted. "Not in this state."

Cassandra considered his appearance. Apart from his hair being slightly ruffled, he looked the same as usual. "You're sure?"

"Quite." He winced as if in pain, then schooled his features and regarded her with the utmost seriousness. "You should go. Right now. Before I lose whatever restraint I possess and do something reckless."

The strain of his voice revealed that he was wound tighter than a new spool of thread, and close to unraveling at any second. Understanding his meaning, Cassandra gave a quick nod and turned on her heel. When she climbed into bed ten minutes later after finding Penelope fast asleep, she could not stop from wondering what it would be like to simply surrender – to abandon her inhibitions and let herself lie with Devlin.

The memory of the kiss they'd shared and the pleasure he'd brought her while holding her in his arms filled her with even more longing.

It wasn't until she woke the following morning that she remembered. For the first time since Timothy's death, she'd forgotten to speak her vow before drifting off to sleep. And nothing could have made her hate herself more.

CHAPTER ELEVEN

A S USUAL WHENEVER HE SAILED, Devlin slept only three hours. He'd gone to bed a while after sending Cassandra back to their cabin and was now awake before her, allowing him the satisfaction of watching her face while she slept. He still couldn't quite grasp the fact that she was his wife or the enthusiasm with which she'd kissed him last night. Yes, she'd been hesitant at first, perhaps unsure, but then, once she'd made her decision, she'd unveiled a passionate side he could scarcely wait to explore further. Hell, it had taken his body a good half hour to accept that it wouldn't be getting what it wanted anytime soon.

Slowly, he reminded himself. They had time – plenty of it in fact – and they'd made a tremendous stride in the right direction. So as long as he didn't push her too hard or make demands before she was ready, he was certain they'd soon be exploring each other more intimately.

A devilish smile curved his lips as he went to wash and get dressed. He couldn't wait to see her naked, to bury himself in her heat and send her soaring.

Dropping his gaze, he groaned. Just the thought of it, however brief it had been, had put him in a state once again. He glanced at the window and the cold ocean beyond. With a sigh, he grabbed a book on common diseases found aboard ships and how to treat them, and prepared to wait for his body – or a certain part of it – to relax.

It was almost four by the time he made his way to the galley for breakfast after checking on Monty, who'd taken over the helm right before Devlin had gone to bed. Once he'd eaten, Devlin would relieve his friend so he could get some much needed rest.

He entered the gun deck and glanced around. Ordinarily, Talbot was already bustling about at this hour, getting food ready for four o' clock, when half the crew finished their watch and the other half rose to start theirs. But all was quiet. The stove wasn't even lit and…

Hell. Were those dirty dishes from last night's meal? A cabin boy would have to be roused immediately to handle this mess, and Mr. Talbot too. Devlin prided himself on taking care of his men and would not expect any of them to work on empty stomachs.

But when he reached the sleeping quarters below deck and approached the cot Talbot favored over the hammocks, he instantly knew his cook would not be preparing food that day or for several days to come. His forehead was damp, his sleep the restless kind caused by high fever, and if that weren't enough indication of Talbot's malaise, the bucket next to his cot made it startlingly clear.

Devlin backed up a step to escape the sour stench of vomit. If Talbot was sick, his assistant would have to take over. Except the young man nicknamed Chopper, who'd so often leapt in to help whenever Talbot was indisposed, looked no better off than Talbot.

Good God! If there was an epidemic on board it would cripple the crew, extend the journey, lead to hunger and lack of fresh water before they reached port. It would be a catastrophe, not to mention he'd no bloody clue as to whom he could turn to in order to feed all these men. Four hundred and eighty souls depended on him and here they were, only three days' sail from Lisbon, and now this! He glanced around at the sleeping men in their hammocks while panic began to set in. Perhaps they ought to turn back.

Perhaps…

A thought struck him.

Before he had time to consider the wisdom of the plan forming in his head, he strode forward and shook one of the cabin boys awake. "To the galley with you," he ordered. "There's a mess there that must be cleaned right away."

The boy, barely fifteen years of age, stammered something incoherent before rolling out of his hammock and landing on wobbly legs. Devlin regretted having to rouse him but knew not what else to do. Talbot and Chopper both looked like death, and if they were contagious, he'd be an idiot to let them manage the food even if he were able to force them into action.

Instead, he woke another sailor and instructed him to help the cabin boy, assuring him he'd be allowed an extra hour's sleep later as compensation. Satisfied something was being done to fix the situation, Devlin then made his way back to his cabin where Cassandra still slept so soundly, the very idea of waking her gave him pause.

But no. He could not afford to let her sleep when she was the only other person on board who knew how to cook well enough to solve the current dilemma. Devil take it, he ought to have learned himself if for no other reason than so he could leap in and help in such situations. But he hadn't and lamenting his lack of culinary skills wouldn't fill any stomachs.

So he sat on the edge of Cassandra's bed and placed one hand on her shoulder. "Cass?" He nudged her a little and she responded with an agitated groan. "Wake up." He shook her more roughly. She swatted him away as if he were some pesky insect.

Devlin sighed. There really wasn't time for this. In another ten minutes or so the bell would signal the end of the watch, and men would rush to the galley expecting something. "Right then," he muttered and promptly yanked the blanket away from Cassandra.

Her eyes flew open on a gasp. "What the bloody hell are you doing?" she asked as she pulled on her nightgown and did her utmost to protect her modesty.

Later, it would occur to him that her blaspheme should have surprised him since he'd never heard her curse before. But in that moment, the only thing his brain was able to process was the fact that her nightgown had crawled almost all the way to her waist, allowing him to glimpse the rounded curve of her bottom peeking out from beneath the fine muslin. Of course, he'd seen all there was to see of her thighs and legs and feet… but her bottom…

He cleared his throat. Time to take charge and remember his reason for waking her up in the first place. "Talbot and his assistant are both sick, so I need you to get up, get dressed, and come with me right now."

She blinked. "But—"

"No time to argue." He grabbed her by her elbow and hauled her to her feet. "The crew will need to be fed in—" The bell sounding the watch shift rang. Feet pounded across the deck above them. Devlin cursed beneath his breath. "Now."

"I, um…" With a yawn, she nodded.

"Good." Devlin grabbed some undergarments from one of the drawers beneath her bed and located a dress cut from practical brown linen. Tossing the lot on her bed, he proceeded to pull off her nightgown without preamble.

Which earned him a shriek.

He stilled. Let her nightgown fall. "Now is not the time for modesty, Cass, but for practicality and haste."

"As if I was not made aware of that when you

woke me in the rudest and most abrupt fashion I've ever experienced."

"Sorry," he muttered, because it was the thing to say, not because he actually felt it. How could he when his brash method had allowed him to fill in some of the gaps that existed in his most carnal fantasies? "I only thought to help."

"I'm sure you did," she told him with cutting force, "but I can manage perfectly fine on my own. Thank you."

He gave a curt nod, deliberately choosing to ignore the disappointment he felt as he moved to the door. It wasn't as if he expected her to profess her undying love for him because of one kiss, but he had, damn it all, expected it to change *some-*thing between them. In his vast experience of kissing, theirs was the most spectacular, the most unforgettable – perfection itself. Yet now, she wouldn't even let him—her husband, not some stranger, he told himself disdainfully— help her dress.

"Fine then. I'll go and inform the crew that their breakfast is going to be late." And with that he left her, before he succumbed to temptation and caused additional delay by kissing her.

"Christ have mercy," he muttered as he stomped off, his mood defined by the problem he faced with Talbot and the unsated state he'd endured for so long he was sure it was starting to wear on his health. Like the rest of his men, he usually found a willing woman to tend to his needs when he was in port, but his betrothal to Cass had happened so soon after his arrival in London, he'd not had the time. And once he'd gotten betrothed, the idea of sleeping with someone else hadn't entered his head. Which meant it was now...he did a quick sum and decided five months fit the bill.

Good God! Another man would likely have forced himself on his wife by now. Devlin winced. He hated himself for having such thoughts – for allowing himself to consider for even one second the fate she'd have had as another man's wife. As if he wished he were able to be an unfeeling bastard and take what he wanted without hesitation.

He couldn't and he wouldn't, which meant he'd have to suffer the repercussions of marrying a woman who still mourned a man she'd never married, thirteen years after his death. She loved him. It made perfect sense that she did, and it would be foolish to think she wouldn't. He was the man she'd picked to be her life partner, her childhood friend, Penelope's father and, and, and...

The truth was Devlin was sick of Timothy and the hold he maintained on Cassandra's heart.

There it was, even if he had to rot in hell for feeling this way about someone who'd earned a halo the moment he'd drawn his last breath. Timothy's character no longer mattered. In Cassandra's mind, he was incomparable, irreplaceable, a martyr of sorts – impossible for anyone else to live up to. And what surprised Devlin the most was not so much the awareness that this was a fact he would have to accept, but rather the pain it caused him to do so.

Feeding hundreds of men was not on Cassandra's list of qualifications. That said, she wasn't about to back down from a challenge or refuse to help in a crisis, no matter how boorish her husband was choosing to be. She did, after all, know how to handle a stove and how to prepare a basic meal. Having spent the past week watching Talbot work, she also had a sense of the routine required for swift satisfaction among the crew. So she rolled up her sleeves and went to work, ignoring the stares and the bated breaths of expectation simmering in the air.

"Porridge," she declared once she'd taken a moment to ponder her options. There was an audible groan from some of the men who'd heard her. But rather than shy away from their criticism, she glared in the general direction from which the sound had come. "Would you rather wait an hour or two in order to eat?"

When nobody answered, she picked out the largest pot she could find and proceeded to add both water and oats. Once the mixture was simmering over the fire, she added some salt, then located some sugar and cinnamon for the final touch.

"This aint 'alf bad," one of the sailors murmured half an hour later. "Better than I expected."

Cassandra accepted the compliment with a smile and without ruining the moment by asking if he'd been one of the ones to complain earlier.

"Well done," Monty told her when he came

down to collect his ration. "Working under pressure on only a few hours' sleep can be a challenge. Particularly when you're being asked to do something you're not familiar with."

And when your husband is choosing to be difficult, she mused. She still couldn't quite believe the brashness with which he'd forced her out of bed or the harshness with which he'd proceeded to give her orders or... She swallowed, recalling her state of undress when he'd pulled back the covers.

It shouldn't have mattered, she supposed, yet it did. Perhaps because of the kiss they'd shared and the aching awareness that had rushed to the front of her mind as soon as she'd opened her eyes and spotted Devlin. Because that was when it had hit her and she'd remembered – the vow she ought to have made, unspoken for the first time in over a decade, because he'd made her forget. And this, coupled with the vulnerability she'd felt as her body was bared to his gaze, the guilt expanding around her with each breath she took, and the pure annoyance any sane person would feel upon being woken after only four hours of sleep, had made her churlish.

Not that she cared. For the first time ever, Cassandra decided she had a right to be out of sorts, irritated even, if she desired. Her world as she knew it had, after all, been set at an angle. So much so that she'd sail right over the side if the world were as flat as some people once thought it to be.

"Mrs. Crawford?"

Cassandra snapped to attention and stared back at Monty. "I do beg your pardon," she muttered and quickly served him a bowl of hot porridge.

He nodded his thanks. "Not to trouble you, but Devlin said I should ask you to plan the next meal once we've all finished this one. It will help get us back on schedule."

Too stunned to speak, Cassandra stared after him as he walked away. She ought to have known, but she'd been too busy to wonder about the upcoming meals and how they'd get prepared. If Mr. Talbot was as sick as she suspected he must be for her to end up in charge of the galley, she'd probably have to cook every meal until he was able to get back on his feet.

Exhausted, she sagged against the work table and scrubbed one hand across her brow. It was going to be a very long journey indeed. Though not nearly as difficult as she'd imagined when Penelope woke with a fever the following morning.

"I'll fetch Bronswick," Devlin told Cassandra while she placed another cool compress on Penelope's brow. She didn't turn to look at him, she merely nodded in acknowledgement. "And then I'll stay with her." He paused before carefully adding, "While you prepare luncheon."

Cassandra glanced over her shoulder then, but he'd already disappeared from the doorway. Lord help her, she couldn't recall ever being this tired. Or worried, for that matter. Having slept in three hour increments since the previous day, she'd made sure food was ready for the crew every four hours, even if it was just soup and some biscuits to tide them over until the next meal. And now Penelope, who hadn't been sick since she'd caught a cold three years earlier, was burning up.

"Is there anything I can do to help?" Trevor asked when he popped his head in one minute later. Concern flickered in the young man's eyes as he looked across at Penelope.

Cassandra shook her head. "No. Thank you."

Trevor hesitated briefly, made an awkward nodding motion, and left.

"Mama?" Penelope's voice was weak and strained.

"Yes, my darling." Cassandra caught her daughter's hand and squeezed it.

"Can you please stay with me today?"

A lump formed in Cassandra's throat, and for a brief second she struggled to keep her composure. "I'm sorry, but I can't." Heaven above, how she hated this, hated herself for bringing her daughter along on this foolish voyage, for leaving the comfort of their home to travel the world with a husband she hadn't wanted in the first place, and for letting desire destroy her principles.

Her voice trembled when she spoke again. "If you'll recall, the cook is also sick, so I have to step in and help as best as I can. But Devlin…" She had to stop for a moment to gather her wits. Just mentioning his name caused a fresh rush of guilt to clutch at her heart. "He'll watch over you. And

Mr. Bronswick will also do his best to make you feel better."

"Promise?"

Cassandra caught her trembling lower lip between her teeth. "Of course." Bowing her head, she dropped a kiss on Penelope's cheek. Behind her, a man cleared his throat, and Cassandra realized Devlin had returned with the physician. "I will see you later. All right?"

Penelope merely nodded.

Cassandra stood and turned to Devlin. "Promise me you'll fetch me if she worsens," she whispered.

"Of course," Devlin murmured, his dark eyes piercing hers with a fierce intensity that set her mind slightly more at ease.

"Talbot is showing some improvement today," Bronswick said, "which would suggest a swift-moving ailment from which your daughter will soon recover."

"Let's hope so." It was all Cassandra could think to say as she glanced down at Penelope one last time before heading to the galley. Devlin would care for her as if she were his own. Cassandra knew this without even having to ponder the issue. But not being able to sit by her bedside herself – it made her heart ache.

Two hours later, Cassandra stumbled toward Penelope's cabin. She scarcely recalled boiling the eggs, frying the fish, or preparing the oranges she'd decided to serve. It was all a blur since her mind had been fully occupied by thoughts of her daughter and how she was faring. At least no one had sent for her, which surely meant that Penelope's condition at least hadn't worsened.

Clinging to this hope, Cassandra turned a corner and quickened her step when Penelope's door came into view. It required an exercise in extreme self-control for her not to fling it wide open and rush to her daughter's side. Instead, she carefully turned the knob and eased the door slowly away from its frame in order to minimize her disturbance.

The first thing that struck her was the air. It seemed fresher than earlier, and when a sudden rush of coolness licked at her skin, she realized the porthole had been opened. Cassandra smiled approvingly and edged her way further into the snug space. And that was when she saw them. Dismayed, Cassandra froze and simply stared while a series of warm, brightly colored emotions filled her heart and expanded it so much she feared it might burst.

She swallowed hard against the tightening of her throat as she watched Devlin sleep, his large body stretched out awkwardly on Penelope's narrow bed while he cradled her in his arms. Her head was cushioned against his chest and she looked more peaceful than when Cassandra had last seen her. A soft snore left Devlin's mouth, and Cassandra could not help but smile. Timothy might be gone but at least Devlin was here, and right now, that was all that mattered. His strength and his ability to make things better, his thoughtfulness and consideration for a girl who wasn't his own. He was being a father to her – the father she'd always wanted – and Cassandra had no right to resent that. It was clear to her that Penelope needed him. And perhaps she needed him too, if she were being completely honest. Far more than she cared to admit.

Cassandra carefully touched her fingers to Penelope's forehead. Her skin was still hot, but her breathing was calmer. And she was sleeping, which would surely aid her recovery. Locating the bucket Penelope had used that morning, Cassandra glanced into it and breathed a sigh of relief when she saw it was empty. Perhaps the worst had passed. She could only hope and… She looked around. There wasn't much she could do right now. Devlin seemed to have things well in hand, so perhaps her best course of action would be to get some sleep as well.

The half hour bell rang, informing her she would soon have to wake again.

With this in mind, she left Devlin and Penelope to their rest and went in search of her own bed. She collapsed on it fully clothed, but rather than finding the sleep she'd expected, her mind was kept busy with thoughts of Devlin.

His goodness went straight to her heart, filling it with warmth and a desperate yearning for all the things she'd denied herself for so long.

She wanted him.

As much as she'd tried to tell herself otherwise, the kiss they'd shared proved it. He'd torn down her every defense and breathed new life into her soul. And it was time – time to consider the future instead of the past, to be the wife Devlin deserved so he could become the husband he wanted to be. It was time to put all her fears behind her and give their marriage a chance.

Inhaling deeply, Cassandra made her decision, and finally slept.

CHAPTER TWELVE

IT WAS DARK WHEN DEVLIN awoke. He squinted, tried to adjust his eyes. A slim arm was draped across his waist, and he gingerly eased it aside so he could sit. Penelope, bless her heart, still slept as soundly as when she'd first nestled her head against his shoulder. The poor girl had been terribly ill after Cassandra's departure, casting up her accounts until she collapsed against him, too weak to sit up or even to speak.

He'd briefly considered alerting Cassandra as promised, but then Penelope had drifted off and he'd chosen to wait. Rising, he rearranged the blanket, tucking it more securely around Penelope's shoulders. His heart thumped hard on account of her suffering, and he leaned forward, driven by instinct, until he brushed his lips across her brow. She was still hot, though perhaps not as much as before. Locating the compress which had most likely slipped from her forehead ages ago, he wet it once more, wrung it, and smoothed it across her skin.

"I'll be back soon," he promised, even though she would not hear him.

After leaving the cabin, he made his way up onto the deck. "What's the hour?" he asked once he'd located Monty. His friend gripped the wheel, holding it steady while shouting occasional orders to the crew managing the sails.

"It was six at the last bell." Monty gave Devlin a sidelong look when he swore. "No need to worry about it, aye? We're still on course, you're well rested and better prepared to captain this marvelous vessel, and your wife, from what I've been hearing, is preparing beef for dinner."

"Christ almighty." He felt awful. "I have to go see how she's doing." The very idea of her slaving away while he slept made him feel like he'd abandoned his duties. And that was without considering his men. "I'm sorry, Monty. I'll be back in a bit to take your spot. Lord knows you can probably do with some rest as well."

"Wouldn't be the worst thing in the world, now you mention it." Monty gave him a hard look. "How's your daughter doing?"

"Better. I think."

"Glad to hear it. Now go see about your wife."

Devlin did as he was told and was pleased to discover Cassandra hurrying about the galley, checking the oven and stirring the contents of various pots as if she'd been cooking on a ship her entire life. He approached her quietly, savoring the moment, the fragrant smell of meat roasting combined with various spices, and her – the woman he'd married.

She was the most capable person he'd ever

known, managing all these years by herself and even succeeding to help others. While he'd made a convincing argument in order to get her to marry him, he was wise enough to know that she didn't really need him. But it hadn't occurred to him until recently how much he wanted her to. Not just physically, but in all aspects of day-to-day life.

With a sigh, he took a few steps closer. "It looks like you're doing well here."

She spun toward him, her eyes widening with surprise and then something else. "How's—"

"She's sleeping. Peacefully, I might add." She closed her eyes and blew out a shuddering breath. When she looked at him again, he said, "I believe the worst has passed. Your prayers last night must have worked."

"My…" She stopped herself and quickly nodded, though not before he noted her frown of confusion.

Odd that.

Dismissing it as inconsequential, Devlin informed her he probably wouldn't be seeing her again until later. "Monty needs to sleep so I'm hoping to give him a couple of extra hours by giving myself a longer shift."

"What about food?" She made a sweeping motion with her arms, and his stomach instantly grumbled in response.

"Well, I certainly don't want to miss the fine meal you're preparing, so perhaps you can bring a plate up once you've checked on Penelope?"

"Of course. I'd be happy to."

He paused to study her face, or more precisely her features, while doing his best to examine her manner and speech. There was something different about her somehow, something less guarded, more open, not quite so… He wasn't sure what but he sensed with a fluttering beat of his heart that Cassandra had changed while he'd been asleep. Regrettably, he had no time to determine what, how, or why at that precise moment. Not when they both had jobs to do.

So he merely nodded and walked away, allowing his feet to carry him to his post even though his heart would so much rather have remained in the galley. But since he'd slept the entire day, there was so much for Devlin to check on, so many updates for him to listen to while maintaining their course, he scarcely noticed the passing of time until Cassandra arrived.

Dismissing the sailor with whom he'd been speaking, Devlin gave her his full attention, although to be fair, his hunger for food caused his gaze to go straight to the plate she carried. She grinned. "You look like a starved man." And without further comment, she stabbed a diced piece of meat and held it up to his mouth.

He ate it, almost sighing in response to the savory flavor. She offered him another bite, followed by a spoonful of peas, then some potato and yet more meat.

"It occurred to me," she said while he chewed, her voice a little unsure, "that you wouldn't be able to use your hands to eat while steering the ship, so I cut everything into bite-sized portions."

"I'm glad." He couldn't care less as long as his stomach stopped burning. "How's Penny?"

"Much better." She gave him another spoonful of peas. "Thank you."

"It's not my doing."

"Hmm." She said nothing more. She just kept feeding him until the plate was empty. "Do you know where we are?"

"Of course." It might be dark, but that didn't mean he did not know their position with perfect accuracy. "We're passing Mauritania."

"Oh."

He grinned. "You've never heard of it have you?"

"I must confess my African geography isn't quite up to par."

"Can't really blame you," he said with a shrug. "It's not exactly the sort of thing you've needed to know. But perhaps you have a sense of where the Sahara is?"

"Yes it's…" She scrunched her nose as if unsure of how to describe its location. Her hand made a swirling motion next to her head. "I can find it on a globe."

"Right." Devlin hid his amusement by glancing off to the side. "Well, most of Mauritania's land is within the desert, so the population is largely con-centrated near the coast. In a week, maybe less, we should reach the Gulf of Guinea."

"Where the continent curves to one side?"

"Precisely." They could manage a few delays here and there if necessary. Devlin always made sure adverse weather conditions and minor mishaps were accounted for. But it was still vital they stuck as close to their schedule as possible since he'd no desire to sail through another Harmattan.

"Devlin?" Cassandra's hand was on his arm. "Is everything all right?"

"Quite." No need to worry her with the prospect of nosebleeds, cracked skin, and burning eyes, which was what he and his crew had suffered during their last encounter with the wind blowing down from the desert. "Thank you for dinner and for handling all the other meals these last two days. I've been told Mr. Talbot is expected back in the galley tomorrow."

Cassandra cleared her throat. "Perhaps I could help him from time to time."

Surprised, Devlin caught her gaze and held it. "You want to keep working?"

She shrugged. "It gives me something to do and… Well, if life at Clearview has taught me anything, it's the joy of accomplishment and sense of purpose one can find by getting things done yourself. As opposed to relying on servants."

He'd always admired and respected her so much he wouldn't have thought his opinion of her could improve. Yet it did. Every day, it seemed. His heart swelled dangerously with an emotion he'd rather not dwell on.

Attempting to hide his response, he gave a stiff nod. "I'm sure Mr. Talbot would be grateful."

Cassandra beamed. "Excellent. I mean, thank you. I…" She looked strangely out of sorts. "I should probably see how Penelope's doing and keep her company for a bit. When I left her, she was reading."

He merely nodded, but his eyes never left her as she climbed down onto the main deck and made her way below. That feeling from earlier, that something had changed, remained, keeping him company and filling his mind with endless questions until he returned to his cabin four hours later.

Given the time, he'd expected Cassandra to be fast asleep. But she wasn't. And the moment his searching gaze found her sitting in bed and reading a book, wearing only her nightgown, the same desire he always felt when he saw her thus struck him like a blow. Clenching his jaw in the hope of stemming his arousal, he shut the door and averted his eyes. Because if he kept looking at her…

The kiss they'd share had been splendid, but something – he knew not what – had wrecked it, tarnished it somehow. And rather than moving forward with her, he'd felt himself sliding back. It wasn't exactly anything she'd said. It had been her manner and tone when he'd woken her and thought to help her dress. Her sharp refusal had informed him that she wasn't ready to be intimate with him, no matter how heated their kiss might have been. And something about that had twisted his heart, because it had made him feel rejected in a way he knew he ought to expect, but had started to hope he wouldn't be.

Until this evening, when she'd seemed closer somehow. It was the oddest thing, considering they'd barely touched or talked throughout the day. Perhaps it was all wishful thinking on his part or maybe she was just grateful to him for helping care for Penelope.

Either way, he dared not let himself over analyze the situation and resolved to let things unfold in due time. So he took off his tricorn and set it aside, then fluffed his hair with his fingers. "I trust Penny is sleeping?"

"She fell asleep just ten minutes ago. Having slept most of the day, she wasn't especially tired, but reading to her eventually helped."

"And her fever?"

"It's almost gone."

"I'm relieved to hear it." He shrugged out of his jacket and hung it over the back of his chair before going to work on his cravat.

"I can help you with that," Cassandra said. "If you like."

Devlin froze. His fingers clutched the cloth wound around his neck. He hadn't heard her get out of bed, and he certainly hadn't heard her creep up behind him. He turned. Slowly. And sucked in a lungful of air. Because she was looking up at him as if…as if… Good God, he dared not hope that he might know her reason for offering to tend to him thus.

Heart pounding, he dropped his hands. "By all

means." His voice was gruff, like gravel beneath a booted foot.

When she reached toward him, he noted the tremble in her fingers. It was slight, but it was there. She was nervous. For whatever reason, she was stepping away from what she found comfortable in order to help him undress.

Words.

He searched for them – some means by which to fill the silence and put her at ease. "What were you reading?" She'd stepped closer, most likely to more easily reach him. But her proximity brought an intoxicating fragrance with it – not her usual scent of roses but something more unique, more elusive, more...

"To Penelope or to myself?"

He caught the note of amusement in her voice and felt some of the tension subside. "Both, I suppose."

"Well, Penelope has always loved adventure stories, so I read a few chapters of *Waverley* for her."

"Excellent choice," he murmured, acutely aware of Cassandra's fingertips grazing his skin. It was either stand as still as a statue or give in to carnal instinct and pounce on her like an animal. "And for yourself?"

Her cheeks turned a delightful shade of pink. "Well, I must confess I've brought all of Miss Austen's novels with me." Having finished untying his cravat, she slid the length of fabric away from his neck while biting her lip. "Her writing is quite good, you know. Humorous too."

"I'm sure it is, although I never would have thought it might appeal to you."

That seemed to get her attention. "Why on earth not?"

"I don't know. Perhaps because I always imagined the women who read such books to be of the day-dreaming variety."

She put both hands on her hips and allowed his cravat to dangle all the way to the floor. "I'm not sure what frustrates me more about that opinion: your willingness to judge a person based on what they choose to read or your inability to imagine I might indulge in a bit of escapism too from time to time."

"I meant no offense," he grumbled. "I just…" He blew out a breath, aware he should probably shut up now before making things worse. "I suppose I always imagined you'd rather read something along the lines of Benjamin Franklin's autobiography or an account of Captain Cook's travels – something more educational, I suppose. Like that autobiography you recently finished."

"Well…" She smiled, much to his relief. "I must confess to having read both of those books." Her palm settled against his chest and when she spoke again, it was with a whisper. "But that doesn't mean I can't sometimes enjoy a bit of romance."

Her eyes were fixed on his and although the room was dimly lit by a singular oil lamp, they'd never looked brighter. Or, he decided, with a flood of desperation, more inviting. "Cass." Her name crossed his lips both as a plea and as a question.

Without speaking, she untied the fastenings at the front of his shirt, so slowly he feared he might soon explode from anticipation. What she was doing…

Did it mean she was ready to let him claim her? Or was she merely performing what she believed to be her wifely duties, without really performing them? The questions were impossible for him to answer. Mostly because he knew what he wanted them to be and feared he might have it wrong.

But then she tugged his shirt free from his breeches and reached underneath to touch his bare skin. Her palm was warm as it slid up over his back, her fingertips gently pressing against his flesh. An unbidden groan escaped him. It couldn't be helped. What she was doing felt so damn good, and by God, he wanted more. He didn't want her to stop. He just…

Whispered her name. "Cass?" Because he had to know – had to understand what was going on between them before she drove him insane.

Except she didn't answer, perhaps because she hadn't heard the question in his voice or understood what it was he was asking. Whatever the case, it hardly mattered when in the next instant she moved her hands to his sides, running them upward, the motion making him lift his arms until his shirt was suddenly gone and she was leaning in, her lips scorching his skin as she kissed him right over his heart.

A shudder raked his spine and his hand instinctively rose to hold her head to him. "Cass?" he asked again, his voice hoarse and his body unbearably strained.

"Hmmm?" She tipped back her chin and met his gaze, her eyes shimmering with something he'd never seen there before.

Raggedly, he forced himself to ask, "What are you doing?" Because he had to be sure, needed for it to be perfectly clear so he'd know precisely how he should act and what to expect.

An uncharacteristically shy smile touched her lips, but she didn't look away. Instead she slid her hand up over his shoulder, along the side of his neck until she caressed his cheek.

And then she said, "I'm inviting you to make love to me, Dev."

He almost tripped over his own bloody feet in his haste to grab her and kiss her and dear God! He'd dreamed of this moment for so damn long, and now it was here and he hardly knew where to start because he wanted to do everything all at once.

With a deep breath, he forced himself to reign in his fervor. This was to be their first time together, and he doubted she'd appreciate it being over in under ten seconds. And also, he realized, he needed some answers — some sort of confirmation that she wasn't acting irrationally or on a whim.

"Are you sure?" The last thing he wanted was for her to answer in the negative, but he needed to know her heart was engaged and that this wasn't something she would regret in the morning.

"Yes." She tried to pull him back for another kiss, but he resisted.

"What about Timothy?" He wasn't an idiot after all. Devlin knew *he* was the reason she hadn't given herself to him yet. Because she'd believed it was wrong, still mourned the loss, refused to move on. The reason didn't really matter, but the power behind it did. Because during the last six weeks, he'd discovered he didn't just like her or respect her or enjoy her company. He could easily grow to love her. And damn it all, he wanted her love in return. He didn't want her loving another man more. Not even a dead one.

She stopped. Just stopped. As if frozen in time.

Devlin scarcely dared breathe while he waited for her to move, to give him her answer. Because he knew it would shape their future. And he dreaded the possibility of it shaping it badly.

"He was everything to me," she finally murmured. Devlin's heart clenched, as if gripped by a fist. Her eyes found his, their shimmer suggesting she fought back tears. "But I think you could be everything too. I think..." She shook her head. "You've always been a dear friend and I know it's taken me forever to realize this and accept it, but the thing is... I need you. More than that, I want you, in a way I haven't wanted anyone for so very long, and while I don't know where this will take us, *you* are my husband." She implored him with her eyes in a way he couldn't resist, then added, "I want to try and make our marriage a good one. For both our sakes."

She wasn't saying she might one day love him, but in her own way, she'd said enough. More than he'd ever expected, really. So he wouldn't ask her for more. Instead, he would simply kiss her.

Chapter Thirteen

Cassandra wasn't entirely sure when she'd recognized this was what she wanted. In a way, it had happened gradually. But if she had to point at one moment, she believed she would choose this afternoon, when she'd entered Penelope's cabin and found her cocooned in Devlin's arms. Because it had served as a stark reminder of his importance. Having his support and knowing she was able to count on him when needed, made her realize that letting him into her heart made more sense than pushing him away. He was family, the closest thing to a father Penelope would ever know, and God willing, the only husband Cassandra would ever have.

And as this notion had cemented itself more firmly during the rest of the day, the guilt she felt and the gnawing pain in her chest that invariably came with the idea of making a life for herself with a man who wasn't Timothy had dissipated. Until it melted away completely.

Allowing Devlin to care for her and letting herself care for him in return would not diminish what she and Timothy had shared. The bond would be different, perhaps even stronger with time, and she finally felt as if that was all right. Perhaps, she mused, because much of the heartache she'd felt had been self-imposed. Not that she'd felt sorry for herself, but she'd been young – so very young – when it had happened. And looking forward at decades of empty loneliness ahead had been horribly depressing.

She'd never thought she would actually marry. Her reputation had been so tarnished she hadn't even hoped. Instead, she'd run away and told herself to stay true to her love, because at least then, she'd have something to believe in.

Except now there was Devlin. She'd never imagined she'd be here with him, on a ship of all places, like this. What she'd done, undressing him as she had, was more daring than she'd intended. But with her decision made and him staring at her as if she embodied his every fantasy, she knew there was only one way to do this: by living to the fullest.

His lips found hers and she kissed him back boldly, tasting his hunger until they both gasped for breath. And then she kissed him again, because she could and because she loved the feel of his lips against her own. Desperate to touch him, she grabbed at his shoulders and held on tight, reveling in the warmth of his skin and the power that lay beneath.

"Christ, Cass." His lips left hers to trail a delicious path down the side of her neck while his hand crept over her hip. "I need to see you." His breath was hot, his voice thick with desire.

And then he stepped back, allowing cool air to encase her.

She stared at him, at his tight expression and the fire burning in the depth of his eyes. His fingers twitched, as if he was desperate to reach out and touch her, but chose not to do so through some force of will. *I need to see you.* There was no question about what he asked. And since she'd seen him – most of him anyway – she understood his reasoning.

So she reached for the hem of her nightgown and, pulling it slowly upward, revealed herself to him.

"You…" His voice caught and he simply stood there, staring at her until she grew unbearably self-conscious. She glanced at her discarded nightgown. Perhaps she should put it back on? Her fingers started to reach toward it.

"Stop!"

She shuddered slightly on account of the order, but did as he asked. Labored breaths filled the air. His, not hers. As if moving through water, she raised her gaze to his and was instantly overcome by the forceful look in his eyes. "Dev?" she whispered and straightened herself for his perusal.

He licked his lips and she shuddered once more. This time, in a far more intimate way. His throat worked and his upper arm muscles flexed.

"You're perfect, Cass." The words were barely audible and yet she heard them anyway. "More beautiful than I ever dreamed possible. And trust me," a wicked gleam touched his eyes, "I have dreamed."

The words – the implication – was scandalous in the extreme. And it did something to her, something she never would have expected. It made her feel wanton.

He moved toward her, then reached out and let one finger trail down her arm. "But none of my dreams compare to this." Setting his palm against her lower back, he pulled her flush up against him. "Reality is so much sweeter."

What followed was unlike anything Cassandra had ever experienced. Even if she'd been given a lifetime in which to imagine what being with Devlin would be like, she would have failed. Because when it came to the bedroom, her husband was quite the scoundrel. He worshipped her with his hands and explored her with his mouth. And he didn't let her get away with anything less, encouraging her to do things she never would have believed herself capable of.

But with every suggestive word he whispered in her ear and with each wicked touch, he made her want to be daring and bold. So by the time they finally joined, both desperate to reach the peak of their lovemaking, she'd either touched or kissed every inch of his glorious body.

"Bloody hell," he gasped once they'd found a shared rhythm. "I can't…Cass…I don't think…"

She rather felt the same way. They'd spent so much time preparing themselves for this moment, during which she'd almost spiraled out of control three times already, she wasn't sure she'd last another minute.

"It's alright," she managed while matching his movements. "Don't stop. Just…" And then it happened. Like an explosion of light ripping through her and lifting her upward, it carried her off to some blissful height.

Faintly, she heard Devlin grunt, felt him tense right before he collapsed on her with a heavy sigh. Her hand settled on his back, lightly stroking across his hot skin.

"Oh my God," he breathed.

She grinned, because she knew precisely what he meant. Oh my God, indeed.

A moment passed and then he raised himself on his forearms. His expression – the look in his eyes – was one she knew she would never forget. "That was incredible, Cass. *You* were incredible."

His hair was adorably mussed but it was the reverence with which he regarded her that stole her breath completely. He shook his head as if unsure what else to say, then he simply leaned forward a little and kissed her lightly on her forehead.

"It surpassed my own expectations," she confessed a couple of minutes later once he'd rolled to the side and pulled her against him. "I never imagined I'd…um…well…" Her face grew hot and words failed her.

Devlin's hand trailed leisurely over her hip. "I'm extremely glad you did," he murmured seductively next to her ear. "And I look forward to helping you further your skills."

She almost choked, because really, this wasn't the sort of conversation she'd been brought up to have. Not ever. Although she suspected it might be a bit late for inhibitions now after everything that had just passed between them. And besides, she secretly liked him whispering naughty things in her ear.

"For instance…" His fingers followed a path that ended between her thighs. "I've had the most interesting thoughts of you bending over my desk."

She gasped, because of his touch and because of his words, and it didn't take long before she was coming apart once more.

"We should probably try and get some sleep," Devlin told her a short while later.

Cassandra's body felt like jelly, and she rather suspected his did as well, considering what she'd just done. She smiled smugly and snuggled further into his embrace. According to the latest bell, Devlin would have to rise in another two hours while she…

She yawned as she said good night.

"You know," Devlin murmured, "you don't have to mind me."

"What?" She'd no idea what he was talking about now.

"I mean, you shouldn't let me stop you from saying your nightly prayer."

Her stomach clenched with immense discomfort. She opened her eyes and stared into the darkness. "It's not a prayer." She whispered the words, almost hoping he wouldn't hear them. But this was the second time he was bringing this up, and if she brushed it aside now or pretended she was indeed praying when she was not, then that would make her a liar.

"Then what is it?"

She closed her eyes, squeezed them shut and wished he hadn't asked. "Can we talk about this tomorrow?" *Please. Don't make me tell you about this now.*

"I don't like putting things off. Least of all when it's important. And something about your voice, the hesitation there and your reluctance to discuss it, suggests it is." He'd risen onto his elbow, removing his warmth from her back as he leaned slightly over her side. "Cass?"

"It's a vow," she said, hating what her confession would most likely do to the bond they'd just forged.

"What sort of vow?" His voice was low, a touch thinner than usual.

"It doesn't matter," she tried. Turning onto her back she reached for him, attempted to pull him down for a kiss, desperate to somehow distract him from what could only be a destructive conversation.

"Considering the fact that you've whispered it every night since we left London, I'd like to argue that point." Pulling back, further away from her, he sat. And then he asked, in a voice devoid of emotion, "Have you been pledging yourself to Timothy while I've been lying right there, in the next bed?"

Put that way, anyone would think her the worst sort of person in the world. And all she could think to say was, "I'm sorry."

There was a pause, a moment of brief hesitation, and then he was on his feet and dressed. She'd no clue how he managed to accomplish the task so swiftly without light to guide him. Under different circumstances, she would have stopped to admire the skill, but at this moment, all she could focus on was the rising panic. It reached inside her and grabbed her heart, squeezing it until she gasped with despair.

"What are you doing?"

"I need to think."

"Devlin, I—"

"Don't!"

She shrank back. The anger infusing that one simple word was like a shot fired straight at her breast.

"Dev…"

She'd hurt him. She'd known she would the moment she chose to be honest. But she hadn't expected this – hadn't thought he'd react with quite so much vehemence toward her.

"You are my wife, Cass. A vow was made in church. To me. Me! And by God I've tried to be patient and understanding with you. Hell, I never expected you to love me. Not after you told me I shouldn't hold out any hope of ever sharing your bed or even a kiss for that matter. But now we've had this – a moment I hoped for but never dreamed possible – and you're telling me that all the while we've been married, you've deliberately stopped yourself from even giving us a chance?"

"No. It's not like that."

"Then how is it, Cass?"

How could she possibly explain what her heart had been forced to endure or the pain she'd suffered every morning when she'd woken and remembered Timothy no longer lived, that another day had passed to increase the distance between them? And how could she make Devlin see that she'd finally found the strength to try and move on without him wondering if she was merely pretending?

"I've been saying that vow for thirteen years."

He responded with a disdainful snort. "How wonderfully reassuring."

"But I haven't said it since you kissed me. The other night on the deck. I haven't said it since then because it felt wrong."

There was a pause and for a second she believed she'd managed to persuade him that she considered Timothy to be her past and Devlin to be her future.

But then he told her with nothing but bitterness lacing his words, "Of course it did. After all, you were being unfaithful to him."

"Devlin please. Let's—"

The door opened, then promptly slammed shut as he quit the cabin, leaving her alone and miserable in the dark.

God damn her!

Devlin could not recall the last time he'd been so furious. Perhaps when he'd walked away from his father and never looked back? No, even then he'd not felt this blinding rage, this need to destroy something with his bare hands. Because it wasn't anger alone that was wreaking havoc on him, but the hurt she'd caused him. After sharing the most spectacular evening together, she'd practically reached for a dagger and sliced him open.

Gnashing his teeth, he stomped his way up to the main deck and muttered a few cutting words of greeting to the crew he found there. They seemed to sense his dark mood without any problem and quickly removed themselves to the parts of the deck where he wasn't. Shoulders tense, he walked to the side of the ship and looked out across the ink-black water. If he could only bring Timothy back from his grave and punch him, Devlin reckoned he'd feel a touch better.

Gripping the railing, he muttered a curse he'd not uttered in years. She was his wife, for God's sake, and yes, he'd practically coerced her into marrying him, but given their history, he'd thought she'd at least make an effort. What he hadn't imagined was for her to do the exact opposite. And why the devil did he care so bloody much?

His heart thumped, forcing a new revelation to the front of his mind.

He shook his head. No. He couldn't possibly be jealous of a dead man, could he?

And if he were, then what the hell did that mean?

Unwilling to give the question the attention it probably deserved, he forced himself to think back on what Cassandra had said and his reaction. When she'd told him she'd stopped speaking her vow to Timothy after their kiss, he'd mocked her for it, but maybe he'd been unjust. Perhaps she was finally able to move on, start fresh, and live. His lungs felt too tight as he breathed in the air. What if this, whatever had happened between them these last few days, was her trying? Did he really want to punish her then? Or would he rather offer support and encouragement?

"Care for a swig?"

He hadn't heard Monty approach and although he'd prefer his own company for the foreseeable future, he wouldn't say no to the brandy. So he took the bottle and set it to his lips, enjoying the bite and the burn as the liquid slid down his throat.

"Thank you."

Monty took a sip himself, then returned the bottle to Devlin. "Is there a problem I ought to know about?"

Devlin's mood darkened. "No."

"So then, the crew has simply chosen to abandon their duties in this particular area because of…nothing?"

"If they chose to leave me in peace then that's their business," Devlin replied. The sullenness he felt belonged better to a five-year-old. His irritation grew.

"Well, it certainly doesn't have anything to do with your sunny disposition," Monty remarked. When Devlin didn't comment, he sighed, shifted his weight and said, "Just tell me it's nothing to do with the ship."

Devlin looked him straight in the eye, because Monty deserved no less. "It isn't. I assure you."

Monty nodded. "Good. That's good." He nodded some more. His lips twisted slightly in that way they so often did when he was pondering something. Finally, he said, "Look, every man on earth who's ever been married has had the occasional spat with his wife. It'll blow over. And if you want it to blow over sooner, just take the blame for whatever it is, tell her you're sorry, divert her with a few kisses, and all will be well. But don't let it distract you from your work or allow it to get in the way of the crew's work. Ensuring the ship runs smoothly so we reach our destinations on schedule, that's all that matters. The rest…is just a part of life."

Devlin waited for him to walk away before gulping down two more mouthfuls of brandy. Blast it all but the man was right. He had one primary goal as captain and that was to get from Point A to Point B safely. He could not allow emotion to drag him down, and he could not allow himself to treat his men poorly because he was angry and hurt.

With this in mind, he strode toward the helm. "The wind is picking up, Mr. Quinn. I suggest you lower the helm and keep your luff."

Monty grinned. "Aye, aye, Captain!"

"Give her sheet," he shouted, jolting the crew into motion. A flurry of activity followed as he continued issuing orders. "Away aloft. Drop the top sail. A-weather!" The bow sliced through the water, and Devlin allowed himself a satisfied smile. This, at least, was something he understood. Climbing up onto the quarterdeck, he planted his feet wide apart, assuming his position of command at Monty's right shoulder. Work would preoccupy his mind and help clear his head. Most importantly, it would give him a reason to avoid Cass until he was ready to face her again.

When Cassandra woke the next morning, she was alone. She'd been alone almost every morning since leaving England, but the solitude filling her cabin on this particular day was far more acute. After finally choosing to embrace a night of passion with her husband, a decision she'd not made lightly, she'd said the wrong thing, or the right thing just with the wrong words, and driven him away. He hadn't returned. If he had, he would have remembered to take his tricorn with him.

Unhappy with herself and with him and the awful feeling of being weighed down by the lead in her veins, she pulled on her robe and went to check on Penelope without so much as bothering to comb her hair. Barefoot, because she hadn't the energy to shove her feet into her shoes, she walked to the next cabin and quietly knocked.

"Yes?"

She opened the door just as Trevor ran past, his eyes going wide at the sight of her. "Um. Good morning, Mrs. Crawford."

She smiled tightly and nodded, then went to check on her daughter. "How are you feeling?"

"Better than you, I should think." Penelope sat, fully dressed with her back propped against a pillow and watched Cassandra approach. A notebook rested in her lap. "Do you suppose you've caught what I had?"

"No. I'm just tired." She spotted a discarded tray on Penelope's desk. It contained an empty plate and a cup. "I see you already ate."

"Dev brought me one of Mr. Talbot's excellent omelets."

"I see," Cassandra murmured. She wanted to ask Penelope how Devlin had seemed, if he'd been in a good mood or not, but she didn't know how.

But then Penelope said, "He asked if I'd like to learn how to plot a course, which I think might be fun." She shrugged. "You should join us."

"I, um…" Cassandra deliberately smiled. "I'm still rather tired. But we probably should try to resume your lessons at some point later today."

Penelope groaned. "Must we?"

"Basic mathematics is imperative to all facets of life. Even to plotting courses, I'll wager." She yawned. "Do you think you'll be all right if I go back to bed?"

"Of course." Penelope waved her journal. "I've two days' worth of journal writing to catch up on before Dev returns."

"All right then." Cassandra reached for the door.

"Mama?"

"Yes?"

"I hope you feel better later."

Cassandra could only press her lips together and nod. If she spoke just then, she rather feared she might burst into tears even though she didn't quite understand why. She was the one who'd hurt Devlin, not the other way around. Right?

Unsure of her feelings and quite convinced the last thing she wanted was company, she returned to her cabin and climbed back into bed. The half hour bell rang five times while she stared up at the wood planking above her head. And then, when she thought she could bear it no more, she finally fell back to sleep.

CHAPTER FOURTEEN

FIVE DAYS LATER, DEVLIN CAME to the startling, or perhaps, obvious, conclusion that he was being an ass. Initially, he'd kept himself too busy to think, which wasn't difficult since there was always work to be done on a ship. But eventually, he'd had to pause. And once he did, he'd allowed himself to examine things more clearly than he'd been able to do immediately after his argument with Cassandra.

He hadn't seen her since he'd stormed out of their cabin, although he did apprise himself of her daily routine and check to make sure she was eating. Clearly, she was avoiding him. Then again, he'd been avoiding her too, perhaps more blatantly since he'd actually chosen to sleep in a hammock with the rest of his crew. His excuse, when one of his men had questioned him about it, was that he woke his wife each time he returned or departed for his shift. But, he mused as he stared out over the blue expanse ahead, his men weren't fools, and he was certain they knew his marriage was not sailing along as smoothly as the ship.

"Full for stays," he shouted, turning the wheel

the fraction required to put The Condor straight into the wind. Favorable weather had allowed them to make excellent progress. According to Devlin's calculations, they would reach the Gulf of Guinea at least a day earlier than expected.

Cassandra was to thank for that. Had she not managed to step in and help as efficiently as she had while Talbot was out of commission, they'd probably be three days behind instead. He sighed and muttered a curse. He shouldn't have reacted as strongly as he had, especially not when she'd told him she'd stopped making her vow to Timothy after she and Devlin had kissed. Surely that meant something – she'd tried to convince him it had. But by then he'd wanted to hurt her as she had hurt him. So he'd lashed out with ugly words that he wished to God he could take back.

He'd wronged her, that much was clear, and she deserved an apology. Plus, he desperately wanted to set things right between them. He didn't like the glumness he'd been feeling since they'd argued. And truth be told, he really missed her. She was his friend and he hated having a wall between them.

"Dev?"

Devlin blinked. He'd been so wrapped up in his thoughts he'd not noticed Penelope's approach. He gave her a cheerful smile. In spite of his falling out with Cassandra, he'd enjoyed spending time with Penelope during the last few days. They would simply chat or he would show her things like how to hoist a flag or use his sextant and sundial compass.

"Want to steer for a bit?" he asked her jovially. Her cheerful demeanor and overall interest in all things served as a lovely distraction.

But rather than step toward him with a nod and prepare to take over, she placed her hands on her hips and scowled up at him. "Have you and Mama had a row?" she asked, ignoring his question.

Devlin's throat tightened and for a second he was forced to look away simply to compose himself. "Why do you ask?" He knew he was being a coward, stalling for time and hoping to find a way out of a direct answer.

"She's not getting dressed in the mornings or setting her hair, so I know she's keeping to either her cabin or mine." Penelope frowned. "Also, she doesn't look happy anymore. And neither do you, come to think of it."

"Are you sure?" He flashed what he hoped was a cheeky grin.

She did not look impressed.

Devlin sighed. "It's nothing that can't be fixed."

"When?"

"What?"

"When will you fix it?" She'd crossed her arms and was now staring up at him with an expectant glare.

This was her mother they were talking about, the person who came first in Penelope's affections. It stood to good reason she'd want to ensure her happiness. And of course, Devlin just loved her all the more for it, he...

He stared down into her serious eyes and drew a sharp breath. He loved Penelope as if she were his own. And Cassandra…

Swallowing hard, he gripped the wheel until he was sure his knuckles turned white. It was almost as if the ship was tilting and he was sliding and oh dear God! He loved her too. And he realized this was why he'd reacted the way he had, because he wanted her love in return and feared he might never have it – feared she would always love somebody else.

"Dev?"

"Hmm?"

"Are you all right?"

"Huh?"

Penelope scrutinized him with inquisitive eyes. "You look a bit sick. I hope you're not—"

"I'm fine," he more or less gasped as if he were being strangled.

"You don't sound fine."

"Trust me, I…" He cleared his throat and took a deep breath. "I'll do it today. Fix it, I mean. I promise."

Penelope's entire demeanor changed from stern to soft. "Good." She moved closer to him and he shifted, letting her take the wheel for a while.

"Penelope," he said after several minutes of silence had passed. "Tell me about your father." He hadn't meant to broach the subject with her, but he'd realized as he stood there thinking of facing Cassandra again that he really didn't want to ask *her*. She'd only get defensive and he would only get jealous and then they'd probably argue again. But it occurred to him that he really didn't know much about the man she'd hoped to marry and that maybe he ought to. Maybe knowing more about him would make Cassandra's position easier to understand or maybe it wouldn't, but now that Devlin had posed the question, he realized he had to know everything there was to know. For his own peace of mind.

She shrugged, the sort of shrug that conveyed detachment. "I never knew him. He died before I was born."

"Of course. But surely your mother must have mentioned him, described him or…something." Penelope tilted her head up at him, her expression startlingly blank. Devlin crossed his arms and considered, then thought of something. "What was his name for instance? I mean his full name?"

It was peculiar to think he would not know at least that much, but Cassandra had only ever referred to him as Timothy or Penelope's father. She'd known him since childhood, for Christ sake, so the informality would have made sense to her, but it also meant that Devlin had nothing on which to form an opinion, no clue as to where the man came from, who his family had been…nothing. To him he'd never been more than a name, and maybe that made it worse. He wasn't sure, but he wanted to figure it out.

"Bertrand Olivier Timothy Dawson," Penelope said with a flourish. "According to Mama, he hated his first two names so those closest to him always called him Timothy."

Devlin felt his brow crease with recognition. There was something awfully familiar about that name. As if he'd heard it once, a long time ago. "Was he titled?"

Considering Cassandra's heritage as the Earl of Vernon's daughter, it stood to reason that she would have gotten engaged to a lord. And although Devlin wasn't as familiar with the British peerage as he ought to be as the son of a duke, seeing as he'd left the country at the age of eighteen and had made no effort to mingle with the *ton* on the few occasions when he'd returned, he was curious.

Penelope nodded. "It's funny how things turned out. If he hadn't died, I'd be a proper lady and Mama would be—" She stopped herself and glanced at him apologetically. "I'm glad she married you."

Devlin's chest tightened. "Me too."

"And I'm glad you don't care about my illegitimacy."

"It's of no consequence. Character is far more important and you have a fine one, Penny. One of the best, in fact."

She grinned and then told him with an impressive amount of pride, "None of my grandparents thought so, you know."

Devlin clenched his jaw and curled his hands into hard fists. It wasn't right and they didn't know what they'd been missing by turning their back on this wonderful girl. "Who are your paternal grandparents?" he asked, realizing she'd not answered his previous question about her father's title.

She tipped her nose up and told him haughtily, "The Marquess and Marchioness of Weatherly." Blowing out a breath, she added, "My father was the Earl of Ludlow."

And while Devlin's heart did not exactly stop beating, he did feel as if the deck opened beneath his feet and dropped him into the ocean.

One hour later, he wasn't exactly foxed, but he wasn't exactly sober either.

He'd needed at least three glasses of brandy in order to think straight. Or perhaps not to think at all, he decided while trying to figure out what he should do.

No.

Strike that.

He knew what he *should* do. The problem was finding the courage required to do it.

His mind whirled. He could scarcely recall what he'd said or done since Penelope mentioned her father's title. Except Monty had shown up at some point to relieve him of his duties, and now Devlin was here, in the hull of all places. Sitting on a crate with both forearms resting on his thighs, he stared down into the half empty glass between his hands.

This was it. He'd never be happy again. And neither would Cass.

Not once she learned what he knew.

And damn it all, he had to tell her, because living with the guilt of not doing so would most likely kill him. "Hell and damnation." He set his glass to his lips once more and drank.

How the devil was he going to let her know what he'd done? Where would he find the words? *I'm sorry, darling, but it seems I may have killed the man you initially wanted to marry.* Or. *My apologies, but it looks like Timothy's dead because of me.*

He groaned. She'd never forgive him. Never. How could she when she'd loved Timothy so dearly and Devlin had been the one to destroy her life? He'd ruined everything for her and, he reminded himself, for Penelope too. He'd caused the death of her father.

"Christ!"

Without even thinking he smashed his fist into the side of a barrel. There was something immensely satisfying about the sting it brought to his knuckles. He stood. Lifted the barrel onto the crate on which he'd been sitting, and punched it again and again and again. And then, when his flesh was raw and his blood stained the deck, he allowed himself to expel the pain and the anger he harbored inside in a primitive roar.

If anyone heard him, they stayed away. Which was just as well considering his current state of self-loathing. The very devil himself would probably find his mood unsettling. Dear God. For thirteen years he'd lived with the guilt of Ludlow's death but this…Good God…this was a thousand times worse. Because now he was able to point to concrete examples of what the consequences had been – the lives he'd ruined. And the pain was only exacerbated by his love for Cassandra and Penelope. He wanted to protect them, not hurt them. And yet he had. He'd hurt them before he'd even met them. He'd…he'd…

Another ferocious growl tore its way out of his throat as he snatched up his glass and flung it straight at the hull. It shattered, the sound too weak, too lacking. Breathing raggedly, he stared at the mess he'd made. He'd clean it up. No one else should have to do it. Not to mention he'd rather not leave his anguish on public display.

Crouching, he began to gather the pieces. *Useless*, his father had said years earlier before Devlin left home. *A disgrace to this family.*

Devlin grunted. The duke had had no idea. None whatsoever. The worst had been yet to come. He winced as a shard broke his skin, then smiled because heaven knew he deserved it. The bell sounded, signaling that his next shift would begin in only two hours. Once again he wouldn't sleep. Not with the weight of the world bearing down on his chest.

Straightening himself, he swayed a little, waited for his eyes to focus and his head to clear. And then he grabbed the bottle he'd brought along with him and made his way up through the ship, each step a dull thud that would bring him closer to hell.

Because he had to tell her. And he had to do it now.

Before he decided to do something awful like

hide it from her forever.

She had a right to know what had happened.

It was the only honorable path forward. And he had no choice but to take it.

For the tenth time that day, Cassandra considered taking the risk of facing Devlin. She was sick to death of hiding away in her cabin and in desperate need of fresh air. She was also weary of the rift between them and wished they could go back to how things had been before they argued. It occurred to her that she missed him. In a way, he was more than her husband. He was, first and foremost, her best friend, and she realized she longed for his company.

Deciding to act, Cassandra dressed. It had become quite clear that Devlin would not be the one extending an olive branch, so it would have to be her. It wasn't ideal, but it was past time. Five days past, she acknowledged with a sharp nod at herself in the mirror. Grabbing a shawl, she strode to the door. And was forced to jump back when it swung toward her.

As if summoned by her sense of purpose, Devlin appeared. He did not look his best, she noted, and although it occurred to her that she ought to take some small pleasure in knowing she had not been the only one to suffer, she did not. Because on closer inspection, he looked far worse than she felt. He seemed tortured in a soul crushing way that instantly put her on edge.

"Cass." His voice was tired and…resigned?

She attempted a smile in spite of the worry creeping up through her limbs. "I was on my way to find you." His eyes seemed to stare straight through her. "I'd like to apologize for—"

A derisive snort cut her off, then he pushed his way forward, entering the cabin and shutting the door. "Apologize," he murmured, then snorted again. He shook his head while she stared at him, unsure how to handle this strange mood of his.

"You have nothing to apologize for, Cass." He swept past her and sat, even though she still stood. And then he dropped his head heavily into his hands and let out a tortured sigh. "I, on the other hand, have everything to be sorry for."

Well. That seemed rather dramatic. She twisted her lips in thought, drew a deep breath and prepared to say something, though she wasn't sure what. Except...

With a gasp she rushed forward and fell to her knees before him. "What on earth happened to your knuckles, Dev?"

Lowering his hands, he turned them over and studied the bloodied flesh. "Self-flagellation." His voice contained a terrifying lack of emotion.

"Why?" She could barely get the question past her lips. How could her confession have made him angry enough to do this to himself? How could she have driven him to such violence? It seemed impossible. Frightening.

He just sat there. Utterly silent. Until she could stand it no longer. She had to say something. For heaven's sake, she'd decided she would apologize to him and so she would.

She started by taking a deep inhalation. And then she said, "I'm sorry it took me as long as it did for me to put Timothy behind me." Needing closeness, she placed one hand on his thigh and continued. "I knew you wouldn't like learning about the vow, and I'm sorry it made you angry, but I've been speaking those words every night since the day he died and I just…" She swallowed. "I needed time to change the habit, to move on and accept that my loyalties have shifted." She bit her lip and quietly added, "My heart has shifted too. I didn't expect it to happen, and I'm not sure when it did precisely, but I—"

"Don't."

She blinked. Her heart began to tremble. "What?"

"I can't bear for you to end that sentence. Not now. Not when you don't know who you're really married to." He sounded both angry and pained. Tormented in a way she'd never experienced him before.

"You're not making any sense, Dev."

He laughed, but it was with bleakness rather than joy. "No. I don't suppose I am."

They were so close, touching even, and yet she'd never felt further from him. And then he stood, pushing her hand aside as he did so. His posture was tense, slightly hunched as if he carried some dreadful weight.

"I ruined your life."

The words were so soft she scarcely heard them.

Except she did and she didn't understand. And because she didn't, she tried to smile in order to offer reassurance. "I married you because I wanted to," she said, settling on the only concern he could possibly have, the only thing that could have, in her estimation, resulted from him overthinking the vow and what it might mean in terms of her feelings. "Yes, it seemed like the best course of action but since then so much has changed. My regard for you and—"

"You don't understand," he interrupted gruffly. "Ludlow would still be alive if it weren't for me."

"What?" She couldn't have heard him right. It wasn't possible. Her ears simply had to be playing tricks on her. She tried to breathe, but her lungs felt frozen. Every part of her body was suddenly cold, and she realized she'd started trembling.

"Timothy," Devlin said as if to confirm who he was talking about. "He's dead because of me, Cass. How's that for a cruel twist of fate?"

"No." She shook her head. "No, no, no. No, that can't be true, it just can't." Her legs went numb and she slid sideways from her crouched position until she was sitting on her bottom. "It was an accident. A terrible, terrible accident. The witnesses said so. He..." She swallowed hard. "Timothy stepped out into the street without looking just as the carriage rounded the corner. You can't be to blame." She shook her head frantically, as if the action would somehow erase the possibility. And then she looked at him hard. The next words she spoke were filled with resolve.

"You weren't even there!"

"No. I wasn't." His face contorted, banishing any relief she might have felt in response to his words. "But *I* hired the carriage. *I* ordered the driver to hurry – to return as swiftly as he possibly could. *Me!*" He pressed one hand to his chest and stared down at her with wild despair, then added more softly, "I even said I'd reward him with another five pounds if he came back within twenty minutes."

Cassandra couldn't respond. She couldn't speak, couldn't think, couldn't act. Dear God.

This wasn't happening. It wasn't. It was just a nightmare from which she would soon awaken. It had to be, because if it wasn't – if this was real…

An unbearable ache filled her chest. Her heart seemed to struggle with each painful beat. Tears filled her eyes, blurring her vision. It wasn't possible. She couldn't be married to the man whose actions had led to Timothy's death.

She refused to believe it.

"I'm sorry, Cass. I know an apology isn't enough. I know you can't possibly forgive me, but—"

"I want to go home." The words left her before she could think, but once she heard them, she knew they made sense. Her world was spinning and she was falling. The only thing she believed might help her feel slightly better was Clearview.

"We can't turn around. I've a cargo to deliver. There are people counting on me to do so."

"Fine." She wiped the tears from her eyes and clambered to her feet. "I'll get the next ship back to London from Cape Town then." Anything to escape him right now.

"Cass." His tormented voice tore her soul to shreds. "I didn't know. I didn't realize until today."

"It doesn't matter." Her voice cracked as it pushed its way past the lump in her throat. "It doesn't change the fact that I married you." The awfulness of it all overwhelmed her. He'd stolen the life she ought to have had, denied Penelope the right to grow up with a father. And worst of all, she'd imagined she might one day love him. "I need to go. I need to…to do something."

He made no attempt to stop her.

She wasn't sure where she was headed when she left the cabin. Her feet just carried her forward, away from Devlin, until she eventually found herself in the galley. "I'd like to help," she told Mr. Talbot. "I want to keep myself busy."

He didn't argue. He just glanced at her and gave a quick nod.

Five minutes later she was sitting at a table, peeling carrots. Her hands moved of their own accord while her mind worked through the problem she faced. Devlin was connected to Timothy's death in the worst way possible. She was now tied to him for the rest of her life. He owned her. And nothing could have made her angrier.

CHAPTER FIFTEEN

IF THERE WAS ONE THING Devlin knew he would never forget, it was the stricken look on Cassandra's face right after he'd made his confession. In that moment, he'd known he'd lost her forever. Hell, she wanted to leave him!

He stared at the door through which she'd vanished with a desperate desire to bring her back, to turn back time and undo all the damage he'd caused. Emotionally exhausted, he pinched the bridge of his nose. Raw skin stretched across his knuckles, causing him to wince. There was work to be done, a ship to sail, and a crew to manage. He was the captain, for Christ sake. He could not afford to take any more time to himself. Lord knew he'd taken enough already.

Grabbing his tricorn, he forced himself to ignore the sharp stabbing sensation behind his ribs as he quit the cabin. After a quick meeting to compare notes on the weather with Bronswick, he returned to the deck. Penelope was there, attempting to fly the kite he'd helped her make the day before. Devlin's eyes stung, not from the blinding sun but from his attempt to fight back tears. He'd killed her father. The only reason he'd been able to reach for the happiness he'd always longed for – the love he'd so desperately craved – was because of the part he'd played in Ludlow's death. And that piece of knowledge was enough to cripple him forever.

"I can't get it to stay in the air," Penelope called. "Will you please help me, Dev?"

He reached back, steadying himself against the bulkhead dividing the main deck from the quarterdeck. His chest squeezed until he was sure his ribs would crack. And yet, somehow, from sheer force of will, his stubborn nature enabled him to straighten himself and move forward.

"You've unwound too much string," he told Penelope. "If you shorten it, we can make another attempt."

She followed his directions while he collected the kite. It was fluttering from side to side as if attempting to leap up into the air. "Ready?" he asked once the string was taut. She nodded and he took a second to assess the wind's direction. "Move a little to your left. That's it. Now here we go." He released the kite and watched it rise above his head. "Unwind the spool slowly. That's it. There you go."

Penelope laughed with delight and for a brief moment, Devlin allowed himself to savor her exuberance. Until he heard a voice at his shoulder quietly murmur, "A pity her father's not able to see her like this. He loved flying kites."

Cassandra.

If she'd sliced him open with a knife, he reck-oned it would have hurt less than the words she'd just spoken. Not that he didn't deserve them.

Dropping his gaze toward her, he half expected to see her face wracked by painful emotion. Instead, she looked shockingly composed. And he was stunned to realize how much he hated her ability to do so when he was coming apart at the seams. If she'd only rail at him or dissolve into tears, he'd understand her response. But this cool expression she'd donned wasn't something he knew how to deal with.

"I'm sorry," he muttered, because it was all he could think to say.

"Why?" She tilted her head up and stared him straight in the eye. Devlin's heart immediately crumpled, because he'd never seen anyone look so hollow. And then she whispered, "You have everything you wanted."

He drew a sharp breath.

Not everything. Not even close.

But he kept the words to himself. Held himself utterly still so she wouldn't see the precision with which her comment had struck its mark. And then, when he finally felt able to move without breaking, he turned away and marched up onto the quarterdeck.

"Mind if I take over for a bit?" he asked Monty.

"You look like hell," Monty said as he stepped aside to give Devlin the wheel. "Dare I ask why your hands look like they've been flogged?"

Devlin stared straight ahead. "Remember Ludlow?"

There was a very distinct pause – a hesitation suggesting Monty was wondering where this was going. "How could I not?"

"Apparently, the woman he was about to marry that day when the carriage hit him was Cassandra. My wife," he added for clarification.

"Dear, merciful God," Monty muttered. "And she knows this?"

"I had to tell her."

"Of course you did." Silence followed and Devlin lost himself in his own thoughts. He almost forgot Monty was there until the man said, "It wasn't your fault, Dev."

"Of course it was. *I* ordered the bloody carriage. *I* told the driver to hurry. If it wasn't for me he wouldn't have been on that street at that hour, nor would he have driven as recklessly as he did."

"Perhaps not. But it's also not nearly as clear cut as you wish to make it." Devlin's head jerked sideways, his eyes snapping onto Monty's. "You weren't there, but I was. I remember precisely what happened."

"I know." Devlin gnashed his teeth and tightened his grip on the wheel's handles. "You gave me a detailed account."

"And yet you still choose to forget Ludlow's part in the accident."

"The man died." Devlin practically spat the words with all the contempt he felt for himself.

"Yes. He did. But only because he failed to check for oncoming traffic." Monty's voice was quiet, deliberate, and full of regret. "Had he done so, he would have seen the carriage coming, for it rounded the corner before Ludlow stepped out into the street. And that's a fact, Dev."

"Nevertheless."

"Nevertheless what?" Devlin had turned his gaze away from Monty, but he could hear the exasperation in his friend's voice. "Christ, man, you have to stop blaming yourself for this. There were too many actions at play that day for it to have been your fault. You only did what you had to, what any other captain in your position would have done."

"Maybe," he allowed, "but she'll never understand that." Not after he'd made sure she thought he was solely responsible for what had happened. It was what he'd been telling himself for thirteen years – what he'd always believed. But what if that wasn't true? What if it wasn't his fault?

"You know, even the driver's role in all this was bigger than yours, and I think, if you explain it to her properly, your wife will see that."

Devlin sighed. "I don't know." The last thing he felt like right now was another discussion on the subject. And besides… "Ludlow was everything to her. My involvement—"

"Hang your involvement, Dev. Have we not just established that it wasn't as profound as you keep insisting?"

"I don't know," Devlin repeated, because frankly, he'd never been more confused or uncertain about anything before in his life. "I simply don't know."

"Right. Well. I suggest you figure it out then." Monty jutted his chin in Cassandra's direction. She'd stepped away from Penelope and was now standing alone, staring out across the water. "Because having her think you ruined her life is no way to start a marriage."

One week later, Devlin was of the opinion that time did not heal all wounds. Occasionally, it just allowed the wound to deepen. He'd given a great deal of thought to what Monty had told him and had to acknowledge there was a chance of his being right. About everything.

Even so, approaching Cassandra with the purpose of explaining it was something else entirely. Mostly because he wasn't sure how to find the right words. So he'd put it off for a day and then for another and now he was here with an awkward wedge between them. It was the most uncomfortable experience. Because he'd returned to his cabin to sleep in order to diminish potential gossip among his crew. Which meant they saw each other, spoke to each other—though not extensively, he had to admit—shared their meals in the dining room with Monty, Bronswick, and Penelope, and even engaged in the occasional pastime activity with each other.

In many ways, it was as if things were normal between them. Cassandra showed no hint of animosity toward him. Indeed, she was always polite. But she was also reserved and horribly distant. And while it might not have been obvious to anyone else, the twisted state of Devlin's insides served as a constant reminder to him that things were not right between them. Far from it.

"How long until we reach Cape Town?" Cassandra asked when he met her later that day on the deck. She'd been sitting on a crate, conversing with Penelope until she'd noticed his presence and come to join him.

"Lessons?" he inquired, deliberately putting off her question.

"French," Cassandra told him with a nod. "She struggles with some of the verbs."

"I don't blame her," Devlin muttered. "It's a beastly language to learn. Hated it myself."

She pursed her lips. "I can't say I'm especially fond of it either, but educated people are expected to speak it. Considering her…situation…it seemed doubly important that she should be as accomplished as other ladies."

"Her situation," Devlin bit out with a sudden flash of anger, "is that she's my daughter. I've given her my name and acknowledged her as my own."

"Yes. She is fortunate to have you. I am not disputing the fact." Her voice was tighter now, more strained. She also, Devlin could not help but note, had not said *we* are fortunate to have you. "However, the circumstances of her birth are no secret, and that means there will always be someone looking to find fault with her, ready to criticize and exclude her for being a bastard."

She spoke the last part so softly there was no chance of Penelope hearing. Still, Devlin instinctively glanced over his shoulder, then grabbed Cassandra by her arm and steered her further away. "For the love of God, Cass, you're her mother!"

"And what?" Something dangerous flashed in her eyes. "My love for her will never change what she is, and I would be either naïve or stupid to pretend otherwise."

Devlin drew a deep breath and expelled it. "Of course." He let go of her arm. "Forgive me. Few things infuriate me more than the asinine rules of society. And knowing Penelope as I do, the idea of anyone treating her cruelly for any reason makes me want to do bloody murder."

Cassandra's face, which had begun to relax at the mention of *asinine rules of society*, immediately hardened, and Devlin belatedly recognized his poor choice of words.

"I'm sorry. I did not mean to—"

"How long until we reach Cape Town?" she repeated.

A shuddering sigh clawed its way through his body, leaving his chest feeling raw. "A month, I expect."

"Right. Well then." Her mouth had flattened into a grim line. "I'm sure you have a great many things to attend to."

He wanted to ask her to stay, but she was already walking away. Her contempt for him was strikingly clear. Hell, she couldn't wait to exchange this ship for another just so she could be rid of his company. The notion grated. Worst of all, it distracted him from his duties.

With a growl, he returned below deck. It was time to inspect the ship's cleanliness and once that was done, the cargo would need checking. If he was lucky, the rest of the day would pass with greater speed than the previous one and, God willing, bring him closer to figuring out what to do.

She'd been close. Half a second away from telling him she didn't blame him for what had happened – from assuring him she understood – when he'd brought reality crashing down over her head with his words.

Timothy's death had been an accident. A horribly tragic one, to be sure, but an accident nonetheless. And although Devlin had chosen to take the blame, he hadn't even been at the scene. All he'd done was hire the carriage and ask the driver to make haste. For her to hold that over his head, for her to allow him to hold it over his own, would be wrong.

And yet she could not rid herself of the pain his revelation had stirred in her breast. She felt as if she were falling apart all over again. Because of the connection, she suspected. It had to be. The irony of marrying someone so irrevocably tied to Timothy's death was simply too much.

Which was why every instinct told her to run. Because if she didn't; if she faced the feelings Devlin awoke within her...

She almost choked on the sherry she'd brought with her onto the deck. It was late evening. They'd eaten supper by rote after which Penelope and Devlin had both retired, allowing her the solitude she so desperately craved.

A quivering sigh made its way past her lips. She cared about Devlin, just as he cared about her, but to think there could ever be anything more was, "Absurd."

She considered the word and was stunned by how ill-fitting it sounded to her own ears. But to suppose there would ever be anything more between them was absolutely terrifying.

She'd lived with Timothy's loss for so long, buried herself in the love they'd once shared, and known she'd never recover. Marrying Devlin for security was one thing. Allowing him the affection she'd always associated with Timothy was quite another.

Except, the feelings Devlin stirred in her heart were real. It would be cowardly and unfair to them both if she tried to ignore them. He was her husband, her fondest companion, the pillar of strength she'd leaned on when she had been lost and afraid. But when he'd needed her to offer assurance and the forgiveness he deserved, she'd threatened to leave him.

The words had been spoken in pain and anger. It was past time she took them back and told Devlin he wasn't to blame for Timothy's death any more than she was. She had to help him, and she needed to let him know that he hadn't lost her.

"It's not easy, you know," a deep voice spoke.

Cassandra turned and located Mr. Quinn. He was standing just two feet away. "What isn't?"

"Captaining a ship. Being responsible for a crew of four hundred and eighty." He stepped up beside her and rested one hand on the railing. The wind caught his hair, whipping a few stray locks to one side. "Your husband's only ever lost one. Has he told you about him?"

"The boy who fell from the mast?"

"Mm… Devlin was quite determined to save Luke although it was clear to everyone else there was nothing to do." Mr. Quinn's eyes were shadowed by darkness, yet there was no ignoring the intensity of his gaze.

"He told me the ship's physician had gone ashore the previous day when they passed Dover."

"That's right."

Cassandra waited for him to say more. When he didn't, she had to ask, "Then what did he do?" Because this was Devlin they were discussing. No matter how bleak the situation, he would have striven to save that boy's life. Good lord. Had he not told her he'd broken his arm attempting to catch him? How on earth could she have forgotten that?

"He put me in a carriage and ordered the driver to take me to St. George's hospital. My mission was to fetch Mr. Mallory, one of London's greatest physicians, back to the ship as swiftly as possible."

"St. George's," she muttered. "Formerly known as Lanesborough House. It's on Hyde Park Corner." She didn't have to say more to know what this meant. Devlin had sent Mr. Quinn by carriage to fetch the only man he believed might be able to save Luke's life. And in order to get there, they'd had to pass through St. James's. It was the shortest route.

Cassandra blinked. Devlin had told her about the accident, he'd even mentioned the order he'd given Quinn, but she hadn't realized this happened the same day Timothy died – that he'd been struck by the very carriage intended to ensure Luke's survival. Devlin hadn't explained it, preventing her from making the necessary connection.

"Why wouldn't he tell me this?"

Mr. Quinn grunted. "It's not his style. Making excuses."

Maybe not, but it did give Cassandra additional solace, knowing he'd not merely issued an aimless command. Although, she reflected, she should have realized this, regardless. Devlin never acted unnecessarily.

"My point is—"

"He's no more at fault than I was, insisting we had to get married in that exact church." Her fingers tightened around her glass. Was this why she'd been so stuck in the past? Because she blamed herself? She hadn't considered it a possibility until she'd spoken the words.

"Perhaps you should tell him."

"I know I should." A sudden gust of wind dislodged her footing. She caught the railing to steady herself, causing her sherry to slosh over the side of her glass. "I've been meaning to do so for several days."

"Really?"

She shrugged. "Even without considering the reason why the carriage was where it was on that particular day, I knew it was wrong to blame Devlin. It was just easier I suppose, than having to face the alternative."

Mr. Quinn nodded. "He's lucky to have you."

She snorted. "He thinks I'm planning to leave him at Cape Town and go back to London."

"But you won't?"

"No. I'm staying. No matter what."

The deck rose at a sharper angle as a much higher wave lifted the ship. "I think you need to go back to your cabin," Mr. Quinn told her gravely. "It appears a storm may be starting and the last place you'll want to be during that is somewhere out here."

"All right." She wasn't foolish enough to ignore good advice. Just foolish enough not to recognize her husband's innocence or to acknowledge her feelings for him, even when the truth stared her straight in the face. She wished Mr. Quinn a good night and moved past him.

"If you'll recall," he told her right before she reached the ladder, "I'm also married. Trusting another person with your heart is a frightening thing to do, Mrs. Crawford. But the reward is, in my opinion at least, worth it."

Cassandra agreed. She'd been shocked by

Devlin's confession, that was all. Coming on the heels of their lovemaking, who could blame her? The problem was how long it had taken for her to decide what to do. The answer should have been simple. She should have told him it wasn't his fault the moment she'd acknowledged the fact. As his friend, she should have tried to ease the pain and the guilt that so clearly consumed him much sooner.

Instead, she'd kept her distance, too wrapped up in her own grief to pay attention to his.

Tomorrow, she decided as she snuck her way back inside their cabin and cast a quick glance at the bed where he lay, she'd do what she could to acquit him of blame. She'd forgive him if that was what it would take for him to forgive himself, and most importantly, she'd tell him she'd no intention of ever leaving his side.

Unfortunately, as it turned out, fate wasn't quite with her.

The cabin was still fairly dark when she woke to a series of thuds. Her body seemed to tilt, then the chair behind Devlin's desk fell over. Men's voices, shouting, accompanied the stomping of feet as they hurried about overhead. Timbers creaked and Cassandra's head dipped down until she was looking up at her feet. Good God! The overturned chair slid toward her, paused for a second, then slid back from whence it had come.

Grabbing onto the side of her bed, Cassandra attempted to sit. The ship rocked so violently she struggled to stay in one spot. One look at Devlin's bed and she saw he was gone. The ship pitched and fell once again with such crashing force, it was a wonder the wood didn't splinter.

"Mama?" The shout was faint, barely audible from the opposite side of the bulkhead.

Cassandra was on her feet in a second, heedless of how impossible walking might be. If Penelope was frightened, she'd find her way to her cabin, one way or another, even if she had to crawl there on her hands and knees just to stop from falling.

She grabbed her robe and shoved her arms through the sleeves while steadying herself against the edge of her bed. The ship lurched and she skidded forward, slamming her hip into the desk.

Muttering an oath she'd never imagined she'd ever speak, she reached for the door knob and hauled herself forward.

"Penny," she gasped, almost falling into her daughter's cabin. "It's just a storm. You mustn't worry."

"I don't feel very good," Penelope groaned. "I really think sleeping in a hammock would have been better."

"Do you think you might be sick?" Cassandra asked, ignoring her comment.

"Maybe."

Cassandra glanced around, furiously searching for something her daughter could use if she had to cast up her dinner. When nothing seemed to avail itself, she made her decision. "Don't leave your cabin, Penny. I'll be right back."

"Where are you going?" Penelope's voice followed Cassandra back into the passageway.

"Make way," a sailor shouted as he ran past her. Before she could think to ask him where Devlin might be or how long he reckoned the storm might last, he'd disappeared up the ladder.

A spray of water landed at her feet. Cassandra held on fast to the brass rail attached to the bulkhead and fought to stay upright while the ship rolled to one side.

"Mama!"

Returning to Penelope's side right now would accomplish nothing, so Cassandra clenched her jaw and made her way forward. She wasn't quite sure how she managed to reach the galley without falling over. Sheer force of will and knowing her daughter depended on her for help were the only explanations. She grabbed a pot from the hook it had been secured to, held on tight, and started back toward Penelope's cabin.

"Here," she gasped when she finally returned. "Use this if you have to."

The ship dove and Cassandra's stomach dropped. Penelope screamed, but she didn't let go of the pot. "I don't like this, Mama." Her voice was strangled. "I don't like it one bit."

"I know. Neither do I." The deck began tilting again, as it did right before the ship began falling. Cassandra braced herself for the inevitable, with her feet wide apart and both hands gripping whatever surface they could find. And then it happened again, jarring her bones. Her side ached where it had made contact with the desk, and her ankle was sore too, though not sprained, thank God. She could at least walk.

"Water," Penelope said. "There's water on the floor."

"It's coming in through the hatch every time it gets opened. You don't have to worry. It's not a leak." Penelope nodded and bent her head over the pot. At least the guardrail along the edge of her bed would stop her from falling out. She'd be safe as long as she stayed where she was. "I have to go back to my cabin, Penny."

Penelope's head jerked up, her eyes latching onto Cassandra's. "No. Please stay."

"I…" Another wave lifted the ship, then dropped it straight back in the ocean. Cassandra's foot slipped and before she could gain her balance, she fell on her bottom. Hard. Pain arced through her, wrenching a groan from somewhere so deep it felt like it came from her belly. "I can't stay here for as long as this lasts," she said once she managed to pull herself upright. "But maybe you can come to my cabin instead. Devlin isn't there right now. He's probably—"

"Up there," Penelope said, her eyes wide with panic.

"He, um…" Dear God. Cassandra hadn't allowed herself to worry about him until right now, but of course Penelope was right. He was the captain after all, and as such, he was probably at the helm as they spoke. She swallowed and told herself to stay calm. "I'm sure this isn't his first storm. It's worse for us because we're not used to it. Come on. I'll help you move, Penny. Let's—"

"Man overboard!"

She barely heard the shout. It sounded so distant and yet she knew her ears didn't betray her in the way her spine stiffened and her nerve endings started to wither. And then, of course, if that weren't enough, there was the horrified look of finality on Penelope's face.

"Stay here," Cassandra ordered. "Don't you dare move!"

"Where are you going?"

"To find out what's going on," Cassandra shouted over her shoulder. But the truth was she had to be sure Devlin wasn't in danger. And God, it felt awful, but she could not stop from praying the man who'd gone over the side was someone else. "Please don't let him die. Please, please, please…"

The ship lurched, throwing her into the ladder. She caught the handrails and yanked herself upright, then started to climb. Saltwater splashed her face and dampened her clothes when she threw the hatch open and climbed out onto the deck, careful to hold on to something. Blinking, she adjusted her gaze to her murky surroundings. Men, more than she could possibly count, scurried about, heaving on ropes, even climbing the rigging to adjust the sails.

"Bring to an anchor!"

Cassandra whipped her head round to see who'd given the order, because it didn't sound like Devlin.

And it wasn't.

It was Mr. Bronswick.

She gaped at him for a full second while trying to comprehend what was happening.

She hadn't seen him steer before.

It was always Devlin or Mr. Quinn.

"Beat to quarters and ease off handsomely at the captain's command!"

Cassandra sucked in a breath and looked about wildly, searching for Devlin amid the crowd of men following orders. A drum started, its hollow signal summoning all hands to their respective stations. Another surge of water spilled over her head. She sputtered and wiped her face with the back of her arm.

"Will someone please get my foolish wife below so I don't have to save her next?"

And that was when she saw him.

Devlin was standing near the railing with two of his men who were busy securing a rope to his waist. Stripped of his coat and boots, he offered only his profile for her consideration. But it was enough for her to see the determined gleam in his eyes.

Understanding dawned and she took a step forward, moving as if through mud in a futile attempt to reach him on time. "No. Devlin, no!"

A strong arm wound its way round her waist and yanked her back. "You'll die out here if you're not more careful," a strange voice muttered next to her ear.

And then Devlin jumped, leaping into the mountainous waves without one backward glance. And all Cassandra could do was scream.

CHAPTER SIXTEEN

THIS WAS NOT THE FIRST storm Devlin had sailed through, but it was the first one to frighten the wits out of him, because this time it wasn't just him and his men. Cassandra and Penny – his entire life – were on board, and if anything were to happen to them…

Well, he probably wouldn't live to know about it, he told himself grimly while doing his best to meet the next wave at just the right angle. Monty had woken him two hours earlier when the wind had worsened and it became clear the captain's presence was required on deck. Devlin had been at the helm ever since, calling orders or relying on Monty and Bronswick to do so for him.

Water was now everywhere, falling from black clouds and splashing onto the deck from all sides. A flash of lightening brightened the sky and illumi-nated the next oncoming wave. Devlin tightened his grip on the wheel's handles and held on fast so it wouldn't slip back. He had to keep the rudder on the port side of the stern-post in order to avoid getting hit from the side.

Devlin glanced up at the sails and frowned.

He'd ordered them furled so they could continue downwind with bare poles. Last he'd checked, they'd looked fine. But now…

The main sail suddenly dropped and a gust of wind caught it.

"Christ have mercy," Devlin cursed as he struggled to keep the ship steady. If he failed to hold the stern perpendicular to the approaching waves, one could push the ship sideways, and if that happened, they'd likely capsize.

"The rope's stuck!" someone yelled. "I can't bring the sail back up."

"I'm coming to help you," Monty shouted, his thick voice cutting through all the noise. "Bronswick, toss me a line."

"Wait for my mark," Devlin called, the muscles in his arms burning with the effort of keeping the rudder steady. Another wave caught the ship and lifted it up. With the sail counterbalancing Devlin's steering, they barely managed to stay on course. "Climb. Now!"

Monty made his way up the rigging with remarkable speed and agility for a man of his size.

"Is he tethered?" Devlin asked Bronswick.

"Aye, Captain."

"All right then," Devlin muttered as another wave approached. "Hold on!"

When Devlin glanced back up, Monty was helping another crewmember secure the sail. The task immediately made the ship easier to steer. And then Monty was climbing back down. He reached the deck and removed the tether, started making his way toward Devlin.

The stern rose as a wave grew beneath it, water spilled onto the deck from all sides, and then a sharp wind whipped across the stern, smacking Devlin straight in the face. When he opened his eyes once more, Monty was gone.

"Man overboard!"

The call confirmed what Devlin's brain had refused to grasp. "Bronswick!" His quartermaster was at his side in an instant. "Heave to using the anchor. I'm going in after him." Devlin rushed forward, shouting instructions as he went for a rope to be readied. "We must make haste," he ordered as he glanced out over the side. Monty wasn't very far and Devlin would bloody well reach him if it was the last thing he did.

A rope was secured to his waist while he pulled off his coat and boots.

"Bring to, an anchor," Bronswick shouted.

The bow hit a wave, soaking the deck and everything on it. Devlin glanced back briefly, intending to signal to Bronswick, except his wife was somehow there now, frantically clinging to a handrail, and Devlin's heart seemed to stop beating. He had no time for this. And what the hell was she thinking anyway, to step onto the deck in this sort of weather? Angered by her foolish behavior and the added concern he now had for her safety, he barked an order for someone – anyone – to take her below.

And then, without further hesitation, he dove into the water, submerging himself in silence.

Until he broke the surface and reentered the storm. Frantically, yet with the control he knew he required, he took a moment to get his bearings. The ship was behind him, which meant that Monty had to be more or less...there...

Thank God they were off the coast of Africa and not in the North Atlantic. He doubted he'd freeze to death, but instead he might drown. Or Monty might if Devlin didn't reach him fast enough. Staying afloat while fighting the waves was a difficult battle, more so for Monty, whose coat and boots would be weighing him down.

Devlin caught a quick glimpse of his head, and then it was gone as a wave swept between them. He started swimming toward the spot where he believed Monty to be. One arm reached forward while the other came up and over. The sea swelled beneath him, halting his progress and pushing him back. Good God, he had to save him, he simply had to.

Already exhausted from handling the ship, Devlin forced his body into compliance and kept swimming until he was sure his arms would give up. Panting for breath, he paused to check his location once more. And then he spotted his friend, arms flailing as he struggled against the waves, his body turned in the wrong direction.

"Monty!" Devlin's voice was frayed by the wind, and he knew there was nothing to do but keep going. He had to. He simply had to.

And so he did, until there was only a yard between them. "Grab my hand," Devlin shouted while doing his best not to choke on a large gulp of water.

Monty splashed around until he saw him. He reached for Devlin, their fingers brushed, and then Devlin felt the hard pull of the tether. "The line's gone taut. You have to come closer."

Gasping for breath, Monty struggled to do as Devlin asked, but the waves were no easy foe to conquer, and it was clear that his strength was starting to fail. Devlin reached out again. Now there were two more inches between them.

No. It wouldn't end like this. It couldn't. Not with Monty lost at sea.

He needed something – an extension of sorts. If he undid the tether, the rope would be longer and he would be able to reach. It was a mad idea, a dangerous one, but Devlin knew he would never forgive himself if he chose not to try. "Keep swimming toward me! Stay as close as you can!"

The knot was tied in such a way that it took Devlin only a second to widen the loop around his waist, grab it by one hand, and pull his legs through. Extending both arms, he held on tight to the loop, prayed it would not come undone, and offered Monty his free hand.

His friend barely caught it before a wave rolled over both of their heads. They went under, tumbling, and with their weight trying to drag them apart. But now that Devlin had grabbed him, there was no way in hell he was letting him go. He held on tight and pulled Monty back up with him into the pelting rain.

Cassandra banged on her door for what had to be the hundredth time even though she knew it was pointless to do so. But it was better than turning hysterical. According to Devlin's orders, she'd been locked away in her cabin, and after insisting she had to be let out to see to her daughter, Penelope had been deposited in the cabin with her.

"I'm sure he'll be all right," Penelope told her hopefully. "He has to be."

Yes. He did. Cassandra agreed with that. She couldn't very well murder him if he didn't come back. But if a mere carriage could end Timothy's life, how could she possibly hope for Devlin to leap into the ferocious sea and survive?

The ship lurched, sending her stumbling. She steadied herself against the bulwark, then made her way to the bed. "How are you feeling?"

"Not much better. Oof! It's when the ship falls…" She hung her head over the pot she'd brought with her. "I feel like I'm going to be sick but then I'm not."

"Maybe you should try to sleep?"

"Lying down only makes it worse."

"I see." Cassandra bit her lip. "I could try and read to you in order to pass the time."

And to stop from thinking of Devlin and whether or not she would see him again.

Her insides had tied themselves into a big messy knot when she'd seen him dive over the side of the ship. It tightened now at the thought of him fighting his way through the water, of waves tumbling over his head, and Dear God, what chance did he possibly have? How would he ever survive?

"Mama?"

Cassandra blinked. "Yes?"

"You offered to read."

"Right. So I did." She wasn't sure how she managed to keep every part of herself in check, how she stopped herself from unraveling completely. But somehow she did. Somehow she managed to read two full chapters of *Waverly* without being aware she'd done so. Absently, her eyes had moved over the words while her mouth spoke them aloud. Until she realized the ship wasn't bobbing about quite as much as it had done earlier. It was settling, the darkness receding, and…

Something scraped against the door, most likely whatever had been used to secure it and stop Cassandra from getting out. It opened one second later and Bronswick appeared, looking much like a half-drowned rat. "The storm has passed. I thought you should know." He disappeared before Cassandra could question him further. Infuriating man! She wanted to chase him and shake him and…

Devlin, sopping wet from head to toe, half stumbled, half fell through the door. His eyes went straight to his bed where Penelope rested, the longing on his face transforming into defeat. Groaning, he staggered around his desk, expelled a long breath, and collapsed in his chair.

At which point Cassandra burst into tears.

Devlin wasn't sure what he needed first. A tall glass of brandy, to get his clothes off, or to fall into bed. Unfortunately his bed was presently occupied by Penelope. And as long as she was in the cabin he couldn't get undressed either. So he chose to start with the brandy.

The bottle he kept in his desk drawer would serve nicely. After fumbling about for a bit on account of his aching hands, he managed to fill a glass and drink. Christ, that felt good! He welcomed the bite and the heat that followed. It filled his chest and made him feel more or less whole again.

Penelope stood. "I'll go back to my own cabin. In case you want to lie down."

"Thank you." He wasn't sure he had the strength to get out of the chair, but he was grateful for her consideration.

She seemed to hesitate. "Will you be all right, Mama?"

Cassandra made a sound and Penelope left the cabin. "I thought you were dead," she said once her daughter was gone. Her voice was hoarse and slightly broken.

Devlin took another fortifying sip of his drink. Ahh. "Sorry to disappoint," he said, aiming for levity. After all, they'd been at odds with each other for weeks now, so it seemed like a natural comment to make.

But then he looked at her, at her blotchy face and red-rimmed eyes, at the tears streaking over her cheeks. His heart made a funny leap, and he straightened himself in his chair. But before he was able to analyze the situation, Cassandra was on her feet with her hands fisted at her sides. The cabin was small, so it took only two steps for her to reach him. Leaning down, she brought her face level with his. Anger, the likes of which he'd never seen before, flashed in her eyes, and for a brief second, he seriously considered jumping back into the ocean.

"I thought you were dead," she hissed, repeating herself. Only this time she followed the statement with a punch to his chest. It hurt. Even though there wasn't much force behind the blow, Devlin's weak body received it with bruising force. And then she hit him again. "I thought I'd lost you as well, Dev." Another punch landed against his shoulder. "I thought I'd never see you again."

He caught her wrists even as she collapsed before him, sinking onto her knees with great heaving sobs. "I had no choice, Cass. You have to understand. I had to save him."

He stared down into her crumpled face and felt his heart wobble. In spite of everything, she obviously cared for him. Why else would she respond like this?

"Never again. Please, you have to promise me, Dev."

"I'm afraid I can't do that. Not as long as I am the captain." This only made her cry harder, so Devlin did the only thing he could think of doing and pulled her against his chest, holding her close, his hand stroking her back until her breaths eased. And even then, he remained as he was, hugging her to him and savoring her warmth for long moments after.

Until she leaned back abruptly, as if she'd just remembered something. "We have to get you dry." Her eyes, still wet with tears, had widened. Her hands reached out, patting his chest. "No, no, no…you cannot survive all of this just to die from a chill." She pulled away and rose to her feet. "I won't allow it."

Devlin gave her an assessing look. "You seem remarkably concerned about my wellbeing all of a sudden."

"Of course I'm concerned. I would have to be a shrew not to be."

He raised an eyebrow. "Really?"

She puffed out a breath. "You are my husband after all, and I do love you." Her hands waved about as if they had the power to speed things along. "Now get up so I can help you undress."

But Devlin couldn't move. He could only stare, and eventually manage to ask, "Could you repeat that please?"

She looked delightfully irritated. Devlin frowned. How could irritation possibly be delightful? Shrugging, he chose not to ponder the issue while waiting for her to respond.

"I said, get up."

"No," he drawled. "Before that."

Her lips curved ever so slightly, into what resembled a secretive smile. "You're my husband."

She crossed her arms as if in defiance.

"No. That's not it either." He stood, forcing her back a step. "The part I'm interested in pertains to how you feel. I'd like to hear you say it again."

She tilted her head at a stubborn angle. "Very well. I love you."

Air rushed from his lungs. "Did I really have to almost die for you to realize that?"

"No." She shook her head. "It occurred to me before the storm started. I wanted to tell you, but you were asleep by the time I returned to the cabin and when I awoke, you were gone."

He blinked. She loved him and he…

He clasped each side of her face, holding her steady while he kissed her. "I love you too," he murmured against her lips. "I'm just not sure I deserve you."

Her hands worked the fastenings of his shirt while he kissed his way down her neck. "Of course you do. You're no more to blame for what happened to Timothy than I or anyone else." Stepping back so he was forced to halt his progress, she stared him straight in the eye. "It was an accident. I was too emotionally wrapped up in it not to find your confession jarring. But once I'd thought it all through, I regretted the way I reacted. It was wrong and you didn't deserve it. Especially not when you were just trying to save that poor boy from dying."

"Just because my intentions were good doesn't mean—"

"Of course not. I know that. But you've carried this weight for so long, and I'd like to help free you from it." Her hand reached up to cup his cheek. "Too many factors played a part for it to have been one man's fault alone. And in the end, the truth is that Timothy didn't look where he was going. I loved him. I'll always love him. But that doesn't mean I cannot love you as well."

"Do you really mean that?" He dared not hope.

She nodded. Just once. "I wouldn't say so if I didn't." The smile she gave him next was almost bashful. She tried to hide it by giving her attention back to his shirt, and in the next instant the garment was pulled up over his head.

Devlin watched as she shook it out and hung it on a hook behind the door. His skin was damp and he suddenly felt much colder than he had before.

"Here. This will help," Cassandra said. She'd produced a towel and was now running the thing up and down his arms.

It was hard not to smirk. Damn him but he was exhausted, though apparently not too much for him to enjoy his wife's ministrations. She loved him. And that made everything better. It also made him want her with a desperation that nearly stole his breath. After the day he'd just had, one would think he'd be too bloody knackered to think in such terms. But his body was clearly responding to what she was doing. And he, wicked man that he was, couldn't help but tease her a little.

"My legs are practically frozen." He tried to give her a pitiful look. "Perhaps you can help me remove my breeches."

She went utterly still. The towel pressed against his chest. "I, um…" He heard her gulp and almost laughed.

"The fabric's rather clingy," he explained.

"A—all right." Nibbling on her lip as if pondering some complicated equation, she stared at the buttons of his falls.

"You do understand how clothing works, do you not?"

Her expression turned into one of pure annoyance. "Of course I do." And apparently that was all the goading she needed. Her fingers reached for the buttons, and quicker than he could adjust himself to what was about to transpire, she'd divested him of his breeches and smalls in one fell swoop.

He gaped at her.

She eyed him with smug satisfaction. "Will that be all?"

"Hell no," he muttered.

A startled squeal was all she could manage before she was in his arms. His mouth captured hers, conveying without the need for words what was in his heart. He loved her. He would always love her. And being with her like this was utter perfection. So he deepened the kiss, held on tight, and allowed himself to believe he deserved this — that he deserved *her*.

She responded with fervor, kissing him back as if she would perish if she didn't.

"My God, Cass." He fumbled with her skirts,

yanking them up until he discovered her warmth. "I need you. Right here. Right now." The whimper she uttered when he turned and lowered himself to his bed was all the encouragement he needed. He pulled her down with him, straddling her on his lap. "Just…" He shifted her slightly, gritted his teeth, and hissed out a breath when she claimed him. He was naked, she fully clothed, and that alone drove him wild.

Gripping her hips, he guided her movements until he was dizzy with pleasure.

She was perfect, her body complementing his in the most intoxicating way imaginable. He could get drunk on this feeling, on this love that had blossomed between them. And he had to tell her, had to remind her of how much she mattered to him.

"You're mine, Cass. I'll cherish you forever. For as long as I live. I—"

"Dev!" His name was part gasp, part benediction.

One second later, he followed her over the edge with a heartfelt, "I love you."

"I love you too," she told him soon after, once they were stretched out on his bed. It was narrow, but cozy. They were lying on their sides, her back to his front and with his arm curled over her waist. Snug and warm.

Eyes closed, Devlin felt himself sinking as sleep crept toward him. A thought, or rather a worry, roused him just enough to ask, "Does this mean you're not leaving me when we reach Cape

Town?"

She grabbed his hand and gave it a squeeze. "It means you're stuck with me, I'm afraid. Forever."

"Good," he muttered against the back of her neck.

Reassured, Devlin inhaled Cassandra's sweet fragrance and finally, blissfully, allowed himself to rest.

CHAPTER SEVENTEEN

"MAY I GO UP THERE?" Penelope asked. She gestured toward the top of the main mast. "Please?"

They'd docked in Sydney harbor two days prior and were due to depart the following morning. Deciding to join Devlin when he'd gone to call on Governor Macquarie, Cassandra had been quite surprised by the colony's development since it had only been established roughly thirty years earlier. Yet she spotted a couple of rather nice churches, a bank, and a series of shops that looked as though they'd been plucked out of Bond Street.

It was surprisingly civilized when considering Sydney's past as a penal colony. Intrigued, Cassandra had taken careful note of the people, aware that many were emancipated convicts who'd been given land and had chosen to stay.

"I don't know," Cassandra said in response to Penelope's question about the climb she wanted to make. "It's very high up." Since leaving Cape Town, Penelope had begun climbing the rigging with Devlin whenever the weather was calm enough to allow it. But she'd only been up in the crow's nest once and was now keen to go up again.

"The view from up there will be stunning," Penelope pleaded.

"You'll have to be tethered," Devlin remarked. "And someone must go with you."

"Not to criticize you for interfering," Cassandra murmured, "but it does sound as though you're volunteering."

"Trevor can take me," Penelope said.

Cassandra narrowed her gaze. "Trevor?" The name left her mouth as if it were foreign.

"Mr. Bronswick's son?" Penelope offered.

"I know who he is," Cassandra said. Locating the youth, she gave him what felt like a much too tight smile. "I'm just not sure if he's…um…I mean…" Grappling for words, she looked to Devlin for help. "Is he capable?"

"You can trust him to bring her back safely," Devlin assured her. He followed the statement with a wink directed at Penelope.

Penelope grinned and Cassandra sighed. She wasn't sure who doted more on whom, these days. "Very well. You may…" Penelope was already off, hurrying across the deck to where Trevor stood waiting.

"I reckon she'll marry him one day," Devlin murmured.

"What?"

"She does seem to favor his company."

"Pfft. That doesn't mean anything."

"Doesn't it?" Devlin caught Cassandra's hand and together they watched Penelope climb up the rigging with Trevor directly behind her, his hands on either side caging her in and keeping her safe.

"She's only just turned thirteen," Cassandra muttered. "It's much too soon to think of her marrying. And besides, he's got to be twice her age at least."

Devlin grinned. "I do enjoy needling you, Cass."

"You're a scoundrel, do you know that?"

"Yes, but at least I am *your* scoundrel." He pulled her closer and dropped an affectionate kiss on her temple. "And he's actually only ten years her senior. I could see it working."

Cassandra wrenched herself away from him so she could give his shoulder a punch. But she was laughing and she secretly loved her husband's teasing, even though she doubted she'd ever admit it.

Chuckling, he pulled her back to him. "Perhaps we should stop our arguing."

"We weren't…" She caught herself, fell silent, and wound her arms round his neck. "You're right," she agreed. "It just seems to get in the way of things, doesn't it?"

He nodded and then his lips were on hers, kissing her fondly while holding her close and infusing her with his strength and his warmth. When she broke the kiss moments later, she leaned against him and glanced up toward the sky. Penelope and Trevor had almost reached the top of the mast now.

"Thank you for bringing us with you, Dev."

"You don't regret coming along?"

"No. It's been an incredible journey in more ways than one."

He didn't comment. He just wrapped his arm around her shoulders and held on tight. Together they waited for Penelope to climb back down. And then they spent the next hour listening to her account of what she'd seen.

That evening, after helping Penelope prepare for bed and tucking her into the hammock she'd finally managed to convince Cassandra she needed, Cassandra returned to her own cabin with more hesitation than ever before. It was time – time to tell Devlin what she now knew beyond any shadow of a doubt. And for some silly reason, having to do so caused her stomach to flutter most uncomfortably.

Sitting behind his desk, he was busy making notes in his log. The tip of his quill made a sharp scratching sound each time he finished a word. Cassandra smiled and lowered herself to the edge of her bed. It was funny how many little details she knew about him now, how much she'd learned during the last four months, like how he pressed down harder on his quill when he wrote the last letter, or how he would tap his foot while trying to gather his thoughts. He was tapping it now while considering what to write next.

Cassandra waited. She didn't want to interrupt him while he was working and usually chose to pass the time with a book. But today was different. There was a restlessness bubbling inside her that caused her to scrunch her nose at the thought of reading. Because that would require sitting still and right now she needed to move.

She stood, fluffed her pillow, smoothed out her blanket, and sat back down. With a sigh she watched Devlin scribble more words. She did a little dance with her feet, tapped a tune on her thighs with the palms of her hands. And sighed again.

He leaned back in his chair, crossed his arms, and directed a frown her way. "What is it?"

"Hmm?"

"You're not usually this…" He looked up as if hoping to find the words he needed printed somewhere overhead. "Agitated."

"I'm just waiting for you to finish writing."

He tilted his head. "Any particular reason?"

"Well…"

"Cass?" He stood and came toward her. Concern marred his features as he sat beside her and took her hand in his. "Is there something you need to tell me?"

"I didn't want to disturb you."

"Too late for that," he said with a wry smile. "What is it?"

"Well, I'm two weeks overdue." She noted the look of incomprehension on his face. Her heart tripled in size, filling with warmth as she held his gaze. "I'm fairly sure, or rather I'm actually quite positive, there's a baby on the way." His jaw dropped and she instinctively grinned because he looked so adorably befuddled, like she'd just swept a rug out from under his feet.

"A baby," he muttered. "I'm going to be a father. I mean, I'm already a father but this…this…" His voice cracked as he pulled her into his arms and kissed her.

She understood him completely. The day she'd learned she was carrying Penelope had been the most precious day of her life, and while Devlin had stepped in and happily accepted the role of being her father, having a child of his own would be extra special.

His lips met hers with reverent tenderness before brushing over her cheeks, her forehead, and even the tip of her nose. She tasted the salt from his tears and felt his hands hug her as if she were dearer to him than anything else in the world. And when she was finally given a chance to gaze upon his handsome face, she knew this was what true joy really looked like.

"How long until…" He gave his eyes a rough swipe and then motioned toward her belly.

"Another eight months, give or take."

He expelled a deep breath. "Thank God." Cassandra wasn't sure what he meant by that and he must have realized as much because he quickly added, "We'll be back in England in roughly five months which means you'll be able to have a proper midwife tend to you."

Cassandra nodded and tried her best not to let the comment dampen her good mood. But it was hard, because it also meant she'd have to remain in England while Devlin went off on another journey without her. They'd be apart and by the time he returned, the baby would be at least six months old. It wasn't a situation she would have minded when she'd decided to be his wife, but her perspective on life had changed a great deal since then. Devlin mattered to her. She loved him with all her heart and could not imagine spending so much as one day apart from him.

His mind was, from that moment onward, focused on far more practical matters, like ensuring her comfort, having Mr. Talbot cook special meals to keep her well-fed, preventing her from doing anything he deemed too strenuous. It was endearing at first, but did not take long to become exasperating. Especially since she wasn't even starting to show yet. And by the time she reached Calcutta two months later, after enduring a horrid month of constant queasiness along the way, Cassandra decided she'd had enough when Devlin insisted she needed a blanket, not a shawl, if she were to spend time outside.

"I am having a baby, Dev, not suffering from some incurable ailment. There is no need for me to confine myself to bed or to have someone take my arm every time I leave the cabin."

"There's always the risk you might fall," he told her as if he were some great authority on all things related to childbirth. "Being precautious won't do any harm, but carelessness might."

She ground her teeth together and practically snarled. "You sound like my father did when I was a child."

"Well, he obviously loved you very much and

was simply trying to protect you."

Cassandra glared at him. "If that were true, he would have stood by my side and offered support when he learned I was pregnant. So don't you ever speak of him or of my mother again as if either of them ever cared about anything besides the very indelicate question of how having a wanton for a daughter and a bastard for a grandchild reflected on them."

"I'm sorry." His face had gone pale. "I spoke without thinking. Cass please, I'm only trying to do what is best."

"I know. I'm sorry too." Her moodiness this past week made her feel like a stranger to herself. "But this is not my first pregnancy, Dev. I have a fair notion of what to expect and what I need. Being treated like an invalid is not very helpful. And besides, I have to be able to manage on my own or it will be so much harder after you're gone."

"Gone?"

She nodded. "Unless you plan on remaining in England for at least three months, you'll be away when I give birth."

His brow creased in contemplation. "You're right," he said, causing a boulder the size of a barrel to wedge itself in Cassandra's stomach. She'd hoped he might tell her he'd stay with her, that he wouldn't sail off and leave her alone. Instead he just smiled and dropped a kiss on her forehead. "I'll try to be more considerate."

"And less domineering," Cassandra said since it wasn't so much the consideration she minded.

"That too," he agreed, though she'd have had to be deaf not to hear his reluctance.

"A cup of tea wouldn't be the worst thing in the world though, if you're willing to bring me a cup."

"Of course not. I'll be right back." His eagerness to help her however he could lent a sparkle to his eyes and a bounce to his step.

Cassandra watched as he strode away. She'd married a sailor – a high ranking one – but a sailor no less, so she'd always known it would be like this. What she hadn't counted on was how much she would hate the idea of him leaving her for long periods of time. She'd worry. She knew she would. After what she'd experienced during this journey, she'd worry about him every second of every day until he returned. It would be unbearable. And she wished, oh how she wished, he would choose not to leave. She wished he would choose her instead of the sea, even though she was aware it was selfish of her to do so.

Devlin loved the ocean. If he gave up his seafaring life for her, she'd always feel like she'd ruined part of his soul. Which meant there was nothing else for it but to accept what she had and be glad for the days they were able to spend together.

It was late May by the time they docked in London's harbor. After helping his men tack the ropes and prepare for disembarking, Devlin went to help Cassandra and Penelope pack the last of their things. "We'll go straight to Camberly

House if that's all right with you," he said.

"I've no other appointments at the moment," Cassandra said with a grin. She tossed him a dress which he stuffed into one of the trunks. "And besides, I rather look forward to seeing Mary again and giving her our good news."

Devlin eyed Cassandra with all the fondness he felt for her. She couldn't quite hide the small bump she'd developed. And he realized he rather loved that. There was something immensely satisfying about being able to advertise the expansion of their family. It filled him with pride and, he had to admit, an overwhelming amount of dread.

For the most part, he'd managed to ignore it. He'd been too busy to turn it over and give it his full attention. But now they were leaving the ship and he'd have more time on his hands for the next four weeks – time enough to go mad with worry.

"Dev?"

He blinked. "Yes?"

"You were staring off into the distance. Is everything all right?"

No. It wasn't. Not exactly.

Instead he said, "Of course," and smiled, then distracted her by suggesting she hand him the book lying on her bed.

She frowned, assuring him she wasn't so easily fooled, but she went along with it anyway, and before he knew it they were in a carriage together with Penelope, their luggage strapped to the top, as they made their way through the busy London traffic.

"I'll send for Mother and Griffin straight away so they can come join us," Caleb said once the greetings at Camberly House had been taken care of and Caleb's children had received their gifts. He gave a few quick instructions for the butler to follow.

"Join me," Mary told Cassandra once the children had scampered back up to the nursery and the butler had gone to dispatch a couple of messengers. She dropped a curious look at Cassandra's belly, "I'm sure you've a great deal to tell me."

"This way," Caleb said once the ladies had disappeared into the parlor. "We can celebrate your return in my study while they talk." He gave Devlin a pointed look. "I'm sure you'd prefer a glass of brandy right now to a cup of tea."

Devlin traipsed after his brother. "I certainly would."

"Now, I don't mean to be indelicate," Caleb said once he'd handed Devlin a glass of his finest brandy and they'd each taken a sip, "but I'm not sure there's any other way to address this." He paused as if waiting for Devlin to leap in and save him, but Devlin just raised an eyebrow and took another swallow of his drink. Caleb sighed and then finally asked, "Is your wife increasing?"

It was impossible to stop a wide toothy grin from spreading across his face. So Devlin just gave up and nodded. "She is."

"Well, congratulations then. I'm immensely pleased for both of you. And for the rest of us too since we'll finally be seeing more of each other."

Caleb crossed to his chair and sat.

"Because I'm going to stay in England from now on?"

"Exactly!"

Devlin scratched the back of his neck. "I, um…I'm not sure that's what I want to do."

"A bit late for that now." Caleb's eyebrows had drawn together in the beginnings of a scowl.

Sighing, Devlin dropped into a vacant chair and stretched out his legs, crossing them at the ankles. He studied his brother. "Having a child doesn't mean I can't keep on sailing. Monty's been doing it for decades."

"True. I'm sure there are countless men who do it. But is that really what you want? I mean, I always thought you left to escape our father. Later, it seemed there may have been other reasons at play, but I would think you now have more reason to stay."

"Maybe," Devlin allowed. But the truth was he wasn't sure. Whenever he stayed in England for extended periods of time, he started to panic. Just being in the same country as his father, even if the man had been dead for six years, tended to make him angry. And having to pass through London, where the memories of his own shortcomings always came back to haunt him whenever a carriage drove too fast, had always made his blood run cold.

Nothing had ever made him feel better or happier than setting sail and leaving England behind.

"What does Cassandra think of your plan?"

Caleb quietly asked.

"I haven't exactly discussed it with her."

Caleb snorted. "My God, you really are a novice at this marriage business, aren't you?"

"What the devil is that supposed to mean?" Devlin asked, disgruntled.

"Only that I'll wager an argument is heading your way." He scoffed and shook his head. "When are you planning to abandon her then?"

"I'm not…" Enough. Devlin was tired. He'd sailed around the world for Christ sake. The last thing he needed was a lecture from a brother who was only older than him by ten minutes. He set his glass on Caleb's desk. Hard. "I never gave her any reason to believe I'll be staying. In fact, Cass knows I won't. She understands that I have to leave if I'm to support her and our children."

"If it's financial aid you require, I'm here to help."

"Thank you, but I don't want to be dependent."

"All right then."

"All right?"

Caleb shrugged. "Seems to me you've made your decision."

"What I told you from the start, if you will recall, is that I'm not sure of what I'm doing."

"So you did." His blasé tone was infuriating. It made Devlin want to leap across his brother's desk and strangle him with his perfectly tied cravat. "Although speaking for myself and for Griffin, with whom I've had a chance to discuss our formative years in great detail since our reunion, I'd hate for my children to be raised as I was."

Something dangerous and dark began twisting and turning inside Devlin. "My children will never suffer as we did, Caleb. They'll never have cause to question their parents' love for them, and they'll never be told they must be something they don't want to be or that they're useless."

"No. I don't expect so," Caleb murmured. "But for them to avoid having parents who live apart, you have to be there, Devlin. And you have to participate in their lives, build memories, and watch them grow. You can't run away as you always do."

Devlin pushed out a heavy breath. "If you must know, I have been considering a change of pace. I just don't want to feel like I'm being pushed."

"Of course you don't. I wouldn't either." They shared a look that somehow stripped away all the years and took them back to the day when they'd all had enough of their father's dogged attempt at controlling their lives, to the day they'd all gone their separate ways until news of their father's passing had reached them. "I'm sorry. I suppose I just want you to have what I have. I'm ridiculously happy, you know."

"I'm glad to hear it." And he was. Truly. During the last nine months he'd managed to acquire a similar joy. But there was still an element of doubt, uncertainty, and a distinct fear that crept under his skin whenever he thought of remaining on land forever. It made no sense, but deciding to marry Cassandra had been remarkably easy when compared with quitting his life as a captain. It was almost as if…

Devlin froze as everything became clear.

It was almost as if he was thinking of relinquishing his identity. If he wasn't a captain, then who the hell was he? And what was he going to do with the rest of his life?

CHAPTER EIGHTEEN

A COMFORTABLE FEELING OF RIGHTNESS SETTLED over Cassandra as she stepped through Clearview's front door five days later. Visiting Mary and seeing Emily had been lovely. Travelling around the world with Devlin had been a grand adventure. But this had been her home for almost fourteen years. In every room and every corner she could see glimpses of the past, memories of all the people who'd breathed life into this place.

"I wish I'd known you were coming," Katherine said once Cassandra and Devlin had removed their outer garments and Penelope had run off to find her friends. "I'd have prepared a feast to celebrate."

"No need for that," Cassandra assured her. She followed her into the kitchen to help prepare the tea while Devlin carried their luggage upstairs. "I feel as though we've done nothing but eat since we arrived, what with Mary planning a grand supper and Emily and my mother-in-law following suit. All three arranged baskets of food for us to take along in the carriage, if you can believe it."

Katherine grinned. "You are meant to be eating for two."

"Yes, but not for two fully grown adults." Smiling, she perched herself on a stool and glanced around. "I see you've painted the cabinet doors over there."

"A necessity after Henry and Clyde attempted to *clean* them." She rolled her eyes and pursed her lips while hanging the kettle over the fire. "They found a piece of chipped paint and decided to give it a tug. By the time I found out what they were up to, the doors were pockmarked."

"Oh dear." Cassandra bit her lip and tried not to laugh. "I presume you punished them for their crime?"

"Oh yes. They were made to tidy up the rice I accidentally spilled." Katherine delivered the most evil smile Cassandra had ever seen, then added, "One grain at a time."

It was impossible for Cassandra to contain her laughter any longer. "How perfectly diabolical of you."

"I thought so." She retrieved a tin and began scooping tea leaves into a strainer. "I'm glad you're back, Cass."

"Me too."

Katherine eyed her curiously. "And will you be staying for a while?"

"Yes. If it's not too much trouble, I'd like to have my baby here since it's where I'll feel most at home without Devlin."

"What are you saying?" Katherine stared at her

and then her eyes widened. "Are you telling me he won't be here for his child's birth?"

"He has to work, Katherine, and besides, it's not so strange really. Plenty of fathers miss out on such things." It was what she'd kept telling herself since she'd realized what his intentions were.

"Certainly," Katherine agreed, "if they're away at war perhaps, in need of a steady income, or simply don't care."

Cassandra sighed. She really didn't want to discuss Devlin's reasons for leaving. Not because she doubted his love for her or worried the birth of their first child wasn't important to him. It was perhaps because he had said he needed to make a living, even though he was the brother of a duke and was quite unlikely to suffer financial difficulties. Surely he could at least skip one journey and send his crew without him. With this last voyage being Monty's last, it might be slightly more tricky, but Bronswick was pretty capable as was Mr. Harris, the boatswain. And Trevor had, on the return from Sydney, started to learn how to captain a ship. Yet Devlin insisted he had to go, which meant there had to be some other reason – maybe one he himself didn't fully comprehend.

Or, she considered, he simply loved the sea more than he loved her.

Now there was a depressing thought.

"You have to tell me everything," Katherine said as she handed Cassandra a mug. "Did you see any sharks along the way? I've read they can cut a man in half with their teeth.

Cassandra grinned and shook her head. "No, there were no sharks." Together, they removed themselves to the kitchen table. Katherine placed a tin of biscuits in the center while asking additional questions about the people of China and if they really ate with sticks.

A movement beyond the window caught Cassandra's eye. It was Devlin who'd apparently chosen to go outside and give her a bit more alone time with Katherine. She smiled as she watched him kick a ball to James who passed it to William. Henry and Clyde were naturally too busy climbing a tree to join in the game.

"Perhaps we should take the tea and biscuits out there," Cassandra suggested. She hadn't even greeted all the children yet and was suddenly eager to do so. Not only because she'd missed them, but because she was eager to answer the pull she felt as she watched Devlin interact with them.

"I think the children would be delighted," Katherine said. "I'll grab a blanket for us to sit on. We'll have a tea picnic of sorts."

Cassandra picked up the tin of biscuits and made her way outside where she was immediately accosted by all the children who stopped whatever they were doing so they could come hug her. And receive a biscuit each as reward.

"We knew you were back," William said while crumbs spilled from his mouth.

"You really shouldn't talk with your mouth full," Cassandra gently chided. She turned her attention to Clyde and Henry. "And you two were supposed to behave, not destroy the house while I was away."

"We know. But the paint had come off just a bit and it was so tempting to give it a pull and then…" Henry gave a big shrug. "We just couldn't stop."

"But we have learned our lesson," Clyde said. "Katherine made sure of it."

"Very well," Cassandra chuckled, "I suppose you may both have a biscuit as well then."

They snatched the offering and ran off, racing each other to the far end of the lawn, their laughter filling the air to mingle with bird song. Inhaling deeply, Cassandra glanced toward Devlin, whose love for her shone bright in his eyes.

How could he go away again so soon?

She did her best to smile, even though she didn't understand it.

"I've been thinking," Devlin told Cassandra a couple of days after their arrival at Clearview. "Perhaps I should look into buying a house – a place we can make our own. It might take time, but as long as I find the right place before I leave, Caleb should be able to finalize the deal after I'm gone and you can—"

"No." The word was tight, Cassandra's expression more so. But then she seemed to relax, her puckered brow smoothing while a smile appeared on her lips. "It's a lovely gesture, and I appreciate it, but Clearview is special to me, so if you're not staying, then this is where I want to be."

"Cass…"

"It's home and then, of course, there's the added benefit of me being surrounded by people. I won't lack company or support."

She had a valid point. It was just that he felt he ought to do more and providing a house for their growing family seemed like a good start. He sighed. "Perhaps you'll reconsider when I return."

"Perhaps." She rose up onto her toes and planted a kiss on his cheek. The weather was lovely, and they'd decided to take the children out for a walk so Katherine could have a few hours to herself.

Devlin put his arm around Cassandra's shoulders and drew her close to his side. She was his wife and he would show his affection for her as publicly as he wished. Propriety, be damned.

"When I grow up, I want to marry a man who loves me as much as you love Cassandra," Rosemary declared. She'd been skipping along silently beside them, but now that she'd spoken, she chose to run off and join Sophie and Penelope, who were picking wildflowers further ahead.

A knot formed in Devlin's chest and his heart starting pounding. This was his family, he realized, as if he'd had his head buried under a rock. Not just Cassandra and Penelope, but the rest of the children too. And he was deciding to leave them because… Well, because that was what he did. He travelled. Gone for nine months and then back for one. It was a routine he'd had for almost seventeen years, ever since he'd argued with his father.

To stop and change his life had not occurred to

him until Caleb suggested it. Or maybe it had, but he'd always shoved the notion aside, deemed it impossible, and buried it, refusing to give it the attention it required. But now, with his departure rapidly approaching, he found it difficult to think of anything else. Ideally, he wanted Cassandra to come with him, but he also wanted to make sure she and their child received the best medical care during labor. And if she didn't come with him and he chose to stay, then there was the question of what his purpose would be.

Except…

He suddenly smiled. Maybe he was complicating the issue, because in the end, life had a way of sorting itself out. Right now, however, the future would be determined by choice. He was choosing to leave, but he could also choose to stay. The decision was his. No one was making demands either way, certainly not Cassandra, who'd simply resigned herself to the eventuality of his departure.

He frowned. "How come you haven't asked me to stay?"

She glanced up at him, startled. She blinked several times in rapid succession. "I suppose I didn't want to seem pushy. You love sailing, Dev. Asking you to give it up felt wrong. Selfish."

"Expecting me to be a part of your life, of our children's lives, would never be selfish."

Her eyes widened. "Does that mean?" They'd both stopped walking and she'd turned toward him, her face tilted up toward his. "If I ask you to stay, will you?"

"I don't know. You'll have to find out."

She grumbled something low beneath her breath and then cleared her throat. "Very well, then." The wind caught a strand of her hair, and she reached up to tuck it behind her ear. "Will you stay here in England with me?"

Instead of the panic he'd always felt at the thought of remaining in England, Devlin's heart started racing with joy. This was what he'd needed. To know his presence was truly wanted. For someone he loved to ask him to stay.

"Yes. I can't imagine myself being happy anywhere else." He took her hand. "I'll give my duties over to Bronswick. Harris can be his first mate, and Trevor can become his quartermaster."

"Are you sure?" she asked, her hesitance evident in her voice and her eyes.

Devlin nodded. "I always sailed to escape and because there was nothing to keep me here, but you've helped me put the past to rest. Now I have you and our children, and Cass…I love you. With all my heart I—"

Her squeal cut him off as she practically threw herself at him, knocking the wind right out of his belly. "Thank God," she said, and then somehow she'd pulled his mouth down to hers and was kissing him with total abandon, as if they were somewhere alone and did not have an audience consisting of seven children.

"Ewe," Clyde said. "They're exchanging spit."

"That's so disgusting," one of the girls muttered.

Devlin laughed against Cassandra's mouth. "Mind if I throttle them?"

"I will if you don't," she said, her lips curving against his until she was grinning.

"All right. It's settled then." Devlin carefully disengaged himself from Cassandra, dropped a quick kiss on her forehead, then raced toward the nearest child with a roar.

Squeals of delight followed, increasing in strength as he caught Henry by his waist and swung him high in the air. The rest of the children eventually got their turns as well, and Devlin's heart grew, tripling in size until it was close to bursting. Somehow, thanks to a mean old woman, he'd found a permanent home for himself filled with laughter and love. He'd have to extend his gratitude to Baroness DeVries at some point, perhaps in the form of flowers.

It was, he decided, the least he could do, considering he'd never been happier.

EPILOGUE

"**H**AS YOUR BOATSWAIN CHECKED THE ropes?" Devlin asked the captain in a no nonsense tone while following him across the deck. "They can fray and tear, you know."

"I am aware," the captain replied.

If Cassandra wasn't mistaken, he was starting to sound quite exasperated. She hid a grin and turned to Penelope, who was even worse at concealing her amusement. "Do you suppose we'll be asked to disembark before we even set sail?"

"Of course not. Michael wouldn't dare ask you to do so. He's much too fond of Dev."

"I think you're right. But I also suspect Michael might regret suggesting this voyage sooner than I'd have expected."

As if on cue, Devlin's and Cassandra's grandson, Captain Michael Bronswick, approached. "You must be a saint, Grandmother. It's the only explanation for your ability to put up with him all these years." He glanced over his shoulder and sighed when he realized Devlin was standing directly behind him.

"And don't forget to inspect the hold," Devlin

said. "It's your responsibility to do so, Michael."

Michael turned to his grandfather with a glare. "There's a chair over there. I would be eternally grateful if you would use it."

"Well," Devlin muttered while Michael marched off to some other part of the ship where his grandfather wasn't present. "I'm only offering the boy some sound advice."

"He's three and thirty," Cassandra reminded Devlin. "I think it might be time for you to accept that he cast off his leading strings some time ago."

"Devlin does have more experience than Michael," Penelope pointed out. "It wouldn't hurt for him to listen."

The edge of Devlin's mouth lifted to form a crooked smile. "I always knew I loved you for a good reason, Penny."

"Well, you've always supported me, so I think it only fair to return the favor, even when it involves my son." She glanced around as if searching for something and when she smiled, it was clear she'd found it. Or him, to be more precise. "If you'll excuse me, I think I'll go and see how Trevor's managing."

"I thought he was securing the main sail," Devlin said.

"Yes," Penelope said. She started forward but Cassandra managed to catch her by the elbow and bring her to a halt. "You're not going up there."

Penelope grinned. "Of course I am." She must have seen the horrified look in Cassandra's eyes for she instantly added, "You mustn't worry though.

I am wearing trousers beneath these skirts."

Cassandra groaned and let her hand drop. "Of course you are," she muttered. She knew by now that her daughter was far more stubborn than she'd ever been and that there would never be any stopping her once she put her mind to something.

"I did tell you she'd marry him," Devlin murmured close to her ear. His hand had snuck its way around her waist, offering her strength and that wonderful sense of security she couldn't quite seem to get enough of.

"So you did. And you've never let me forget it."

"Why should I? It's the most precise prediction I ever made. Besides the one about you falling madly in love with me, that is."

"Really?"

He smiled with a hint of bashfulness that went straight to her heart. "Well, no. But I did hope. And I never stopped wishing."

"You're a lucky man then." Cassandra looped her arms around his neck and locked her eyes with his. "Because it does appear as though your wish came true."

"I love you, Cass."

"And I love you, my seafaring scoundrel." No words were truer. He'd been her best friend and constant companion for four long decades and now they were off on one last adventure.

During their marriage, they'd been blessed with three daughters, Alexandra, Theodora and Lavinia, none of whom enjoyed sailing. Not that Devlin hadn't done his best to encourage them, and later their husbands, but it had been a struggle and eventually they'd all given up. Of course, there might be hope yet for the girls' sons, but until they showed an actual interest, Devlin contented himself with the fact that Michael adored the sea as much as his father and grandfather did.

The transition from seadog to landlubber had been trying. It had taken time for Devlin to find a satisfying routine, to adjust, and accept his new role. Until Cassandra had encouraged him to pursue a new dream by using some of his savings to purchase two additional ships. Within one year, he'd turned them and The Condor into a profitable shipping business. Now, forty years later, The Crawford Company's fleet numbered more than one hundred vessels.

Cassandra squinted against the morning sun and considered her husband's face, so dear to her she was sure she could gaze upon it forever with pleasure. It was perhaps slightly more creased than it had been when they'd first met, but he was still a striking man. The arm he'd once broken pained him on occasion, especially when the weather was damp, and his once dark hair was almost entirely silver now. But he was still as handsome as ever, and he always made sure to tell her that she was the most beautiful woman in the world, even though she knew there were wrinkles around her eyes and mouth and that her body wasn't as slim as it had once been.

Together, in the years since Devlin had stopped sailing on a regular basis, they'd raised their children in a modest cottage Devlin had purchased for them near Clearview. For although Cassandra regretted leaving the house she'd called home for so long, it had gotten overcrowded with the expansion of their family, and she'd realized she and Devlin required a place of their own. But she visited the orphans Clearview continued to welcome over the years as often as she was able, advising the management and keeping abreast of the goings on.

There was no denying that it was time for both her and Devlin to accept their age now. They no longer had the energy of their youth and had decided that perhaps the time had come for them to stop pushing themselves so hard.

During the past forty years, they'd gone on five additional voyages together, but this one was Michael's idea because, as he'd put it, "What better way is there for us to spend time together than by doing something all of us love?"

Standing beside Devlin with her head resting on his shoulder, Cassandra watched the coastline recede until only the wide open sea lay ahead. This was perfection, this moment piled on top of all the others that came before, to create a lifetime of memories for them to look back on. A sigh of contentment escaped her as Devlin's warmth seeped through her clothing and dove right under her skin, heating her from within.

She smiled at him and he smiled back.

No other words were needed.

All that mattered was that they were together.

THANK YOU SO MUCH FOR reading *Her Seafaring Scoundrel*. If you enjoyed this story you're sure to enjoy the first books in the series as well. Grab your copy of *No Ordinary Duke* and *More Than a Rogue* today to find out how Mary and Caleb fell in love and how Emily and Griffin found their own happily-ever-after.

Or if you're looking for a longer read with a rags to riches trope, you might consider trying my Diamonds In The Rough series, starting with *A Most Unlikely Duke*.

You can find out more about my new releases, backlist deals and giveaways by signing up for my newsletter here: *www.sophiebarnes.com*

Once again, I thank you for your interest in my books. Please take a moment to leave a review since this can help other readers discover my books.

And please continue reading for an excerpt from *No Ordinary Duke*.

No Ordinary Duke

CHAPTER ONE

R AIN STREAKED DOWN THE CARRIAGE windows while Caleb Maxwell Crawford traveled from the London docks to his family home on Grosvenor Square. Dusk had turned to night since he'd stepped off the ship on which he'd sailed from Calais yesterday afternoon. Jaw set, he tightened his grip on the leather satchel beside him on the bench. It held all the evidence he needed to prove how wrong his father had been when they'd parted ways ten years earlier. Filled with letters of praise and articles heralding Caleb's architectural abilities, it would show the old bastard he'd made a success of himself. It would prove that refusing to join the clergy and being cut off financially had not led to his downfall, as his father had claimed it would when he'd railed about Caleb's ungratefulness.

Peering out past the heavy rivulets of cascading water, Caleb narrowed his gaze on the murky darkness. He couldn't wait to gloat and see the astonished look on his father's face when he showed him the lithographs printed in the Paris Gazette. They illustrated in fine detail the mansion he'd designed for the Duke of Orléons. Building had commenced six years earlier and had just been completed last month. Inhaling deeply, Caleb tightened his hold on his satchel. The carriage drew to a jarring halt moments later, throwing him slightly off balance. Muttering a curse, he opened the door and climbed out into the unpleasant downpour, satchel in hand. The driver helped him retrieve his valise from the boot.

"Here you go sir," the man said while water streamed over the brim of his hat.

"Thank you." Caleb paid him and walked toward the imposing Mayfair mansion that loomed before him. The heavy front door with its massive brass knocker was less than inviting.

Rain gushed down the curved slope of the roof and pelted against the ground. Pulling his hat down over his forehead, Caleb drew the collar of his greatcoat up to protect the back of his neck and climbed the slick stone steps.

He still owned a key and withdrew it now from his pocket to unlock the door. It swung open and gave way to a dim interior. Entering the foyer, Caleb paused to listen. All was silent. Not even the longcase clock ticked away the progression of time.

Shivering, Caleb nudged the door shut behind him. It closed with a resounding thud. Where the devil was everyone?

He sighed and muttered another oath. He didn't like the idea of having to hunt down his family at one of the country estates. But even if they'd left town, there ought to be servants about. His parents had never left a house completely empty.

A soft snick caught his ears, and then the sharp click of approaching footsteps filled the air. The sound accompanied a man whom Caleb instantly recognized, even though his features were far more drawn now than when he'd last seen him.

"Murdoch," he said, addressing the butler. "It has been a while."

The old man drew a sharp breath. The candelabra he carried displaced the darkness. "I thought I heard something, so I came to investigate." Moving closer, he peered up at Caleb. Light from four guttering candles flickered across his face, accentuating the creases there. "Is it really you, my lord?"

Caleb drew his hat from his head and swiped back the wet strands of hair that clung to his forehead. "Yes. I have returned." He set his valise and satchel on the floor and proceeded to take off his gloves. "Where are my parents?"

Murdoch stared at him as if he could still not believe he was actually there. "Your mother is upstairs in her rooms." Breaking eye contact, he proceeded to help Caleb off with his coat.

"And my father, the duke?" When Murdoch failed to reply, Caleb knit his brow. "Is he not at home?"

"No, he is not." The butler busied himself with hanging the coat and setting Caleb's hat and gloves aside. "But your mother will be pleased to see you, I'm sure. Please, follow me." He led the way up the stairs while Caleb followed behind, his curiosity piqued by the servant's unwillingness to supply him with details. Perhaps his parents had quarreled during his absence and were now living apart?

They reached the top of the landing and turned left toward the duchess's apartment. Caleb knew the way well enough, but was glad the butler would be there to announce his arrival. After all, he doubted his mother would be as pleased to see him as Murdoch believed, considering he'd left without saying farewell. But he'd been too angry to do so at the time, and his decision to leave had been made in haste without consideration for anything besides getting away.

Arriving in front of the door leading into his mother's sitting room, Murdoch paused to knock. A maid answered seconds later, her eyes widening when she noticed Caleb.

"Please inform Her Grace that her son, Lord Caleb, is here to see her," Murdoch said.

The maid nodded and the door closed, only to be opened again moments later by the duchess herself. "Thank God you are here!" She stared up at him with shimmering eyes, and then, in the next second, her arms were around him, and she was holding him to her as if he offered necessary support.

Unaccustomed to such a display of affection from his mother, Caleb hesitated briefly before wrapping his arms around her as well. He hadn't expected such a warm welcome and was slightly thrown by the effect it was having on the resentment he'd harbored for the past ten years.

Placing a kiss on his mother's cheek, he listened to her uneasy breaths until she was ready for him to release her.

"Shall I have some tea sent up?" Murdoch asked, reminding Caleb of his presence.

"Please do," his mother said. She opened the door to her sitting room wider and invited Caleb in. Unlike his mother, whose youth had departed during his absence, the space looked unchanged. "Come sit with me, Caleb. There is much for us to discuss."

He wasn't even sure where to begin. This reunion wasn't going at all the way he'd imagined it would. Since leaving Paris five days earlier, he'd pictured himself storming into his father's study and shoving the evidence of his success under the man's haughty nose. Now, inhaling deeply, he approached the sofa and lowered himself to the vacant spot beside his mother. There was so much to say. Too much, in a way.

Perhaps the best place to start was with an apology. "I am sorry," he told her and reached for her hand. "I should have written to you, but the more time passed, the more difficult it became."

"I know."

He looked at her and was swiftly accosted by guilt at the sight of her watery eyes. Christ, he'd been awful to her. She hadn't deserved it, but his pride had been wounded, and he'd only been able to think of himself and of getting away from the life he'd come to despise.

"At least I am not your only son," he murmured. She had three besides his older brother, George, the heir who'd received all their father's affection.

"You haven't been in touch with Griffin or Devlin?" she asked in reference to the brothers who'd been born only minutes after himself. He shook his head. "They left shortly after you, for similar reasons, I suspect. Now, after everything that has happened, I am hoping they will return as well. I've sent out letters, but it will take time for them to reach your brothers." She met his gaze. Her brow puckered ever so slightly. "I'm surprised you are already here since I had no idea of your actual location. I suppose the agent I hired to find you was good at doing his job."

Unease traversed Caleb's spine. He tightened his hold on his mother's hand. "No one came to find me, Mama. I returned of my own accord."

"But then..." She swallowed and closed her eyes. Her lips trembled and it became suddenly clear to Caleb that she was making a stoic effort to maintain her composure. "You do not know." The words were only a whisper.

"Know what?" he asked even though he sensed he had no wish to hear whatever it was she would say in response.

"Your father is dead, Caleb. A fire broke out at the Everly stables last week," she said, referring to one of the dukedom's larger properties. "He and George went to inspect some repairs. They were supposed to be gone only for a few short days but now…" A sob cut off her words, and her free hand rose to smother the sound.

Caleb's heart thudded against his chest. "And George?" he asked, already dreading her answer.

"When your father didn't come out, George went in after him." Tears streamed down her cheeks. "They're both gone, Caleb. I buried them at St. George's this morning."

It was as if time slowed to a halt. A distinct feeling of disappointment and deep regret trickled through him, numbing his veins. Slumping back, he tried to make sense of it, to accept what his mother told him as fact, only to find that he couldn't.

The door opened after a quick knock, and Murdoch returned carrying a tray. He placed it on the table, exchanged a few words with the duchess, and departed once more. Caleb's mother withdrew her hand from Caleb's and dabbed at her eyes. She then busied herself with pouring tea while he watched with a strange sense of detachment.

He shook his head. "No. It cannot be true."

She sniffed and took a sip of her tea. "You know what this means," she said, as if he'd not spoken. She waited for him to meet her gaze before saying, "You are the Duke of Camberly now."

Caleb stared at her in dismay. "I don't want to be." It was the first thing that came to mind. He liked his uncomplicated life, free from all the responsibilities his father and older brother had faced. He'd never envied either of them. But he had cursed the way his father's sense of duty and obligation had affected his life.

"Unfortunately, that hardly matters. With your father and brother gone, the title falls to you."

He instinctively shuddered and bit back the comment that threatened. To say that he ought to have stayed away would only cause his mother pain. She was happy to have him home and probably quite relieved with the prospect of him taking over the day-to-day running of things. And for her he would do it, or at least he would try.

He drew a deep breath and felt his chest tighten. "Very well. But if I am going to do this, I will need something stronger than tea. Please tell me you still keep a bottle of sherry in that cabinet over there."

Her wobbly smile tilted as if trying to find its balance. "Yes. I dare say I could do with a glass myself."

Raising her hand to his lips, Caleb pressed a tender kiss to her knuckles before going in search of their fortification. He was conscious of his heart beating a dull tattoo, like a drummer marching him off to the gallows. Recalling the satchel he'd left downstairs, he closed his eyes briefly and muttered a curse. Everything he'd worked for these past ten years had been for nothing. His father would never know of his success. How ironic that the son he'd named his greatest disappointment would now be continuing his legacy.

As had become his habit in recent weeks, Caleb arrived at White's shortly after nine in the evening to enjoy a drink and possibly a game of cards with his friend, Robert Moor, Viscount Aldridge. The two had known each other since childhood and had been sent off to Eton together as lads. The moment Caleb's return to London had been announced six months ago, Robert had immediately come to call, and the two had spent an hour washing away the years wedged between them with a few glasses of brandy.

Since then, Robert had offered invaluable advice and support. He'd invited Caleb out for rides and to Gentleman Jackson's boxing saloon whenever he'd needed to lose himself in something besides accounts, ledgers, investments, and his mother's most recent obsession – his need to think about marriage.

He'd cut her off and walked away the first time she'd made the suggestion and every time since. But when the Season had been well underway and she'd produced a list of potential candidates she considered appropriate for courtship, he'd had no choice but to listen, even though he detested the extra pressure it placed on his shoulders.

"You look more somber than usual," Robert said when Caleb found him. "Trouble with the dukedom?"

Dropping into a vacant chair, Caleb frowned at his friend, who poured a large drink and handed it to him. Caleb took a long sip, enjoying the powerful flavor and the heat it exuded as it slid down his throat. "I cannot stand it any longer." Leaning back, he cradled the glass between his hands and stared at his friend as if he had the power to save him. "It is awful, Robert. I just…" He sighed and scrubbed one hand across his jaw. "I hate being a duke."

Robert had the decency not to argue. Instead, he watched, his eyes increasingly somber until he finally said, "Then don't be."

Startled by the comment, Caleb grinned, the expression so foreign to him now it actually hurt his jaw. "As if it's that simple, but you know as well as I that it is not."

His friend inclined his head, paused for a moment as if on the verge of divulging some piece of information, but then set his own glass to his lips and drank. "Is it not getting any easier?"

Caleb thought back on the endless hours of work that held him hostage in his study. There had been little reprieve and no time at all to consider his own wants and needs since his return. Even now, the satchel holding his architectural designs remained unopened. He'd had no opportunity to share them with anyone or to dream up new ones.

"No," he told Robert with unwavering honesty. "If anything, it is getting worse. The demands on me are increasing with each passing day. Women I've never met are showing up at my home, intent on praising their daughters' charms. Meanwhile, every business in Town is paying me court, and every hostess wishes to make me her guest of honor. And that's not considering repairs I am asked to fund and approve at my various estates and the tenants who all have concerns they've decided to air in a steady stream of letters I receive daily."

Robert's lips twitched as if struggling to contain his laughter. He cleared his throat. "I see."

"Do you really?" Caleb wasn't certain. "You were groomed for this sort of life from the day you were born, while I was largely ignored until I was dropped in the middle of it."

"I also have the added benefit of being happily married to a woman who helps me endure the burden of the responsibility I carry." Robert considered Caleb for a long moment before saying, "Maybe your mother has the right of it. Perhaps marriage is precisely what you need."

Caleb groaned. "Don't be daft. The last thing I need at the moment is another female to coddle." He winced, aware he'd just referred to his mother in rather disparaging terms, but the truth of it was that as much as he loved her, her constant weeping and insistence he fill a mold he didn't quite fit had driven him to the point of madness.

"Then what do you need?" Robert stared him straight in the eye. "Do you even know?"

It took a moment for Caleb to turn the question over in his head and find the right answer. "Yes," he finally said. "I believe getting away for a while would help."

Robert studied him with increased interest. "Where would you go?"

Caleb snorted. "I have no idea. If I head to one of my country estates, all the problems I'm trying to escape will surely follow."

"So you want to go somewhere where you won't be bothered."

"Just long enough for me to find my bearings again." Because he could not believe this was all there would be to his life— now until he drew his last breath. There had to be more to it than sitting in a study, going over numbers. Somehow, he had to rediscover himself, recover from the shock of losing his father and brother, and find the means to stay true to himself while being a duke.

"Is your secretary capable of running things without you during this absence?"

"I believe so," Caleb said with conviction. The man had worked with his father for the past two decades. He knew everything he needed to know to handle things efficiently, which made Caleb warm to the idea of taking a break. Perhaps it would be more possible than he'd dared to believe.

"In that case, I have a proposal I'd like for you to consider." A smirk made Robert's mouth tilt with a hint of mischief. "I have a modest property in Cornwall. Clearview is its name. It's a decent place, but the money I've sent for repairs has, as I understand it, been spent on other things."

Caleb frowned. "If you think your servants are stealing from you, it might be prudent to go and investigate the matter."

"And so I would if I had the time, but with Vivien's pregnancy, I am reluctant to leave her side at the moment, so I thought perhaps…"

Understanding dawned. "You want me to go in your stead?"

Leaning forward, Robert rested his elbows on his knees and pierced Caleb with a direct stare. "I believe a man like you who enjoys working with his hands might take pleasure in seeing to some of the repairs himself."

"You could be right," Caleb said. The prospect of mending a leaking roof or a crumbling wall held a lot of appeal. "I can also hire new servants for you, if you think that might be helpful."

A flicker of amusement brightened Robert's eyes. "There are no servants there, Caleb. Just my sister, her friends, and the orphaned children they offer sanctuary to."

Caleb blinked. "Your sister?" Robert had several, some younger, some older.

"Cassandra, to be exact. She's five years younger than us, so you might not recall her. She debuted after you left England." His expression cooled a fraction as he added, "She made the scandalous choice of bedding her fiancée before they were married. Poor devil died on his way to the church, struck down by an oncoming carriage."

"Jesus!"

Robert nodded. "Cassandra sought my help shortly after. Apparently, that one indiscretion had gotten her pregnant. When she refused to pass her child off as another's, which was what our parents advised, they threatened to turn her out of the house. So I secretly bought a place for her to live. When two other girls encountered similar hardships, Cassandra invited them to come with her. During the last five years, they have taken in several children, who cost more to keep than they can afford with the measly donations they receive from friends and family."

"In other words," Caleb said slowly, "these three spinsters are mismanaging funds in an effort to run a make-shift orphanage?"

"More or less," Robert said with a shrug.

"And you have allowed this to continue for five years?" Caleb could scarcely believe it. It wasn't that he didn't approve of the kindness these women were showing toward the less fortunate, but if they let the house fall into complete dis-repair, the day would come when they wouldn't even have that. And then what?

"She's my sister," Robert said. "I have tried to help her as much as I can while keeping her scandalous circumstances at bay. She and her friends have been hidden away and mostly forgotten, but they are constantly in need of assistance, and I simply don't have the time or the resources to keep ensuring they're well looked after. I have my own family to consider, estates to tend to as well as investments and parliamentary responsibilities. You know how it is."

Wasn't that the truth of it? Caleb flattened his mouth and considered his choices: stay in London, tied to a desk and with endless demands placed before him, or ride off to Cornwall for a breath of fresh air and the physical activity awaiting him there.

He knew which he preferred, but there was still one problem. "It would be unseemly for me to live in a house with three unmarried women."

"Spinsters, Caleb, not debutantes. Makes all the difference, you know. But I actually agree, which is why I suggest you stay in the caretaker's cottage."

"There's a caretaker's cottage?" How big was this place?

"It's nothing to get excited over since it's only one room, but if you want to stop being a duke for a while and pretend you're a…" he waved his hand between them before settling on, "laborer instead, then you're welcome to it."

Uncertainty settled between Caleb's shoulder blades. "How come no one's living in this cottage right now?"

"Because the caretaker I hired to keep things in order had a massive row with my sister's friend, Mary Clemens."

"About?"

Robert sighed. "Using the funds I sent for repairing the roof."

Caleb gaped at his friend. "So this…Miss Clemens, is the real problem I take it?"

"She's part of it," Robert agreed. "She's certainly not afraid of speaking her mind. This is the third caretaker she's frightened off in just over a year."

Raising an eyebrow, Caleb stared at his friend. He was no longer entirely sure he was up to the sort of change he offered. "I will have to think about it." Long and hard and then a few times more to be absolutely certain.

But when he arrived home and found three Society matrons waiting for him with their very eligible daughters, Caleb quickly retreated to his study. He spent the next three hours discussing matters with his secretary and ensuring that the man was indeed capable and willing to handle all his affairs if Caleb chose to remove himself to the countryside for a while.

That settled, he went in search of his mother, who was not the least bit pleased with his decision. He understood her of course and promised he'd soon return, assuring her that when he did, he'd be ready to focus on finding a wife.

Grab your copy of *No Ordinary Duke* today and continue reading!

ACKNOWLEDGMENTS

I would like to thank the Killion Group for their incredible help with the editing and formatting of this book. My thanks also go to Chris Cocozza for providing the stunning artwork. And to my friends and family, thank you for your constant support. I would be lost without you!

ABOUT THE AUTHOR

Born in Denmark, Sophie has spent her youth traveling with her parents to wonderful places around the world. She's lived in five different countries, on three different continents, has studied design in Paris and New York, and has a bachelor's degree from Parson's School of Design. But most impressive of all – she's been married to the same man three times, in three different countries and in three different dresses.

While living in Africa, Sophie turned to her lifelong passion – writing.

When she's not busy dreaming up her next romance novel, Sophie enjoys spending time with her family, swimming, cooking, gardening, watching romantic comedies and, of course, reading. She currently lives on the East Coast.

You can contact her through her website at *www.sophiebarnes.com*

And please consider leaving a review for this book.

Every review is greatly appreciated!